of Sterling Quality

Book Four
A Woman
of Sterling Quality

Barbara L. Wyckoff

To order additional copies of this book, contact:
Xlibris Corporation
1-888-795-4274
www.Xlibris.com
Orders@Xlibris.com
98013

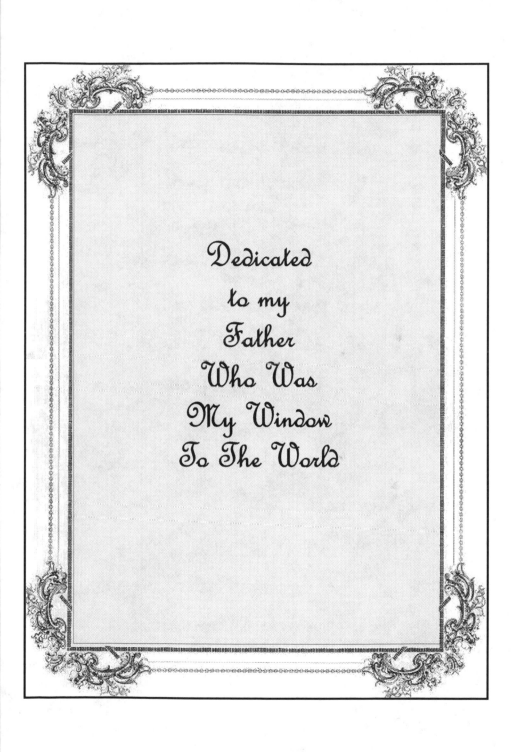

Dedicated

to my

Father

Who Was

My Window

To The World

Where did it go,
My days of youth,
My days of young,
When I laughed and ran
And played in the sun?
It was swept away
By the greed of some
And the arrogance of others.
Love, honor, dignity and pride
Saw me through as a woman
of quality in love with a man
who only in spirit
could stand by my side.

Book Four
"of Sterling Quality"

A Woman
of
Sterling Quality

Chapter One

The quality of civilization can be defined by the standards of those who live with it. Or in some instances—without it.

It was doubtful if those who traveled the iron rails, in the early mid-1880s, considered that final golden spike driven at Promontory Summit, Utah in 1869, which had connected Eastern civilization to the unruly Western frontier, an act of civilized men.

The joining of those rails was merely an act which highly relieved the travel concerns of the entrepreneurial businessmen, the politicians who would try to keep civilization connected, along with the casual traveler who had definite destinations in a country which obviously belonged to the civilized.

Among those traveling west on the Union Pacific Railway in the spring of 1882 was a young lady with dark hair and dazzling blue eyes. Many of the passengers had the distinct privilege to see this astonishingly beautiful woman usually in the Pullman Dining Car during the dinner hour. Although not rude, she held herself aloof speaking with very few as she kept her thoughts to herself. Those who did see her, when she was not in her own small drawing room, could not help but notice her attention was focused out the windows of the belching, smoking iron horse which carried them away from Missouri across the prairie to the grasslands of the great plains.

Not that it would have mattered to her traveling companions, but after almost two years of arduous training in a strict finishing school for refined ladies, Lillian Anne Sterling was going home.

Her mother, in a most 'civilized way', had forced her to leave her home to attend a school of refinements. A place where her wild Western, uninhibited childhood had been connected to Eastern civilization and proper protocol during the years from late in 1880 to the early months of 1882.

Just as the connecting of the East to the West by means of rail had proven to have its construction difficulties, and required years to complete, the connection between an unruly, willful childhood to the refinements of a proper young lady had proven to be extreme, challenging and difficult requiring time for the proper nurturing of a spirit not wishing to comply. It was the civilized thing to do, and after all, she was civilized.

For her privacy, and a certain sense of security, one of the Pullman compartments had been procured for her train travel. This time, she required no chaperone and entertained no thoughts of running away as she was returning to where she had wished to be all along.

After the excessive time away from the only home she had ever known, the same insensitive rails that had taken her away from that home were bringing her back to Denver, Colorado, and the Sterling House.

She remembered, when leaving Denver, she had looked back at every bend, every turn, taking every opportunity to lock and hold the backdrop which had been her home for 16 years.

However, when she had left the Wibscott Finishing School of Refinement for Ladies, and the strict tutelage of Madam T. Margaret Wibscott, she had not once looked back at the cold, stark gray walls of the building that had confined her body for the duration of her schooling. Nor had she taken the slightest interest in the mean streets of St. Louis, Missouri, where the pretentious school was located.

There was no doubt in the eyes of the many who saw her this was not only an exquisitely beautiful woman, but a proper lady of extreme refinements possessing manners and mannerisms of an impeccable status.

Her mother had been accurately correct to send her to such a school of refinement; but Lillian Anne Sterling had learned more than just the social graces and elegant refinements of what was considered to be acceptable in her modern day society. She had learned survival of the mind, her soul and her spirit. All of which, although connected to her social refinements were, intricately separated in her humanity.

They could not change or confine her Rocky Mountain spirit, no matter what they had tried. Some things, within her spirit, were kept very private, secreted away from the powers of change and control at the Wibscott Finishing School of Refinement for Ladies.

Using her gloved fingertips, she tried to clear the film from the train window, but quickly realized her efforts were futile as most of the grime was on the outside of the pane.

She recalled this same gesture close to two years prior as she had watched her father walk away and her mother became smaller and smaller on the platform of the train station as the train slowly pulled away. There had been no smiles to grace her cheek and no giggles bubbled up from inside.

As she lowered her hand, she also recalled the grim, unsmiling face of Mrs. Torbin, her traveling chaperone. She had sternly warned her to sit up straight on the train seat, not slump like a common child and not stare out the window as it did not present proper decorum.

The other three girls, also being taken to the Wibscott Finishing School of Refinement for Ladies did their best to please the stern Mrs. Torbin as they straightened their little spinal columns in compliance.

Lillian recalled she had stared at the woman, with no expression in her blue eyes. She also remembered how she had deliberately let her back rest against the seat and refused to sit perfectly straight. Mrs. Torbin had leaned forward, frowned with a tight harshness and said, "That is not 'Accuracy of Personality'. I see we have much to address with your schooling."

That had begun a very dour relationship between Mrs. Torbin and Lillian Anne Sterling which had extended to a very strict relationship with Madam T. Margaret Wibscott, proprietor and head mistress of the school her mother had so laboriously selected for her to attend. Lillian, along with the other young ladies in attendance at this select school, had fared better with some of the various tutors because some were not quite as rigid as others.

All elements of writing were taught with strong emphasis on delicate penmanship, readings of current literatures to include the writings of Bronte, Crane, Emily Dickinson, Browning, Oscar Wilde and Mark Twain. They learned the proper ways to sit, stand, walk, enter and leave a carriage, hold a parasol, the train of one's skirt, and even how to lay one's head on a pillow to preserve delicate curls. There were lessons on how to relegate household duties. What to shop for in the markets and what to leave for the household servants to procure.

Other fields of study included pet grooming, flower cutting along with floral arrangements, to say nothing of hours of tedious lessons and lectures on proper table settings from a tea and crumpet morning to a full coursed meal late in the day, none of which were to touch the lace gloved hand of the mistress of the house.

The young ladies had to learn the tortuous stitches of stitchery, along with what colors complimented each other. All the while, instructors tapped them sharply between the shoulder blades if they neglected their posture.

Husband pleasing, child rearing, servant hiring and dismissal, all designed to keep the proper woman properly in her considered proper place were also part of the curriculum. All of this was always tempered with "Accuracy of Personality."

Some of the young ladies failed miserably. Amidst many tears, they were dismissed from the only too proper dignified school. Others left of their own volition. Lillian held her stay, determined to learn all that was set before her to learn. She realized to return home without her graduation documents would only mean being sent off to a similar school to continue on this road of learning her mother felt so important for her well being.

The earliest letters from her mother had informed her of this in no uncertain terms. After the first three to four of these letters of disciplinary acts if she returned prematurely from the Wibscott Finishing School of Refinement for Proper Ladies, Lillian refused to open the letters from her mother. Her Paw Paw did not write, but in her heart, she forgave him. What could he say? He was undoubtedly, and for some unknown reason, at Abigale Westmoreland Sterling's mercy.

Lillian was angry, but she would stay in the school and learn all that was presented to her. With a bitter determination, she had excelled and actually enjoyed the camaraderie with the other young ladies in attendance.

As she had quickly learned, she had more skillfully kept her inner thoughts most private counting the days until she would return to the Sterling House.

Lillian felt a degree of satisfaction as she recalled her graduation day. Along with her excellence in academics, a popular vote selected her to give the valedictorian speech. She had carefully chosen her words and her inner pleasure deepened as she remembered her confidence as she had stood behind the gaily decorated podium.

She recalled letting her blue eyes move quickly from one side of the room to the other, noting the bright array of pink and orange flowers in every window, the first real brightness she had seen in this structured sanctuary for young ladies during her residency.

17 young ladies were properly seated in 17 velvet trimmed, wooden chairs. Each lady was properly posed, both feet on the floor with gloved hands folded demurely in their 17 respective laps. Their backs were straight as ramrods, with not a curl out of place on each slightly tilted head.

Her parents were not in attendance due to the extreme distance, combined with the business of the Sterling House. At least that is what her mother had written on the returned engraved invitation her parents had received. Many other sets of parents, brothers, sisters, a few cousins, aunts and uncles, plus well wishing friends were in attendance. In her private opinion, she felt 'the' Mr. and Mrs. Sterling did not need to be in the clustered groups of those expressing one accolade after another.

Pastries, sweet cakes, fresh fruit, tea and coffee urns filled to capacity were all carefully placed as they silently waited to become the focal point of palate refreshment. Each lace trimmed linen napkin was properly folded with the perfect silver service catching the afternoon sunlight as it filtered through the open windows.

Lillian had turned and curtsied toward Madam T. Margaret Wibscott, Head Mistress, the right and distinguished Mrs. Torbin, who had taught so many "Accuracies of Personality" and other various instructors. These ladies had been those responsible for strict indoctrinations into those states of poetry and prose, histories of the world, arithmetic as applied, reasoning as was reasonable along with all the proper approaches to caring for and living in the most proper delicate Victorian society of moral taste and conduct.

Executing perfect balance with her curtsy being held the proper number of seconds, Lillian rose and turned to face the assemblage. She then did the more than expected by delicately cleaning her throat as she straightened her note cards. However, these cards were useless to her as they were devoid of words. With deliberate intent, she walked from behind the podium into full view of all present. She knew precisely what she was going to say. There was no need for gilt edged cards to prompt her words.

"My sisters," she began in a voice clear and firm which was many degrees from the soft, demure, perfect ladylike voice she had been trained to use when addressing publicly.

Madam T. Margaret Wibscott gasped and caught her hand to her throat, but it was far too late for that.

"I have been requested to speak today as the young woman who has demonstrated excellence from this school for proper ladies, where we all have endured much these past two years.

"Like all of you, I was made rudely aware of every "Inaccuracy of Personality" which I ever possessed. The cost for this proper schooling has been tremendous for some of those who aspired to have proper daughters for entry into the upper echelon of the elegant society they wish them to enter."

"Miss Sterling, that will be quite enough!" Madam Wibscott said in a voice strained with control as she had quickly recovered her decorum and had risen to her feet in an effort to take control of what she knew was rapidly becoming an out of control issue with this young woman who for all intent and purpose was still rebellious.

Lillian turned. The intensity of her demeanor forced the only too proper Madam T. Margaret Wibscott to sink quietly back into her chair. When Lillian was sure the woman would remain seated, she returned her attention to the anxiously waiting young ladies of

7

inaccuracies as each was addressed and reset in accordance to the Wibscott values of accuracy. The head mistress had failed to check her footwear on graduation day.

*　　*　　*

Lillian closed her eyes to let the motion of the train invade her senses. Not all the days had been terrible for her. She had gained many truly wonderful, valuable personal assets which she felt confident she would carry with her the rest of her life.

Above all else, she was a fit, proper lady with all the mannerisms befitting one of her standing. Just what that standing was, she was not sure at this point in her life.

Although it had not been openly discussed, she was very much aware what her father did for a living was not held in the highest of esteem according to the Wibscott School's standards. However, the money for her tuition, books, hoops for needlepoint, tatting shuttles, delicate threads for the same along with all her schooling, no matter how tainted its origin, was not refused. This fee helped allow the self serving, self righteous M. Wibscott to maintain her place in St. Louis society as a firm, rigid instructress with all the graces that would cover any "Inaccuracy of Personality" a young lady might possess.

The spur from Cheyenne, where she had left the Pacific Rails on the Denver Pacific Train finally slowed as it pulled into Denver's Union Station, creaking and groaning to a slow, hissing stop as the steam escaped and the engines began to cool.

"Denver, Denver City, Colorado," came the booming voice of the conductor. "Miss, this is Denver City." he said more quietly as he stopped beside her where she sat in the traveling coach.

"Yes, sir. I am very much aware as this is my home," she replied, smiling warmly at him as he offered her an assisting hand to rise from her seat. She deftly took his arm instead of the offered hand as she rose to her feet.

She, Lillian Anne Sterling, had returned to her home.

*   *   *

Andrew Wesley Sterling, a long time resident of Denver, waited on the platform of the newly remodeled Union Station. He was, to the best of his recollection, about 40 years old. He had seen much, he had done much and had conquered much in the 20 some years he had been in this sprawling, screeching, howling city on the plains.

One of his proudest hours would be the return of his most precious daughter with all the refinement, elegance and charm that would be to her benefit in the days to come. What had been the words Abigale had used to convince him that Lillian needed extreme, almost foreign schooling in far away St. Louis, Missouri?

"She is awkward, gangly, unkempt an' certainly unmannered. She needs proper schoolin'," Abigale had argued, "An' she will have it!"

Andrew felt adequate schooling could be obtained in Denver, but proper Eastern schooling was what Abigale had her stubborn mind and heart fixed on for their daughter. So, for one more time, against Andrew's better judgment, he had given in, convincing himself that the two years without his baby girl would pass quickly. The ending result would be worth more than the sacrifice of not being with her.

When Andrew Wesley Sterling saw the beautiful woman he knew had to be his beloved daughter being escorted from the train by the conductor, he could scarcely believe what he saw and knew the time without her had most certainly been worth it. She was breathtakingly beautiful.

Chapter Two

As a child growing up in the Sterling House, much to her mother's chagrin, Lillian had raced and romped up and down the swirling spiral of the double staircase as she had played the growing up games of childhood. But it was the grown woman, Lillian Anne Sterling, a woman of sterling quality, who descended the same spiral staircase on the steady arm of her father. Unlike the moccasined racing feet, of the wild prancing girl, each satin slippered step was precise and exact to allow the satiny train of her ivory colored, elaborately bustled evening dress to trail perfectly behind her on each step she left behind.

She titled her head ever so slightly to the side as her eyes swept the room below her. She recalled many of the faces she saw below her in the common eating area of the Sterling House, which had been changed to accommodate her homecoming reception. Many were in attendance who remembered her as a child. They were the miners, the gambles and the regular patrons of the Sterling House. There were also those who recognized a free meal and a few drinks when they saw it all laid out before them. These strangers to the Sterling House raised their glasses to honor the beautiful woman descending the stairs and wished they did know her.

Suddenly, as if with no force of her own, Lillian stopped her descent, causing Andrew to question this faltering step.

"Lillian?" her father questioned. "Are ya all right?"

For a moment, locked in time, and to be forever captured in her heart of hearts, the room was no longer filled with laughing, applauding, smiling friends of the family and those wishing her well on her return.

Directly in her line of vision was a man like none she had ever seen before. A man with black hair and dark eyes and a smile more radiant than any sunrise. For that moment, she saw only him as he saw only her. Lillian felt as if her breath had been momentarily taken away then suddenly given back.

Just as quickly, all the sounds came back to the room. All the people were still applauding, holding their glasses high in her honor. Try as she might, she could not find the strange man who had captured and held her heart for that intense moment.

"Yes, father," she answered. "I am . . . I am wonderful" she answered, smiling at him not letting her eyes stop their searching of the room for the man she had seen. Or had she imagined him? *No, he is still in this room,* she thought, feeling warm and incredibly more beautiful than she had just a few moments before. He had not left and she would find him before the night was out.

At the bottom of the stairs, she stopped in front of her mother and greeted her with all the decorum she had been so laboriously taught. "Mother. How beautiful this honor is for me." she said indicating the room, the fine elaborate trappings with food and drink all exquisitely displayed. "In two years my home, and all of the Sterling House, has changed little except for the addition of those electric lights."

"My daughter," Abigale said, kissing Lillian lightly on one cheek and then the other. "All in yur honor, my dear. The electric lights are so new ta Denver City. I jist had ta have 'em fer tonight. It all comes from a contraption called a battery an' some wiring. "I do not understand any of it. All thet matters is thet it provides us this exquisite lighting.

But come," she flustered. "We must greet all yur guests." Abigale's emotions were spilling over as she fussed with one of Lillian's perfect dark curls. "Yur poppa an' me are so glad ta have ya back in our graces an' finally home from thet school."

"It is good to be home again as well," Lillian responded moving away from her mother's fussing hands and ignoring her insensitive remark about Lillian's finally being home.

"Do I still call you Baby Lily?" came a voice from behind her.

Lillian Anne turned to face the voice. It was Charley Gaynor, whose smile was as she remembered it with teeth still as white as the pure snow.

"Her name is Lillian Anne," Abigale hastily interrupted.

"Uncle Charley!" Lillian said, holding back her squeals of laughter and completely ignoring her mother as her arms reached for him.

Charley demurely took one of her gloved hands and, with an elegant gesture, kissed her on the back of the gloved hand while he bowed very lowly and properly in her direction. "My good Lord, woman," he exclaimed as he stood back up. "You are Beautiful! If an uncle can make such a bold remark?"

Lillian winked at him, regained her poise and said, "A lady never refuses a compliment from an uncle, or otherwise, provided it is expressed in the proper manner." Charley slapped Andrew on the shoulder. "My friend," he said, "I can see right now, better build a big, high fence around this one."

"Stop it, both of you," Abigale scolded in a very tight lipped manner. "Anyone with good sense can see she is a perfect lady an' there should be no hint of anything ta the contrary."

"Mother, they are quite within proper boundaries," Lillian said as she noticed a red haired, young man who shyly held back. "Erwin?" she asked and then stepped toward him. "Oh, Erwin! I have missed you the most," she said, going against all proper etiquette as she wrapped her arms around him. His face promptly turned as red as his hair.

"My Miss Lillian" he said, tears welling into his eyes.

"Lillian," she said to him. "Just Lillian, like it was and always will be."

As he stood there grinning at her, Erwin found himself embarrassed, unable to speak. Yet on this night of nights, his happiness knew no bounds. His Lillian was home. "Something to drink?" he shyly offered trying to overcome his awkwardness.

Lillian smiled kindly toward her childhood friend and protector, who would probably always be shy, and nodded her head yes. "Where is Jonas Gregory?" she asked recalling the quiet man who had brought Erwin Frederson into their lives.

"Tending bar, Miss Lillian," Erwin answered. "Do want me to get him for you?"

"Maybe a little later, Erwin." She was a little overwhelmed by the number of people around her wanting to wish her well. Some had no words as they just wanted to gaze into her face to admire her. "Maybe a glass of champagne, if don't mind?"

"Yes, Miss Lillian," Erwin said and disappeared across the room to just as quickly return. He handed Lillian a crystal stemmed glass of bubbling champagne. "I have something for you," he said between people congratulating her and complimenting both Andrew and Abigale on the issue of her return to the Sterling House.

"What would that be, Erwin?" she said, delicately sipping the light yellowish liquid in her glass. If his heart had not been stolen by the baby Lillian and the wild, young Lillian he had tried to take care of, he was captivated by the woman she had matured into. "A piano piece I composed just for you."

"Erwin," she exclaimed with great enthusiasm, "when may I hear this composition of yours?"

champagne in hand, his blue eyes sparkling as he brushed his curly, gray streaked blond hair off his forehead.

As he watched this stunning young woman, who in his opinion was of the finest and most beautiful Sterling quality, walk toward him, Andrew was without any doubt the proudest father in all of Denver.

He also experienced a twinge of protective jealousy when he saw how proudly the young Spaniard friend of Charley's walked beside her. For an instant his mind clouded with the memory of another woman he had so proudly stood with and sensed for a moment there could be great love between this handsome young man and his beautiful daughter. He wondered if anyone else saw the radiance between them?

Then it happened! It happened quickly from the darkness behind the spiral stairway into the light, through the crowd and across the room as the man wearing the blue lensed glasses, the man forgotten, the man known as Simon Pails, made his well planned assault on Andrew Wesley Sterling.

"You can't have it all an' never will!" the man screamed as his pent up anger drove the knife he was wielding in an upward vicious thrust.

A shot rang out. Simon Pails was violently shoved aside and fell to the floor, moaning in abject agony as the lone shot from Charley Gaynor's pistol ripped into his body. The blood began oozing between his fingers as he clutched at the gaping hole in his chest. In a moment he relaxed his hand and the moaning stopped, because Simon Pails was quite dead.

No one seemed to notice as all eyes and all attention was on Andrew Sterling where he had crumpled to the floor and was being held in the arms of the man who had tried to shove the knife and Simon Pails to the side.

Abigale had screamed one time and fainted. Several ladies were waving fans in her face and patting her on the wrists in an effort to revive her.

18

Lillian had stifled her own screams by placing a hand over her mouth as she dropped the glass of champagne her father had just handed her. She knelt on the floor beside the strange man from Hispania who was cradling her father in his arms.

Andrew's eyes fluttered open and he said one thing, "Charley?" He held his hand against his side where the knife had penetrated his body.

"I'm here, Andrew. I'm right here," Charley said also kneeling beside his fallen friend. "Get back!" he demanded of the crowd of curious onlookers who seemed to be pressing so close as to steal the very air from those on the floor.

With the efforts of the ladies, Abigale had regained her senses and was trying to push her way through the crowd which was rapidly growing in numbers as word of the stabbing rumbled through the Sterling House. "My husband! My husband!" she was screaming. "Let me pass! Let me see my husband!"

The crowd parted enough for her to stare down at her fallen husband, uncertain as what to do.

Lillian looked from her father into the dark eyes of Paris Jacob Montoya, who still cradled him. She looked back at her father. "Paw Paw?" she asked. "Uncle Charley?" she implored him with her eyes. " Senor Montoya?" she questioned.

"Someone get a doctor," Charley demanded, as he helped Paris Jacob pick Andrew up. "Abigale," he demanded, "Get up to your rooms and get a bed ready and be quick."

Abigale just stared at him. In the confusion, she was not certain what to do. Lillian started to rise and Erwin helped her to her feet. "I will go," she said, glancing at her motionless mother and then at Erwin. "Erwin, help me," she commanded leading the way. The silent crowd parted as Paris Jacob LaRoche de la Montoya carried the very still form of Andrew Wesley Sterling toward the spiral stairs.

Lillian saw her mother regain some of her composure and meekly followed them up the stairs. Her mind was reeling in a million directions as she tried to find a reason for what she had just witnessed.

Who was that man lying dead on the floor below them? She stopped for a second to catch her breath and Erwin said, "Come on, Miss Lillian."

She brought her attention back to him. As always, as from her childhood, he was being her strength.

"Yes, Erwin," she said and looked back to see the Spaniard man, with the incredibly long name, gently carrying her father across the room and toward the stairs. Her Uncle Charley was right beside him forcing people out of the way. She could also see her mother being assisted by Jonas Gregory to ascend the stairs. This was a nightmare in the slowest of motion and she thought they would never reach the third floor of the Sterling House.

*   *   *

It was uncommonly hot and quiet on the third floor sitting room of the Sterling House. Lillian waited with her Uncle Charley, Erwin, Jonas Gregory and her mother, who had not said a word since the knife had flashed through the air to find the destination Simon Pails had intended. They were all silent, waiting for the doctor to come from the bedroom and tell them just how serious the cut had been.

Lillian saw her father's blood on her dress and carefully touched the dried and drying spots.

Everything seemed to move in slow motion all around her. The heaviness in the room pressed on her every nerve. *Take a breath,* she thought. *Breathe. My Paw Paw must be all right.*

With demanding eyes, Lillian looked at her mother, who was fussing with the ruffled lace fronting of her dress. *Did she have some hidden knowledge about what had caused this to happen? Someone knew. Someone had to know what this was all about.* Abigale could not bear to meet her daughter's gaze. Neither could she look at Charley, who stared down at the floor in front of him. Jonas and Erwin had stepped back into the shadows of the room where they whispered to one another.

Abigale's hands stopped fluttering and she let them rest in her lap. These moments would pass and her life would resume in ways she was accustomed to. This was nothing more than a bad dream from which she would waken at any moment, but the intensity of her daughter's gaze frightened her into the reality of the moment. Her husband was fighting for his life. This was no dream. She was truly sitting in this dreadful room waiting to find out if Andrew Wesley Sterling, her husband, would live or die.

Charley's mind could not adjust, would not adjust, to what had just happened. He had witnessed the only man he had ever trusted, the only true friend he had ever had, the one person he trusted his life to being assaulted, stabbed, and could possibly be dying. He closed his eyes. All he could see were those hideous dark lensed glasses, the flash of that unforgiving steel and the insanity of Simon Pails as he had lunged across the room through the crowd of people to seek the revenge he thought was his. He could hear the pistol shot. Knew he had fired the gun. He thought the man to be dead but was not sure. At this point, he did not care.

Lillian broke the unnatural quiet, her voice low. Her words measured. "Who was that man?" she asked.

"Yes," Abigale added, finding her own voice and then with a demanding tone, said, "I have a right ta know. I demand . . ."

"Mother!" Lillian said, cutting her mother's words more sharply than the knife that had cut into her father. "You can demand nothing at this time."

Charley walked to the window to stare down onto Larimer Street below and then up into a dark, moonless nighttime sky. "Simon Pails," he began, "was a loathsome man who tried competing with us at the River House Saloon where we both dealt Monte before the Sterling House was built. Seems this Pails challenged Andrew to a grudge match the night we all found out about the war starting. Andrew beat him in the game. Beat him fair and square with the bet being that whoever lost the game would leave Denver City forever. This is also how Andrew came by this land and the start he got for the Sterling House. It all originally belonged to Simon Pails."

He stopped talking for a moment letting his mind drift back to the miners tent, the painting of the nude and those horrible rotted eggs they had encountered the first time they had set foot on this property.

"Seems the deeds to this property was in that bet too along with the lock, stock and barrel of it. Pails lost it. He lost it all with the turn of one card to my partner but seems his leaving forever did not last." He sadly shook his head and turned back to look first at Abigale and then at Lillian.

"Lillian," he said in her direction and then looked at Abigale. "Abigale, what can I say beyond this. I think I killed that man, but it was not quick enough. This is bad. Where is PJ? He tried, I saw him try to stop Pails. Where is Senor Montoya?" Charley knew his words were irrational, but he could not seem to stop himself.

Erwin spoke up, "He excused himself. Said this was family matters, but I reckon he is probably downstairs. Do you want him, Charley?"

Charley looked at the shy, quiet boy he had taken to raise. "No, son, I will talk to him later. I just want to know what is going on behind that closed door. But maybe," he added. "you and Jonas should go downstairs. See if can clear the people out. Close the place up for tonight."

Both young men nodded in agreement, glad to be out of the room and have something to do besides stand and wait to hear words from a doctor as to the condition of Mr. Sterling.

The intense heaviness fell back into the room as Abigale, Lillian and Charley continued their waiting.

What seemed like hours was in reality only a few minutes more until Doctor Safford, one of the local doctors who had been summoned, came from the room, setting his black bag on a table and availing himself of a cup of lukewarm coffee from the table urn. Everyone had risen to their feet but the doctor motioned them to sit back down. "Mrs. Sterling, your husband has been gravely injured."

Lillian held her breath.

"At this point, I am not sure he will live."

Abigale's hand flew to her mouth and she visibly began trembling.

Lillian sank back in her chair, stunned beyond words.

"What do mean, he might not live?" Charley asked, his voice sharp.

The doctor resumed his explanation. "I have stopped the bleeding, but the cut is deep. Missed his lungs as his breathing seems to be all right and he is not spitting up blood.

"But I fear an internal organ was damaged. No real way to tell." He addressed Lillian. "Your father is a strong man. He needs quiet and a lot of rest. If he moves around, the bleeding will start again. I don't know," he stated and shook his head. "I have given him something so he will sleep but he is asking for you, Miss Sterling," he said, still looking at Lillian. "I will return tomorrow to see to him again."

"Ya mean he does not want ta see me?" Abigale asked, anger touching her words. "He has asked for his daughter," Doctor Safford replied.

Abigale started to take a step toward the bedroom door, but Charley's hand on her arm stopped her. "Let Lillian go. You can see him, too, but later," he said, trying to be gentle with her as he urged her to sit back down.

Glaring at him, Abigale jerked her arm away from his hand and sat down crossing her arms over her chest and exhaling sharply.

Lillian ignored her mother's actions and behavior as she quietly crossed the room and just as quietly entered the bedroom where her father was resting, his eyes closed, his grayish blond curls sticking damply to his forehead. Lamps were burning low and light also flickered from the new fangled installed battery powered electric lighting Abigale had insisted be in every room of the house. It all seemed to cast a strange yellowish gloom into the room.

Pulling up a chair next to the bedside, Lillian sat down. "Paw Paw," she said, smoothing back his damp curls.

Andrew opened his eyes and smiled into the anxious face of his daughter. "Boss Girl, seems I kinda spoiled yur homecomin'."

"Shhhh," she said. "The doctor said you need to rest, not to be worrying about some party for me."

He tried to focus on her but the laudanum was beginning to lull him to sleep. "There are so many things ya do not know 'bout this family an' things ya should know. What they did. What I did an' how this all come about."

"Later, Paw Paw. You should sleep."

"Do not take unkindly ta yur mother. Promise me ya won't." he said, his speech becoming more slurred. "Promise," he said again, "Prommmis." And his words floated away as the laudanum closed his mind away from the pain.

Tears streaked down her face as she leaned to kiss him on the forehead. "I promise, Paw Paw. I promise. I will promise anything. Just don't die."

Chapter
Three

Steady rain dripped and drizzled from a moody unrelenting sky turning the streets of Denver to its noted sticky gumbo mud. Cherry Creek rose but posed no threat. The South Platte moved lazily on its northeasterly direction, placid in its intent. After three days, the storm shuddered, gave up a steady downpour through the night, and passed on its spent way.

The early morning saw cloudy skies with a damp chill hanging over the city. The storm, the mud or the rising of the infamous little creek did not stop Denverites with their variety of jugs and bottles to contain and carry home the highly desired water from the numerous artesian wells in and around Denver. The most frequently visited was the fountain in front of the court house at Court and Tremont Streets.

Many attempts were made to drill for more of the prized artesian water. Commonly the wells produced petroleum and even traces of silver. It was even rumored that one drill site lost its drill bit to a pool of quicksand. That rumor was quickly squelched as there was no need to have downtown Denverites feel they were residing and working over pools of something that could suck them into the ground.

The Indians, who had been invited to be on display as an exhibit at the National Mining and Industrial Exposition at the new exposition hall at South Broadway and Exposition Avenue, were warm and dry inside the teepees they had set for their comfort in the street in front of the massive new building.

The fear of these native inhabitants of the land, which had at one time fiercely controlled the attitudes of Denver's populous, had produced a mixture of curiosities by the local gentry, who were convinced the savages were quite subdued.

The Indians sat in their lodges, warmed by their fires, listening to the stories of old being told in a tongue only they could understand. Once in a while, one of them would peek out the lodge door and look with a strange and soulful disdain at the monstrosity of a building which housed the white man's strange displays.

This was a place where once only prairie grass grew. Now nothing lived or grew but the white man and his strange buildings. The door flap would be dropped back into place and those looking out would retreat back into worlds only they understood.

Simon Pail's body had been unceremoniously taken away from the Sterling House. His remains were claimed by no one. The acting Chief of Police, D. J. Cook, had sent two of his marshals to investigate and interview several eye witnesses to the stabbing which had resulted in the ultimate killing of Pails.

Charley had gone, most willingly, to the jail and Cook had personally assured him that, although a small hearing would be conducted, it was obviously a matter of justifiable homicide.

Simon Pails was a homeless drifter who had gravely assaulted one of Denver's citizenry. In light of all who had witnessed what had happened, and testified to the same, there would be no charges pressed against Charley Gaynor for the death of Simon Pails.

Just as unceremoniously as Simon Pails had been carried out of the Sterling House, he was just as unceremoniously buried in the old city cemetery with no one in attendance.

Charley Gaynor was not in the least concerned about the mining exposition, the somber and sober Indians who were on display outside just one more ostentatious building in Denver, or the fact that someone had lost a drill bit into what appeared to be quicksand under a building while drilling down for yet one more artesian well.

At the moment, Charley felt as if he was sinking into a quagmire of quicksand of his own as he sat watching his friend try and recover from a very dangerous stab wound. He would have gladly gone to jail and only wished he had killed the man faster. Then none of this would be happening to them.

"Charley," Andrew said, "ya look tired, my friend."

"Haven't slept much." Charley responded concern clouding his face.

"Reckon ya be thinkin' thet be my fault?" Andrew asked, managing a smile.

"Reckon so," Charley answered, putting another pillow behind Andrew's head as he saw him struggling to sit up a little straighter. "Doctor Safford said you are not to be moving around too much."

"I do not give a damn what the doctor said," Andrew answered. "Got ta sit up a bit here, so I can talk ta ya better 'bout some things."

Charley saw Andrew wince with some pain and then catch his breath from his efforts.

"Partner, I may not make it this time. I feel it inside an' it don't feel good," Andrew said, still struggling against the pain.

"Nonsense," Charley said.

"No, I do not feel right inside. An' whatever I feel goes beyond this knife cut pain."

"Want some more laudanum?"

"No," Andrew answered. "Makes me too sleepy an' I got things I got ta say. An' one a them is to say thank you. Thank you fer all we have been ta each other. What ya have been ta me."

"I don't need thanks for what was the natural order of things between us," Charley said, fighting back his own emotions.

27

"My family is gonna need someone ta look after 'em an' take care a the Sterling House. It is all they will have left an' the only home they have."

"You will be taking care of your family, Andrew," Charley said with a strong firmness in his voice.

"No," Andrew said just as firmly. "Listen. Ya must hear me an' it is you thet must stay with 'em after I am gone."

Before Charley could say anything more on Andrew's recovery and the issue, Abigale and Lillian both came into the room followed by the doctor.

Abigale opened one set of the velvet drapes and tied them back before she came to the bedside. "Andrew," she said, kissing him lightly on the forehead and taking the chair where Charley had been sitting. "Are ya better? Ya look better. Do ya want something ta eat? Maybe some soup? Soolie would know what would be best. Oh, how I wish she was here ta tend ta matters," she babbled, "but Doctor Safford is here," she said looking at the man. "I am sure he will do everything jist fine."

Doctor Safford walked past the prattling woman to where Andrew lie in the bed. He removed his coat and rolled up his sleeves in a most professional manner. "Mr. Sterling, how are we feeling?" he asked, placing his hand on Andrew's forehead and a stethoscope on his chest.

"I have seen better times," Andrew answered.

"You are feverish. Have been taking the laudanum as prescribed?"

"Oh, yes he has," Abigale interjected straining to see what the doctor was doing.

"Mr. Gaynor, will you be so kind as to help me turn him over just a bit?"

"Sorry, partner," Charley said as he could see the pain on Andrew's face as he was held over on his side and the doctor tapped on his side, listening more with the stethoscope. A frown creased between his eyes.

"Lay him back without the pillows," the doctor said and then placed the listening instrument on Andrew's stomach. "Are you sick to your stomach? Been throwing up?" he asked.

The effort of moving around had caused Andrew to break out in a sweat and he nodded yes. "Can I sit back up a bit?" he asked, feeling the nausea increase by his lying down flat.

"Yes, by all means," the doctor answered.

Charley helped hold him up and Lillian arranged pillows behind her father until he was comfortable. She could not help notice how pale he was and how hot he was to the touch. "Doctor?" she questioned.

"I fear some Peritonitis," he said beginning to check the dressing on the wound.

"Perri . . . what?" Abigale asked.

"Mother, please," Lillian said. "Let the doctor finish. I am sure he will explain." She, too, wanted to understand what the strange sounding word meant as they all seemed to be at the medical mercy of this man who was tending her father.

Lillian watched as the doctor closed his little black bag recalling a time when these little doctor bags held magic. This time, she feared there was none left. At least none for her father.

They all listened quietly while this stranger, someone they had not known before, tried to explain in proper medical terms what was causing the sickness that had taken over the stab wound.

Lillian watched her mother dab at her dry eyes with a lace trimmed handkerchief and nod her head at the appropriate times. She silently accepted what the doctor was telling them, but Lillian was not impressed by him or his clinical explanation of this thing called Peritonitis, which he said was some kind of infection of a membrane lining the abdomen which had resulted from the knife's penetration into her father's side. In unspoken words, Doctor Safford was saying her father was dying and there was virtually nothing anyone could do.

"He must rest," the doctor said. "By all means remain calm. No physical or emotional exertion of any kind. This will only spread the infection. Thin clear soups. Green teas if have them and have him drink water. And mind you, no alcohol of any kind."

Lillian looked at the two dark brown bottles standing side by side on the wash basin stand.

"Oh, and this," the doctor added gesturing toward the bottles. "Do not fail to give him one spoonful of each three times a day, morning, noon and night along with the laudanum for the pain. Do you understand me, Mrs. Sterling? All of this is very important if we are to keep your husband alive. I will send a nurse to assist."

Abigale picked up the two small bottles and looked down at them. On one was written the words "Ganoderma lucidum" and on the other, "Olea Europeca." She had never seen, let alone heard such strange words, but these brown bottles contained tinctures of hope.

Lillian walked to where her mother stood and took the bottles of medicine from her. "I will do this," she said. "And I will take care of my father. There will be no need of a nurse in the Sterling House."

"But, Lillian . . . ." her mother protested.

"No, Mother," Lillian said, firmly, "he is my father and I will take care of him."

"As you say." The doctor rolled down his sleeves and put his coat on as he spoke. "If there are changes, inform me immediately. I will call back tomorrow to check on Mr. Sterling's progress. Good day, Mrs. Sterling, Miss Sterling."

"I will show you out," Abigale said, glad for an excuse to leave the room. She looked once at Andrew's still form lying in the bed, acknowledged her daughter and quickly followed the doctor from the room.

Charley frowned, letting his eyes follow the doctor's departure. Not sure exactly what to do or say, he also left the room trying to let his mind accept what they had just heard. A death sentence pronounced by a man wearing a black coat, carrying a black bag filled with bottles of seemingly limited to no hope.

Lillian sat down in the chair which had taken a permanent place beside the bed. "Are they gone?" Andrew asked, opening his eyes.

Lillian reached, took his hot, moist hands in hers and said, "Yes, Paw Paw. They are gone."

"Good," he said, struggling to get more upright.

"You are supposed to be resting, not trying to sit up." Lillian said, as she again adjusted his pillows.

"I can rest when I am in my grave, which sounds like it could be more sooner than later. There are things ya must know an' things thet ya must take care of. Open thet window an' let some air in this room. I do not want ta die the way my momma did in some closed up room."

"You are not going to die," she responded as she got up and opened the window to let a cool breeze come into the room stirring dust motes with its first passage. Andrew inhaled as much as his bandage would allow and motioned for his daughter to sit beside him on the bed. The fresh air seemed to abate the nausea and he relaxed.

"My lil' girl," he said, smiling at her and stroking her cheek. "My baby girl, born the night of the great fire." He let his hand fall, closed his eyes to recall that night, and another image that would be forever in his mind. It was all coming to an end and he knew it. *How much should I say?* He wondered.

It took all of Lillian's strength to stay quiet but she knew that whatever it was he wanted to tell her was of great importance and that she needed to let him tell it in his own way.

"Yur mother will never tell ya the way it really was an' how it is between us. Ya have a right ta know thet I shamed her in a most disgraceful way. Back in Georgia, afore the war, when I was so young, I kinda loved yur mother an' it was expected fer us ta marry an' we did. Lillian, it was wrong from the very beginnin'.

"An' when something is wrong, there ain't no way a makin' it right. I had a dream an' it was ta find the gold thet I jist knew had ta be out here." Andrew closed his eyes and drifted. He saw it all. A time when he had stood on his own. Lived in one room as he saw fit and made his own way. He opened his eyes. "I never found the gold, Lillian. I found something more. Meant more ta me than the gold. I would have died fer her if'n I could." he added still letting his thoughts wander.

"Paw Paw, I know about that Indian woman who lived here with you before mother came here. Long before I was born."

Andrew came back to the moment, questioning her with his eyes.

Lillian was kind. "Even a young girl can hear street gossip. Charley Paul told me most of it. I believe he learned it from Grand Paw Paw. How could I have not known what with that Sterling quality I always wanted. One would have had to be blind not to see that blond hair and be certain who the father was."

He reached up and touched her dark hair. "Does yur mother know this?" "Mother never got past her hatred of Charley Paul, and of Denver City, to realize I was learning many things. Sool Sool and Grand Paw Paw took Charley Paul and left here because of that hatred and her meanness toward my brother. I was aware of that too. Now, Paw Paw, that you know I know, will you tell me tell me about that

Indian woman?" Andrew sighed, relieved. "Lillian," he began with tears flooding into his blue eyes, "I loved her more than life itself. She was my life. She was every thing ta me." He took a little halting breath and regained control.

"Pale Star Rising came ta me when I was cold, alone an' not sure of my future here. Not a wantin' ta go back ta what was in Georgia. It wasn't like they all said an' promised afore I came out here. I was scared ta try an' go up in those mountains alone by myself ta find thet gold cause it wasn't jist lyin' around in the streets an alleyways here in this wild town.

"I swear ta ya, Lillian, I wanted ta make a home here an' then bring yur mother out here. Give her everything. It was the winter a '61 when Pale Star came ta me from off the streets a old Denver City. Lillian, I knew, I knew the moment I saw her I loved her an' would love her until my day's end. It was wrong, I knew it was wrong, but I forgot about yur mother back in Georgia. I forgot about everything thet once mattered ta me an' then when Pale Star gave me my son, your brother Charley Paul Standing Horse, my life was complete. I was a proud man an' I wanted it ta stay the way it was but, it could not. It all ended when I got the letter from yur mother a sayin' she an' Soolie was on their way here. I thought I was goin' ta die when I had ta tell Pale Star she had ta leave 'cause my rightful wife was on her way." He stopped and caught his breath.

Lillian gave him a drink of water, but did not speak. He had to finish this story in his own way.

He leaned back on the pillows, holding his hand against his side where the knife had entered his body. "Lillian, I tried, I tried ta love her an' be kind ta her an' even made love ta her but my heart was not in it as it was out there somewhere on the plains, in a teepee with a woman I could only long ta be with.

"An' then ya was born in thet Arapaho village thet night a the big fire. We ran from thet fire an' Buckland took us ta a safe place. It was a village of her people. An' I saw her, so beautiful an' so proud an' my heart broke again. Soolie knew. Soolie saw her with me, but she never said a word. Never, an' I loved thet ol' slave woman even more than I ever did before." Andrew was out of breath from his efforts.

Lillian got up and wet a cloth in the wash basin to cool his moist forehead. "Paw Paw, you need to rest. The story can wait until you feel better to finish telling me." she said, as she tried to be firm with him.

"No, " he said, grateful for the cool cloth on his forehead. He felt he was more feverish and sicker than what that doctor had said. Many things needed to be told while he could still tell them. "Thet was the last time I saw her." he continued. "I prayed ta God thet she had escaped the butchery a Sand Creek an' thet madman, Chivington, but . . ." and he faltered, his face contorted with the pain of the memory.

"Paw Paw!"

Andrew took another more shallow breath as he let the harsh memory fall away from him. "Buckland brought Charley Paul back ta me an' thet was the end of any kind a relationship with yur mother. She tolerated me, an' made me spend money on what she wanted. Out a guilt I did. I tried, but I could not love her. I could not! I loved Pale Star." There was still great sadness in his heart and it showed from the very depth of who he was. He was dying and he knew that too. He saw his daughter brush away the tears. He waited for her to regain her composure.

"There will come a time in yur life, an' ya will feel it like no other time when a man will come an' take yur heart away with his. Hold on ta him, Lillian, hold onto thet men an' love him with every part of what ya are. He will take ya fer his own an' ya will love him fer thet.

There is no power stronger than the love a man an' woman can have fer each other." He coughed and fought down the nausea brought on by drinking the water.

"There is somethin', my lil' Boss Girl, thet I want ya ta have." he struggled to sit up a bit straighter and reached for the ivory snowflake which still hung around his neck. "Yur Uncle Leon, yur mother's brother who died in thet hateful war, gave this ta me the day I left Westmoreland so I would never forget our friendship. I gave it ta Pale Star the day she had ta leave me so she would never forget my love fer her."

He stopped for a moment, recalling the bloodstain that was also on this piece. "I killed Tom Smith ta git this back from him after I knew he was the one who killed my Pale Star out there at Sand Creek cuz he stole it from her an' he stole it from me.

"He was wearin' it the night he came ta the saloon braggin' 'bout what he had done. I killed him Lillian! I killed him dead!" Andrew stopped himself and let the anger subside. "It belongs in the Sterling family an' I want ya ta have it so ya will always remember thet yur of the finest quality a person could ever be."

"Yes, Paw Paw," she whispered, holding the ivory snowflake in her hand and feeling the smoothness of it with her finger tip.

Andrew knew his strength was all but gone. He had more he wanted to say. "Yur mother will not understand this. I want ta be buried with certain things. I trust you an' Charley will see to it. Ain't never been one fer too much sentiment, but hidden in a niche in the picture of the nude downstairs are two old shot glasses an' two pouches filled with lil' rocks. One set belongs ta me an' one ta Charley. Would mean a lot ta me if'n my set could go with me."

"Yes, Paw Paw, I will do that." She did not question him as to the meanings of his requests, as she knew the stories about both items. He weakly held up a hand indicating he needed to say more.

" More important, there is an old trunk over there behind the stair casing kinda out a sight. The key fer it is hidden in thet same picture frame down stairs." Andrew smugly recalled how he had hidden the key there where it would be safe from Abigale's finding it as she would never have gone near that painting.

Lillian frowned slightly as she remembered finding that trunk years before. She also recalled trying to open it but the secure lock had proven beyond her efforts.

"The things inside are the things thet Pale Star an' I shared. I want ta be buried in thet blanket an' I want those moccasins on my feet. Promise me," he said and then said no more as he knew his wishes would be honored.

"I promise," Lillian whispered and let him sleep, still touching the snowflake with her fingertip and felt a strange warmth from the woman who had worn it before her. Somehow it did not matter if there was a memory of blood connected to this strange piece of jewelry.

Going to the window, she looked out over a very busy Larimer Street. People were riding back and forth, walking back and forth, some standing still perhaps wondering where they were going or questioning where they had been. It was bright outside, brighter than she had ever seen it.

She suddenly sucked in her breath and just as quickly let it out. She had just heard her father admit to killing a man over this piece of ivory she held in her hand. Or, more importantly, a matter of honor. Had this Tom Smith killed Pale Star at Sand Creek? How had all of this come about? Would she ever find out all there was to know about this Sterling family? Did it matter? Lillian Anne Sterling quietly fastened the necklace around her own neck, vowing not to remove it until something of a great value of Sterling quality would cause her to do it as it had her father.

A few more days passed. Doctor Safford came and went. Andrew refused food, allowing only a little water which he would vomit back up just about as quickly as it slid down his parched throat.

Abigale would enter the quiet, darkened room to look at Andrew lying in the bed. She would then stare out the window and quietly leave, saying nothing to anyone. Lillian refused to leave her father's bedside, keeping her thoughts to herself, only going out to relieve herself and then be right back beside him, praying for a miracle to bring him back to her.

Charley Gaynor would stay for hours, speaking in low tones to his friend, and then leave for a few moments only to return, praying to a God he, too, did not understand.

Jonas and Erin would come into the room, stand about, saying nothing, not certain what to do. Neither of them stayed long feeling this was a close family time. They thought they could both be of better benefit if they took care of the business, such as it was, downstairs trying to answer the questions of the curious.

It was late in the afternoon and cool on the third floor of the Sterling House.

Sounds drifted up from the busy Larimer Street but the Sterling family did not hear them. All was silent in the room except for the slight fluttering of the lace covering the windows where the velvet draping had been drawn aside. The windows had been opened again to allow fresh air into the room.

Andrew's eyelids fluttered ever so slightly and he opened his eyes just enough to allow light into his mind. For a moment, he was disoriented. Then he remembered. *Had she been with him?* No, she was only in his weakened thoughts. He moved his lips to speak and Lillian bent closer to hear what he would say. "Pale Star, " he whispered, "Pale Star."

He exhaled one more time, closed his eyes and Andrew Wesley Sterling stopped breathing.

His beautiful daughter, Lillian Anne Sterling, took his relaxed hand in hers, put her head on his chest and wept. Not a sound escaped her but the tears ran from her eyes which were as blue as her fathers.

"Paw Paw," she whispered as she removed her hand from his and allowed Charley to help her slowly stand up.

Abigale stood at the foot of the bed with absolutely no expression on her face as she watched her husband take his last breath. She watched her daughter pull away from the dead man she, in so many ways, had never truly understood. Yet had loved and hated during the short span of time they had shared.

"What did he say?" she quietly asked.

Lillian looked at her mother for a long time before she answered. It would be a lie. The first of many she would tell.

"Nothing." she replied, withdrawing her thoughts to the privacy of her own mind.

Chapter Four

Where men live, men die. Where they die, they are laid to rest. Where they are laid to rest, sometimes depends on the circumstances of how they lived.

When General Larimer jumped the claim of the St. Charles Township, and platted his own town, he did not fail to include a place of burial for those whose lives would end in his City of Denver.

Even though the whole region still spiritually and morally belonged to the Arapaho, General Larimer plunged forward and set aside 320 acres east and a little south of the platted city to receive the remains of the dead. He called this grandiose addition to his scheme—Mt. Prospect Cemetery. On the crest of a hill he laid out several plots where only the affluent were to be interred, the middle class to be buried down the hill with the outer most areas reserved for the criminal and those of little to no means.

The first to require the intended serene calmness of Mt. Prospect was a man who died of a lung infection, or possibly the first was a man hung for murder. No one seemed to recall for sure as no accurate records were kept. It was highly rumored; however, that both the hung man and the victim, his brother-in-law, were buried in the same grave on the edge of the cemetery which created sensational gossip.

Larimer may have had high expectations for the Mt. Prospect Cemetery, but the graveyard slowly became the unexpected final

Sterling could keep her husband away from the woman he had loved. Truly loved all his life.

Behind the veil, Lillian was happy as she realized her father was finally at peace and he was where he had longed to be. Due to his honor, only his death could free him and take him there.

Chapter
Five

Two mourning wreaths hung on the front doors of the Sterling House. One for the saloon entrance and one for the dining entrance. Charley said he would open the saloon the day after the funeral, but it was questionable when Abigale would reopen the restaurant. Lillian did not understand how to attend to the kitchen or see to reservations, let alone serving meals. Those tasks were not among the many outstanding attributes taught at the fine school she had just left. Abigale had summarily dismissed the hired help with no apparent plan as to when their services might be required for a reopening.

Lillian was not thinking about any of these things as she allowed Erwin to help her from the carriage after the ride back from Riverside. She and her mother had declined a formal reception. The steady stream of those who expressed sorrow, grief and meaningful condolences had become too much to bear. Both she and her mother had expressed a desire for solitude after the burial of Andrew Wesley Sterling.

When they entered the darkened lower rooms, the smell of cut flowers assailed Lillian's senses. She found herself ill to her stomach as she thought if she lived to be 100, this was one smell she never wanted near her again. She realized people meant well, but this was overwhelming. A modest "I am sorry" would have sufficed. All around her, were dead and dying flowers which would have to be discreetly thrown out.

"Ya have no idea what it was like, comin' here an' bein' here on these godless plains waitin' fer first one disaster after another ta happen," her mother sharply retorted. "Livin' with a man who in name only was a husband. A man who forced his husbandly attentions on me akin ta rape 'cause I never consented ta what he did ta me. An' then when the truth of how he had lived with another woman was thrown inta my face, he forced me ta live with issues of embarrassment."

She sucked in her breath and stopped herself, feeling flush from what she had just said. She quieted her tone and continued. "Ya want the truth, young lady, I will give ya the truth. Here in this horrible place, I was nuthin' more than an inconvenient truth. An obligation he had ta meet. I had a home an' a beautiful lifestyle in Georgia but yur precious Paw Paw did not see fit ta stay there on either a the plantations. Westmoreland or Ironwood."

"What about the war? The South lost or have forgotten?" Lillian interrupted. "Those plantations, and that beautiful lifestyle, are gone."

Abigale held up her hand to stop her daughter. "I have not forgotten anything," the Widow Sterling hatefully snapped. "We could a won thet war, if'n more men, like yur poppa had a stayed ta drive those Yankees off our land. But he, like hundreds of others, maybe thousands, was a coward an' he ran away usin' his dreams a gold an' glory as an excuse ta leave. My poppa an' my brother, Leon, died hideous deaths tryin' ta preserve our rights as Southerners while yur poppa scratched around out here in the dirt, searchin' fer God only knows what, 'cause what he found was not decent. An' it was thet indecency what kept him here. A saloon an' an Indian woman off the streets a this wretched town.

"She would a still been here if'n I had not come out here an' took my rightful place with my husband. Mine, Lillian. Not hers. Yur poppa deceived me. Led me ta believe all was right out here an' right fer me ta come here. When I got here, I had ta learn how ta survive in a most inhospitable land. There was the fire of '63, when ya were born an' the flood a '64, the blizzards an' the cold an' the rains thet could turn everything ta mud. Then those same mud holes turn ta dustbowls an' the dirt everywhere.

Then there was these savage people out here. These godless Indians thet were here," she continued, her voice raspy as she saw things in her memory that Lillian could not recall in her own mind.

"They frightened me so badly. They would come beggin' at the back door of this very Sterling House. Beggin' fer scraps a food or cups a coffee. They smelled bad an' looked worse with those filthy blankets wrapped around 'em an' thet grease in their hair. I knew they hated me by the way they would stare. I wish Col. Chivington had been left ta do what was necessary an' rid the plains of 'em forever. He was a God fearin' man who knew what should a been done. Sand Creek was jist a start."

It was as if a dam of all the pent up emotions, angers and rages Abigale had felt for so many years, along with the grief on her shoulders, came rushing from her. All of this bitterness spilled into the room to lie in a tangled heap on the floor between her and her very silent daughter.

"An' then," she continued, her voice quieter, "there were the people who first came ta yur poppa's saloon. Filthy, nasty dirty miners smellin' of the very ground they grubbed around in an' the trappers reekin' of animal hides an' unkempt bodies with the worst of 'em bein' thet, thet, thet . . . Buckland man who took my Soolie away from me. Soolie was mine, even though we gave her freedom papers long before thet cur of a man Lincoln, freed her. Thet devil worshipper could not realize what he was doin' by releasin' thet Negro plague on society. An' cuz he is dead too, he will never know the damage he has done. Those animals destroyed my home an' killed my family. When the war was over, there was nothin' left ta go back to or for. Ya think I don't know, Lillian? Well, I do. Westmoreland was burned an' the land finally sold fer taxes to 'em carpetbaggers.

"Ironwood was parceled out ta sharecroppers. It has all been lost forever an' I had no home ta go home to." Abigale stopped in her tirade to see if her daughter was truly listening.

"Fer all the years I have spent in this world of hateful hardships I have never stopped missin' an' longin' fer the gentle, sweet smellin' men of home with their gentle words an' genteel ways.

"Andrew Wesley Sterling, of such Sterling fine quality, made me come out here an' I adjusted, Lillian. Adjusted ta a world where I did not belong. Thet is why the dinin' establishment of the Sterling House is the way it is. I created my world away from yur poppa an' what he had. His saloon. But then," she added, her dark eyes narrowing to mere slits, "He brought thet boy here. He let thet nasty, vile lil' animal stay here an' he jist expected me ta turn the other way an' pretend I could not see thet blond hair an' know about his immoral indecency with some Indian woman. I had heard the rumors an' gossip but I ignored it all until thet boy came here. I hated 'em both, Lillian.

"Do ya understand what I am sayin'? An' I will tell ya this will happen ta you too in time, if'n ya trust a man, any man, with any part of yurself. I am a woman shamed by the vile, indecent acts of a man with no morals. He is gone. Now I will be the proper, grievin' widow fer the rest a my days. Perhaps then society will accept me in spite of him an' his sinful ways."

Lillian held back, strangely quiet, trying to let her mind absorb all she was being told. It was as if two sides of morality and decency were being presented to her. The one where her father had walked and the one where her mother had, according to her, been forced to live. Her father had spoken of love, honor and forgiveness. Her mother spoke of nothing but bitterness and hatreds.

Abigale crossed the room to stare at her reflection in a wall mirror. She did not admire what she saw staring back. Instead she saw the reflection of a woman drawn and bitter by circumstances brought into her life not of her choosing. Turning her head slightly, she stared past her own image to see that of her daughter which was reflected in the same mirror.

"The Sterling House will survive. I am sure ya will see ta thet." She faced her. "Am I not right?" she said, allowing veils of reclusiveness to fall into place. "I believe I will go ta take my rest. It has been a wearisome day an' I require a bit of tonic fer my nerves."

Abigale turned to walk out of the room. She stopped and looked back at her still very quiet daughter. Her eyes narrowed again as she said, "I warn ya, Lillian, ya will rue the day when ya trust yur heart to a man."

She closed the door and quietly sought the comforts of her own bedroom chamber.

*   *   *

Lillian sank onto a small fainting couch, stared at that closed door for a long time, allowing all she had just heard to find its place in her logic. She was angry and confused. Feeling as if the weight of two worlds was resting on her. As a child, she had sensed there was much which was wrong between her mother and father but had no idea as to the truth of the matter.

Her father had told her that love was the right thing to feel, to seek and to have. Her mother was telling her it would lead to ruination. All of what she had been told was about their lives, their circumstances, and not hers. She was of Sterling quality and would seek only Sterling quality to be a part of her life. There would be no lies and no deceptions. She had lost her father to a horrible and untimely death. It was possible her mother as well to the torturous memories consuming the woman's mind.

mother was in no mental state to do these things. At least not right away.

Out of respect, Abigale would be consulted, but Lillian seriously doubted she would be that helpful until the bitterness and grieving period was over for her, if it ever would be.

She went to her father's office room, but saw it much differently than when she used to run into this room and beg for his attention when she knew he was attending to business.

Lillian stared down at her father's leather topped desk. She was seeing past the tidy piles of papers, odd files of paid and unpaid bills of lading and other documents of an alien nature to her. It was all strange and foreign to her. This was her father's domain and the true heartbeat of the Sterling House. But, she was also shrewd enough to know that without her knowing it, and by a severe stroke of fate, she had become the heartbeat and it would be up to her to manage and control the family business.

First of all, she had to determine just where the Sterling House stood from a financial standpoint. Where was the money coming from? The saloon? The gaming? The general food area downstairs? The private dining rooms on the second floor? It has all grown out of necessity and need but was it all necessary? Even before she had gone away to school, she had seen money being spent by many patrons in the Sterling House. She had seen her father, and on some occasions her mother, counting money in this very room and knew of one secret place where her father had kept a lock box and now she wondered if there had been any kind of bank accounts? The Sterling House obviously had a monetary standing or it would not still be standing.

For a moment, she wondered if she was possibly too young to assume so much responsibility and was only too aware she would have to be cautious about her abilities in this man's world of finance and business. However, Lillian Anne Sterling was stubborn. More importantly, determined. The house would stand and it would stand under her direction.

"Uncle Charley!" she called out. *He will know,* she thought and this was where she would begin with logic and questions about what to do with the Sterling House. Her home and their home as well.

Chapter
Six

Death, dying, graves being dug or funerals did not stop the passing of days. Business had to stay alert if people were to survive life and the living of it. As Lillian and Charley had directed, the Sterling House was reopened and fully operational. Profitability walked back through the doors.

Much to her chagrin, Abigale was fully aware her daughter and Charley Gaynor had taken over the management of the Sterling House. She was uncertain as to what she should do; however, felt it prudent she let her feelings be known.

"Yur father would not approve a what yur doin'." she said to Lillian as they sat in an upper dining room at what was intended to be an enjoyable breakfast.

"What?" Lillian questioned as she touched the corner of her mouth with one of the Sterling House monogrammed linens.

"Ya know what I mean." Abigale responded as she moved back slightly in her chair.

"No, mother, not exactly." Lillian was cautious.

"May I remind you," Abigale continued, her lips tight against her teeth, "Charley Gaynor has no legal say in this house an' yur only 18 years old. Not old enough ta assume the business of this house."

Lillian paused in her thinking. She chose her words carefully as she responded.

"First of all, mother, may I be so bold as to remind that Paw Paw was only 20 when he started the Sterling House. Furthermore, what better business arrangement than to have the man who began the business with him oversee the general well being of this house."

Abigale let a darker veil of anger set into her thinking as she snapped her mind shut to the words she wanted to say. What Lillian had said might be the truth although she wanted to refute it. With grimness in her tone, she calmly said, "Have it yur way, young lady, but remember this. Ya will rue the day ya have taken the Sterling House away from me."

With that remark, Abigale silently rose from the table and staunchly walked out of the room leaving no room for discourse.

Lillian sat there for a long time, staring down at a china plate filled with its cold ham and eggs. She had not taken the Sterling House away from her mother. In her opinion she had stopped it from floundering when her father had been killed. She and the Sterling House had no other choice.

All that mattered was that the experienced cooks were back in the kitchen. The serving girls worked long hours. The dish washer did her best to keep up with the wiping, drying and polishing of the silver, china and crystal.

Out of curiosity about what was happening in the Sterling House, along with her penchant for control, Abigale was beginning to make more and more appearances on the lower levels. She had foregone the mourning veils, but still wore her somber clothing as she greeted diners and attempted to keep order with the reservations.

The Widow Sterling ordered more elaborate mourning dresses from the fashionable House of Worth, Paris, France. She had made it quite clear she had every intension of wearing them for the rest of her days. Dressed in this subdued attire, she once again gave strict orders in the kitchen where the cooks politely listened and then quietly ignored as they were quite practiced to the recipes of the Sterling House. The hired help stayed out of the way of this brooding woman in her black dresses who leaned on a cane, which served no valid purpose other than to make her seem more foreboding. They much preferred their orders coming from the young Miss Sterling who was firm but gracious with them.

Jonas Gregory, when not serving drinks in the saloon, was quite busy overseeing the renovations necessary for his move to the Sterling House. It had been decided, much to Abigale's dismay, that there needed to be a man on the premises at all hours and Jonas was the obvious choice. To allow him privacy, one of the private dining rooms was being converted to sleeping quarters. It was logical and it made sense for the safety of the Sterling woman. Abigale had finally, after much argument, sullenly agreed.

Erwin would stay at the Big House with Charley, but would continue his piano playing as he helped in the saloon. He had also shown a fair sense of figuring the numbers, balancing the Sterling House accounts while keeping ledgers and inventory. Lillian had rapidly agreed to let Charley manage the affairs of the saloon, while she learned the nuances that made, and would keep, the Sterling House a place of refinement and quality. That primarily meant that Soolie's old recipes were followed to the last grain of sugar and sprinkle of cloves or cinnamon. She was extremely glad these old recipes had been written down.

It quickly became obvious Abigale was not the only one with keen intelligence for what was above the average when it came to pleasing the senses while one was dining. The crystal glittered, the china gleamed and the silver glistened perhaps even more than under her mother's direction. She had learned more than she knew while at the Wibscott School.

*　　*　　*

It was early in the day, with Lillian and Charley having coffee in the kitchen area. Both felt pleased with the recovery efforts of the Sterling House after closing for the funeral days.

"Baby Lily," Charley said, "you have done well. But I reckon you are not Baby Lily anymore."

She smiled, recalling some of her first memories of this man and how much she loved him. "I will always be your Baby Lily." she said, stirring her coffee, blowing across the top of it before gingerly sipping the steaming liquid.

She kept her gaze on the dark liquid. *Do I dare?* She wondered. It was not the first time the priorities of proper mourning had been, or would be, set aside in the Sterling household. Although it was considered improper by upper society's standards for ladies, especially the unwed ladies, she could not stop herself from asking.

"The man, Uncle Charley, the one who carried Paw Paw up the stairs that night?"

Lillian cautiously questioned, "I saw him at the funeral, and he was most respectful of the family, allowing us our grieving time. What has happened to him? Where is he now?" Charley took a toothpick out of his mouth and was glad his Spanish friend had not left. In fact, PJ had been asking him about her and now she was asking about him. Conditions had been right for them to meet, but circumstances and the violent actions of another had kept them apart. It was time for that to stop and let life move on for them. Had he, too, not stayed silent for far too long when he should have spoken up regarding what should have been an affair of his heart? Andrew would never be forgotten, but he was gone and laid to rest. Let Abigale continue with her sanctimonious grieving. Lillian needed to live a life with the living. "He is still here in Denver City and I have seen him on several

57

occasions. He has asked after your well being each time I have seen him."

"I feel I need to properly thank him for his assistance." She stopped, not sure how to phrase further comments about this man, who was a stranger to her. She felt certain many would think it brash or imprudent of her to inquire of him especially so soon after her father's death.

Charley could not help but note caution and poised restraint. Lillian Anne Sterling was not only beautiful, but certainly a young lady of extreme qualities In time, they would not be practiced but perfected.

"I could arrange a formal introduction, if would like." He saw a quick sparkle come into her blue eyes, but she quickly dropped her dark lashes over those intense eyes so he could not read her thoughts.

"Yes, Uncle Charley. Please do so if the gentleman is agreeable."

You little scamp, he thought. *Of course he is agreeable and more than a little interested, young lady.* But he said, "As soon as possible."

"Thank you," she said, as she quickly dismissed the conversation she had rehearsed over and over in her mind. Her heart pounded with an unexplainable anticipation that threatened to expose her true thinking as she tried to maintain her composure.

*　　*　　*

So it was that Paris Jacob LaRoche de la Montoya found himself once again in the upper rooms of the Sterling House, but under much more pleasant circumstances than the first time he had seen these rooms.

Out of respect, the drapes were drawn, the wall pictures were still heavily veiled and cut flowers in a variety of arrangements graced the room. He now had opportunity to fully assess the grandeur of this

room and knew, as it was quite obvious, that much money had been
invested into a wealthy lifestyle for the Sterling family.

He was properly groomed and balanced his tea cup, perfectly, on
his knee, as he knew would be expected. From evaluating the Sterling
women, he suspected the expectation came from the mother and not so
much from the daughter.

Mrs. Sterling was seated across from him, dressed in a proper,
somber mourning dress including a thin black veil covering her face.
She had obviously been a most beautiful woman at one time, but he
sensed a bitterness in her that went far beyond the grieving of a recent
widow. Lillian Anne, on the other hand, although dressed appropriately
for a daughter still in mourning of her father, sparkled with a radiance
the dark clothing could not disguise. He also noticed, when she turned
her head at a certain angle, there was a modest jeweled pin in her dark
hair.

Jonas, who had brought the tea, had walked over to the door and
now stood there, awkwardly, not sure what to do.

"Thank you, Jonas," Abigale said with an air of superiority which
she hoped would convey her command of the room. "Ya may leave us
now."

"Yes, Ma'am," he said, quietly, and quickly left the room. The
only places he was truly comfortable was behind the bar downstairs,
over at the Big House or his own sleeping quarters. He insisted on
keeping it all modest, not wanting elegance even though he was
surrounded by it.

Lillian poured the tea. Despite the horrible incident the night she
had met her intriguing guest, she still recalled his affect on her. It was
the same only stronger with strange urges rising in her she could not
explain. She had to fan herself and breath very slowly to control her

speech. "Uncle Charley, will you also take tea this afternoon?" she asked, addressing her uncle.

"No thank you, Lillian," he responded and took a seat close to the window. Inwardly he was amused. PJ was on his own with these women and something told him, the young Spaniard would fare well. Very well.

"Senor Montoya, thank you fer comin'," Abigale said, releasing her veil to sip her tea, letting it fall delicately to one side of her face.

"Thank you for receiving me, considering the grief of this family due to your recent loss. I wanted to express my condolences as my business will soon take me away from here. I also wanted to be properly introduced to your daughter, Senorita Sterling."

"Yur condolences are gratefully received, Senor Montoya," Abigale said, shrewdly studying the man. In her mind, his intent was more than obvious and it had nothing to do with his expression of condolence. "Yur conduct is duly noted an' greatly appreciated."

"Senor Montoya," Lillian said, hearing and seeing the tenseness rise in her mother, wishing she was not in the room with them, "what is the business that will take you away from our fair city?"

"Senorita Sterling," he said absorbing every facet of her being from where he sat. In Hispania, his homeland and California as well, he had seen many blue eyed, dark haired Spaniard women of beauty, but never had he beheld such a woman of beauty as this one. "My poppa has great interest in the cattle business from California to Mexico, Texas and into your Colorado. I am about his business but must return to California soon as he is called elsewhere on family matters."

"You are from California?" Lillian asked, feeling his presence move all around her, and though her as he held her thoughts touching

60

her heart with a warmth she did not understand but was fully accepting.

"As I have stated, my homeland is Hispania, Cordoba, Spain, but my family now resides in the Southern part of California near San Diego. Might I inquire the same of you? Is the Sterling family originally from Colorado?"

Before Lillian could respond, her mother broke into the generous warmth she saw and felt radiating between her daughter and this interloper. "The Sterling family is from the South, a state known as Georgia; however, Lillian was born here." She studied him for a moment, feeling this introduction had been in error, but would have to be graciously abandoned. "We owe ya a great debt of gratitude fer yur efforts on our tragic night." She did not want to appear rude, but perhaps if she kept the conversation formal, he would leave sooner.

Paris Jacob lowered his gaze to the tea cup and the dark liquid in the cup. With measured words, he carefully said, "Senoras, I am so sorry I was not quick enough to have stopped the knife." He was strangely quiet as he looked first at Abigale and then at Lillian. He had lived those moments over and over in his mind, and knew he could not have stopped what happened. But it did not stop his wishing he could have.

Charley said, "It was all so fast. We both tried." He, too, recalled that night and would forever hear that pistol shot. He fell silent, not wanting to talk about it any more than necessary.

Lillian cleared her throat. "We are grateful, Senor Montoya." She carefully watched him and, although not proper under the circumstances, felt her lips forming a small smile.

Abigale also was watching him, but she was not smiling.

For a moment, a very strange quiet gripped the room.

Lillian held her posture a little straighter realizing she had to guide them out of the moment's gloom. She had so many questions and it was becoming obvious her mother was not going to ask the socially polite questions when one needed the socially polite answers. Plus, she did not wish to talk about her father's death.

Lillian proceeded. "Forgive my awkward curiosity, but your name is so unusual. Paris Jacob LaRoche de la Montoya." she repeated and hoped she had said it all and said it correctly.

Her mother shot her a disapproving look. Lillian ignored her and Charley had to stifle a chuckle. Abigale certainly had her hands full with this young woman, who had gone away from them sassy and saucy. She had returned with elegance, poise and charm along with a refined sass and sauce.

"No forgiveness is necessary." Paris assured her and Lillian felt herself being drawn closer to the warmth of the man as he explained. "I am Spanish from my father and French from my mother. LaRoche from the French and Montoya from the house of the Spanish bloodline. My mother was born in Paris, France. To her, it is the most beautiful city in the world. My first name for where she loved the most, and," he concluded, "Jacob from one of my mother's favorite stories in the Bible, Jacob's Ladder."

"Most impressive," Lillian said and then asked, "But how do I address you? Do I call Senor Montoya or Monsieur LaRoche or your Christian names which are also quite formal."

Oh, please do tell us, Abigale thought as she was certainly not impressed, barely able to wait to hear his answer.

The man with the very formal long name, turned his dark eyes toward Lillian and her blue eyes favorably met his. "When we are in politest of society, call me Senor Montoya, polite society, Paris Jacob," he said, never letting his gaze leave her face. "When we are alone, call me Paris."

She heard her mother take in a sharp breath and Charley muffle a snigger. " Senor Montoya, are we to have private moments?" Lillian asked, unable to stop herself as she met him equally with her words.

"Senorita Sterling, that is my intent."

Abigale set her tea cup back in its saucer with a slight clatter on the china. She stared at the man with her disdain growing. This was a most distressing situation which needed a father's firm touch. For a moment she directed her attention toward Charley who very quickly averted his gaze.

Abigale cleared her throat. " Senor Montoya, I must ask. Are yur intensions toward my daughter honorable?" She felt the question critical to protect her interest.

Lillian cut her eyes toward her mother, uncertain what to think but said nothing as she too waited for the answer from this man of dark mystery and a fire which was touching her very soul.

"Senora Sterling, that they are."

After that statement, Abigale became partially reticent during the time Paris Jacob Montoya remained. Lillian did not want him to leave, listening to his every word as she felt his slightly accented voice surround and hold her.

The socially acceptable amount of time passed. After all polite conversation had been exchanged, Charley Gaynor escorted his young Spanish friend from the Sterling House, congratulating him on his approach and success with the Sterling women. Other than Buckland Kavanaugh, he had never seen anyone so deftly walk around Abigale with words to leave her rebounding for something intelligent to say.

As Charley walked him out of the Sterling House, Paris Jacob quietly confided to him, "Upon my return, it is my intent to ask for that woman's hand in marriage. I feel you will support me in this matter?" he ventured.

Charley Gaynor smiled the biggest smile he had felt since Andrew's death, rolled his eyes up to a darkening evening sky, then back at Paris. He enthusiastically shook his hand and said, "Hallelujah, yes! Can't say that I know of a finer young man to court the Miss Sterling? As her male guardian, I wholeheartedly approve."

"My many thanks to you, Charley. I will return when my family is properly cared for, the Sterling grieving is fully over and the time is right." he said getting on his horse and riding away into the gathering twilight of one more beautiful Colorado night.

That evening, two women watched Paris Jacob LaRoche de la Montoya ride away from the Sterling House.

Lillian Anne Sterling who saw him as a man she had great emotional curiosity about; a man who had aroused her awakening passions; a man who without her overt knowledge, had entered her heart. Those emotions had come about with a keen, unspoken promise to explore her passion as they had become aroused. She had committed to her memory every detail of his handsome face, his light olive complexion darkened by the sun, his very dark eyes, and certainly black hair. There was even a tiny mole on his right cheek. A sound in his voice like no other and sensuous lips that seemed to invite her to explore places she had never been.

Abigale Westmoreland Sterling breathed a sigh of relief as she saw him mix with, and disappear into, the crowds of Larimer Street. No matter what his breeding, background or origins, this was not the man for her daughter.

Spaniard, indeed! In her opinion, he was nothing more than a common Mexican trail hand, following cattle from one place to another while he shirked the duties of home and hearth. In so many words, he had admitted this was what he was doing. Trailing cattle out of Mexico into Colorado this season and God only knew where he would be the next season.

This man could never be faithful, never be true, never abide with holy wedding vows. Vows he might take while his heart would be elsewhere on the end of some dusty trail with some dark skinned woman. Paris Jacob LaRoche de la Montoya might have some fancy name but he held little to no sway in Denver and certainly not at the Sterling House. Abigale Westmoreland Sterling would see to that. That was if he ever returned.

Chapter
Seven

In the high country of the magnificent Rocky Mountains, the snows receded, bears awakened from long slumbers, green leaves came back to the aspens and the meadow flowers bloomed. On the western slope of Colorado, near the confluence of the Gunnison and the Spanish named Rio Colorado, the newly established town of Grand Junction received its railroad lines that forever linked it to civilization.

On Larimer Street, in Denver, under the watchful eye of Charley Gaynor, the bar keeping skills of Jonas Gregory, and the piano entertainment of the quiet Erwin Frederson, the Sterling House Saloon continued to prosper. Cards were dealt, money exchanged hands, drinks were poured and drunks staggered out the front doors.

Yet the pulse had slowed. All along Larimer Street were so many other drinking establishments for men to frequent. Although there were loyal patrons to the Sterling House, it was obvious that many who had came there before had been there because of one person. Andrew Wesley Sterling. Without him behind that long cherry wood and dark brown mahogany bar to pour drinks and pass the time of day, or night, the atmosphere had changed. Jonas Gregory poured a decent drink, but he was introverted when it came to conversing with the patrons.

Erwin played the piano well and many came to be entertained, but his audience was not enough to fill the Sterling House coffers with their monetary contributions for drinks or food.

Charley still dealt a decent and more than generous hand of Spanish Monte. However, many said his heart was not in the game as it once had been.

For the first time since the Sterling House had been built, the restaurant along with the private dining rooms were doing more business than the saloon. During the winter months, Lillian had learned the business well and was aware of the sensitivity of every aspect of the Sterling House.

She was apprehensive and concerned. Their livelihood depended on serving many drinks, dealing many cards and, of course, serving many meals.

As she had learned the restaurant business from her mother who was, even in her bitter, belligerent state, still a shrewd business woman, Lillian quickly grasped that if they were to survive, they must change to follow the times.

Lillian realized that one of her greatest, and closest, food competitors was Charpiot's Delmonico of the West. She had taken dinner there, just for comparison's sake, finding their roast duck to be succulent and well flavored.

She could smell the juiciness of the sizzling steaks as they passed by her table to be served to other diners, and was delighted by the Delmonico Potatoes fricasseed in a creamy mushroom sauce. She had tasted the pastries; however, in her culinary opinion, although excellent to the pallet, could not be compared to the desserts and pastries of Soolie's which were still being prepared using the old recipes. Many restaurants and saloons competed all along busy Larimer as well as surrounding streets. Still the Sterling House was held its own with the foods, desserts and liquors being served.

It was, however, just one block away at the 1800 block of Larimer where there stood the greatest nemesis of the Sterling House.

The world famous, and infamous by odd reputations, Windsor Hotel. This five-story monstrous building was constructed of rhyolite lava stone which had been railed in from Castle Rock, a settlement south of the city. Within its massive walls, it seemed to contain a small city. The main entrance was at least 20 feet wide and the Sterling House could have fit inside the main lobby of this building. Inside one could find, it was reported, seven miles of yard wide Axminster Brussels carpeting leading to over 300 rooms.

The pompous, sturdy walls surrounded parlors, bedrooms, restaurants, saloons, shops, offices and utility rooms. The Windsor was extremely proud of its separate dining rooms for men only, men with women and one for women with children as well as the very popular ladies ordinary rooms kept intensely elaborate for the haute ladies of Denver's elite.

"I will not enter thet place of abomination," Abigale very rudely stated when her daughter suggested they take a tour and a meal in one of the ordinaries to judge their competition.

Lillian studied her with great questioning in her eyes. It was true, the building was ostentatious, almost garish with its dimensions.

The building had Otis Steam elevators for those daring enough to ride them. The rooms hosted diamond dust mirrors, black walnut bedroom sets and gold plated door knobs in the bridal suites. Steam heat and hot and cold running water was an amenity in each room.

Lillian did not consider it to be an establishment of abomination unless one considered the stories of those who privately visited the Windsor through the tunnels that reportedly led from the Union Rail Station and the Denver City Cable Railway Company. It was also rumored that thirsty gentlemen could place their well polished boots on a barroom floor with 3,000 silver dollars embedded in the floor. That still did not make it an evil place.

"Closer to 4,000, if I had my guess," Charley said, as he had seen the legendary barroom floor. He excused himself and grinned as he walked away from where the ladies sat drinking tea. The number of coins did not matter. The fact they were there—did.

"An' I suppose it all comes from the ill gotten gains of thet lecherous Horace Tabor." Abigale called after him.

Charley chose to ignore her as he knew only too well where this conversation would go if allowed her the reins.

She dropped another spoonful of sugar in her tea and stirred it a bit too vigorously, as a few drops splattered over the rim of the teacup. "Never could git this black tea a Soolie's sweet enough," she said as she laid the porcelain handled teaspoon in the tiny tea spoon rest.

In my privacy, I would have my laudanum with my tea, she thought, *or maybe a drop a sherry*. "Thank you for joinin' us, Mr. Gaynor," she called after him.

"My pleasure, Mrs. Sterling." Charley caught Lillian's eye and winked, as he walked out of the room, glad to have a saloon downstairs to require his attention. He had agreed to mid-morning tea with the Sterling ladies primarily because Lillian had asked him to join them. Abigale Sterling seemed to grow worse with the passing of each day but he would not slight Lillian Anne's request even though the duration of time, in this case, was the drinking of one cup of tea.

"Mother, I don't know what mean by ill gotten gains. Mr. Tabor is rich from his silver mines and has invested well. His building is strong competition. We as restaurant and saloon owners, should know about our competition." She enjoyed her tea savoring the rich darkness of it.

"Oh, I know only too well what thet man is about," Abigale said, seizing on only part of Lillian's words. "He has illegally divorced thet lovely wife a his, Augusta Tabor, an' sought this illicit love tryst with . . . with, what is thet harlot's name? Baby Doe? "'Baby', indeed!

She is nothin' more than a blonde home wrecker, takin' thet which was not hers ta take. They parade around all of Denver City in thet shiny black carriage with the gold trim. Then return ta thet house of debauchery they call a hotel where he keeps her. Jist a place fer 'em ta hide what they do. At least the rightful Mrs. Tabor was spared public humiliation by a child out of wedlock."

Lillian dropped her gaze to the teacup, bit her lower lip to let the moment pass. Her mother certainly had a way with words. Lillian also knew where a lot of them were being learned.

"Mother, I think spend far too much time with the ladies who come here for their afternoon tea and cake. Especially Hortence Wilson. Do you have nothing better to do with your time?" Although very busy with Sterling House business in the early and mid-afternoons, she had not missed seeing the tea drinking hour of her mother's with several known ladies of the Larimer Street's upper echelon when this band of pea hens sucked up the gossip as readily as they did the tea.

Abigale glared at her daughter, her dark eyes narrowed. "Do not speak poorly of Mrs. Wilson. The poor dear lost it all in thet dreadful fire the night ya was born.

Furthermore," she added, "it was only by the generous grace of her brother, who took her in after she lost her millinery shop in thet fire, thet she has a roof over her head. She might be a mere guardian in his house but she is still a great lady of refinement an' a righteous addition ta this, our community." She set her cup down, picked up a cake and slowly bit into it knowing her daughter could not refute what was being said about Hortence Wilson. *She dare not,* Abigale thought, most confident in her stand.

"I know of Mrs. Wilson's fate that night," Lillian said, "and I know she knew Paw Paw before you came here from Georgia. I am aware, she has not had an easy life. I merely wish you would not talk with her quite so much about the past and the business of others."

"We will talk about what we choose ta talk about. I go nowhere. I see no one. How do ya think I find out what is out an' about in this city of cities?"

Lillian fought to remain calm. Reasoning with her mother was beyond the capabilities she possessed. She started to say something when Charley came back into the room, slightly breathless from his climbing the stairs.

"Baby Lily," he said, "have a caller."

"Ya always have callers which ya jist keep on turnin' away. An' Charley, it would be most pleasin' if'n ya would stop callin' her 'Baby Lily'. She is no longer a baby," her mother said as she rose to her feet. "I am gonna go ta my room. I am sure it is no one I care ta see this mornin'." Without consideration, or further concern, as there was always someone who wished to call at the Sterling House, she left the room.

Abigale did not wish to defend her stand with Hortence Wilson. She also felt certain Lillian's fears from the Windsor were unfounded. They were prosperous and doing well as far as she was concerned. Besides, the thought of a few drops of sherry did strongly appeal to her. This required the privacy of her room.

Charley waited until Abigale was out of the room. He then very carefully placed the silver tray in Lillian's hand. He watched with quiet anticipation as she picked up the silver edged card, turned it over. She blinked hard as she read the silver embossed name.

Paris Jacob LaRoche de la Montoya

Lillian Anne Sterling could hardly believe the name she had read on the elegant little card. Although she was trembling inside and could barely keep her thoughts in logical order, she managed to say, "Please, Uncle Charley, show the gentleman to the front sitting room. I will receive him there. Will you please serve tea for us?" Although the business of the Sterling House had consumed her days and wakeful hours, she reserved a secret, sacred place in her heart which had been held silent, waiting for the return of this man.

Time had shadowed his physical memory, yet her spirit still felt the intensity of her hours with him. She walked with sure steps to the front sitting room of the Sterling House reminding herself to breathe as she took a seat and waited for him to be escorted to where she waited. She had dreamt of this moment along with the words she would say. The moment had came so quickly, she felt her throat was dry with her mind empty of words. Lillian closed her eyes, forced herself to breath steadily, as she waited what seemed an eternity for the door to open.

*   *   *

If Lillian Anne Sterling thought she was experiencing confused emotions of anticipation, Paris Jacob Montoya was now intensely aware of every emotion he, too, had felt. His anxiety of waiting had only been quelled by his family matters. Many times, he had faced the rising sun and wondered if she had waited. Soon his questioning mind would be satisfied.

In silence, Charley escorted him up the stairs to the sitting room. Beyond the moment of his walking into the Sterling House Saloon, greeting Charley and expressing his desire to once again be presented to the Senorita Sterling, he had no words to say other than the ones he wished to say to her.

72

Charley reached for the door's handles and then stopped. He winked at Paris. "It may not be proper protocol, but I will leave to your own."

Lillian Anne Sterling was seated; however stood when he entered the room. They both stopped. She waited in front of the richly tapestried Rocaille chair and he quietly stood just inside the mahogany doors that Charley had closed behind him.

Just as the first time, it was a memory captured between them when blue eyes first met dark brown and two hearts knew of an infinite destiny. In a heartbeat, they knew it was to be the last of innocent moments between them.

Lillian extended her hand and Paris took it. He leaned forward but instead of kissing the back of her hand, he turned it over and kissed her palm. He straightened up and slowly pulled her to him folding her into his arms to hold her to him.

No words were needed. He had dreamt of this from the time he had left the Sterling House until this moment when he could hold her close to his heart, breathing in the complete essence of this woman.

"Forgive me, Senorita Sterling," he said, "but I have thought of little else since our parting."

Lillian caught her breath and pulled away a little from him. "Senor Montoya, you have a way with you but I too wished for this," she quietly said, feeling that unexplainable power once again move through her.

Before they could pursue the moment further, there was a light knock on the door. "I have requested tea for us," she said and called out, "please come in."

They parted and Lillian sat down, fanning herself to try and relieve the flush she was feeling.

Charley was not fooled for a moment. No one could miss the blush on Lillian's cheeks or the satisfaction spread across PJ's face. Charley Gaynor was exceedingly pleased. This was right for both of them. "Your tea, Miss Lillian," he said bringing in the tray and setting it on a side table. "Allow me to pour." He was smiling, unable to contain his own joy and happiness.

Charley poured the tea and excused himself. Although it might not be properly acceptable, he felt there was no need of a chaperone for these two young people who needed to be left alone to decide their own destiny. He paused for a moment outside the door and then walked away, refusing to eves drop. At the moment, this was a private affair.

*   *   *

Lillian watched every move Paris made, from the stirring of the tea, the dropping of a dollop of cream in the steaming liquid and the adding of sugar. She was nervous, yet strangely calm as all of this seemed so very natural to her.

Paris equally watched her as he set the tea aside fully accepting what he felt was true and from his heart.

He was not certain how or why it had happened. But he had fallen in love with her without finding out who she truly was or even being with her. This was part of what he had every intension of changing, being only too aware both their family circumstances seemed to stand in the way of their being together.

"Senor Montoya, you do me honor by coming to see me while you are visiting Denver City," Lillian said, initiating the conversation.

"Lillian," he said dropping the 'Senorita Sterling' formality. "As I requested before, please call me Paris or Paris Jacob. Have you forgotten?" he said in a teasing manner. "I assure you, the privilege is mine to be here with you."

"And I assure you, Paris," she said, "I have forgotten nothing," she responded with a twinkle in her eyes. "I am so pleased you are here," she said with a certain boldness in her remark."

Realizing her boldness, she questioned, "Are you again on your family business?" She hoped to cover what could be considered a social blunder. She was trained to begin with light conversation, although her mind and senses were racing to complicated places which were far from a light nature.

He was delighted with every aspect of her. *Ah, the pleasantries*, he thought. "Yes," he responded, allowing her the recovery time. "However, this time I am not trailing the cattle. More so hoping to attract investors."

"Investors?" she inquired.

"There was a time when California was a good place," he continued, "with much opportunity for the Mexican people and we Spaniards who live there. But circumstances have changed much which we, my family and others of the great Spanish land grants, have taken for granted.

"It seems the United States government does not honor that which Spain and Mexico once possessed. Although it has been several years since California became a state, sadly, internal boundaries have changed greatly which has affected many.

"It seems even the weather has frowned upon us as there is also much drought in California. Our cattle must have water and good feeding areas to survive. I am hoping to take the main herd back to Mexico before it is too late. That too is costly which requires an investor.

"However, I did not come here to talk about my family business." He stopped to stare at her seeing where a little of the youthful innocence she had possessed the first time they had met, had fallen away from her. She did not appear older yet somehow wiser behind those intense blue eyes.

He picked up his tea and drank. "Good," he said indicating the tea and set the cup back down.

"It is the black teas we serve at the Sterling House. Something brought here from our Southern home by a freed slave woman named Soolie who was a part of our family for many, many years." She let every intimate detail of this man find a place in her mind vowing she would not allow them to ever fade again.

"Am I to take it your family held slaves?" he asked, letting the conversation travel in that direction wanting to discover everything he could about her.

"Yes," she responded, thankful to let her mind go away from the intensity of how she was feeling. "Both the Westmoreland family of my mother and the Sterling family which was my father's."

"Do you still have land holdings in the South?"

"No, the war destroyed it all from what I am told. The carpetbaggers, the banks and attorneys claimed the land for back taxes doling it out to the share croppers and freed slaves after the war. My father was very wise in his decision to leave and come West when he did."

"Then he did not fight in the war between your states?"

"No, sir, he did not," she said. "He struggled with other issues of survival here when Denver City was very young and unsettled." She looked around the room and his gaze followed hers.

"All of this began in a dingy high wall tent with, as I am told, the nude painting which still graces the saloon, and a jar of rotted pickled eggs." She said as she warmly recalled the stories she had been told.

"In the beginning, it was not easy for him, or my Uncle Charley, to keep a business prosperous. They managed by their own means. My beautiful home and the Sterling House business is the end result of that work. The saloon, where it all began, and the dining areas which my mother added when she arrived here from Georgia"

"I have seen the painting and knew it was very old," he commented. "But rotted pickled eggs?" he questioned.

Lillian laughed and let the question drop.

"Because you are still here and because I saw patrons downstairs when I arrived, I am to understand the Sterling House has fared well this past season?" he questioned still taking in every detail of this woman who sat before him, calmly sipping her tea with only flickers of emotion in her intensely blue eyes.

Have I been wrong? he questioned, but then noticed her hands were trembling slightly and her breathing was quick and shallow as she too was searching for the proper and correct words as she kept her eyes shielded from him beneath her dark lashes.

"Learning the business of my father has not been easy. I have had excellent help from Mr. Gaynor, Jonas Gregory and Erwin. They are all supportive.

"My mother is not fit in such affairs as there is much more to keeping the doors open than just understanding what kind of beef to procure for the plate, which champagnes to have in abundance for the wine pallets which are so tempted, and where the best cinnamons are imported which grace the sweet cakes.

"Like you, we have governmental problems, not state or federal so much, but the City of Denver, which allows those in prestigious and lawful places to extract money in order for us to remain operational." She stopped, waiting to see if he would catch the direction of her words.

"Bribery of officials is nothing new," he said, feeling his own frustration being powerless to stop what was happening to his

California home and also sensing she was facing angry issues of survival as well.

Lillian was most understanding and waited for him to direct the course of their conversation. She knew he had not come here to talk of this yet did not wish to appear too forward in their conversation.

Leaning forward, he said, "Lillian, I am most respectful of your family and of mine. If that were not true, I would not have stayed away in California the past year attending to mine. Also seeing you have wisely attended to yours here."

"Yes," she replied and leaned forward slightly.

With a firm, clear voice, he said, "I should speak with your family first but your circumstances dictate I speak with you. What passed between us a year ago is still strong in my mind. I must know, is it also strong in yours?"

Without immediate comment, she rose, crossed the room to let the street below be her focal point for the moment. Although these were words she wanted to hear, she did not want to appear too eager to answer.

A Tivoli Brewing Beer Wagon clattered past. Lillian barely saw it as her mind and senses reeled with wanting to have this man hold her, touch her in the ways she had only imagined. "Yes." she responded. "The memory of you and the desire for your return helped me surmount the many difficulties I face here."

She turned to find him standing right behind her. "I truly know nothing of you. I am not aware of the feelings of love. My own feelings are strange to me in ways I have yet to understand. All I am aware of is that I have them."

"You will learn," Paris said. Without taking her in his arms, he kissed her lightly on the lips, holding back the urgency that was in him.

Lillian felt her knees weaken and he caught her in his arms, holding her to him as he kissed her neck, shoulders, face and found her willing lips.

It was all she had dreamed, imagined and wanted to have happen since she had first met him. Strange, new fires kindled to fire her emotions. She pulled away. "Is this what love feels like?" she asked him.

Paris gently led her to a fainting couch where they sat down. "Yes," he answered, his dark eyes searching her blue ones. "I am not clear what we should do. I can assure you, we have your Uncle Charley's blessing, but should I speak with your mother? I will not disrespect you or your family."

With a firmness in her voice, Lillian responded. "I would not recommend you speak with my mother." She paused. "She has her difficulties."

Paris nodded, not exactly sure what Lillian was meaning by difficulties as he recalled Abigale Sterling and how he had felt when he had sat in the Sterling House parlor before. He had a feeling the woman could be very unpleasant if it suited her. Although he said nothing, he would consider Lillian's words to be a warning. Still yet, the woman would have to become aware of his intent to marry this young woman who he was convinced had stolen his heart.

"Your thoughts, Paris Jacob?" she asked, touching his face with the palm of her hand.

"Might I suggest we have dinner tonight and discuss how we feel?"

" Senor Montoya, that would be lovely." she said. "There is a place I would enjoy going, if I might be so bold as to suggest."

"By all means, my love," he said, taking the liberty with his expression.

Lillian blushed. She had not missed what he said. "I am told the Windsor has fine dining," she said quickly regaining her composure.

"Amazing," he said, smiling broadly. "That is where I am staying. As much as I don't want to leave you, I must attend to some business this afternoon, but will call for you at eight."

Hand in hand, they rose together. He put his arms around her, stared lovingly into her blue eyes, but said nothing more before he left the room.

After Paris Jacob left, Lillian had to sit down and collect her thoughts. She felt happy, giddy and silly. Just as she had been as a young girl, she wanted to take off her shoes so she could run barefoot down to the river.

She felt like that little girl. Yet like a woman just embarking on a great adventure. She touched her lips and remembered the warmth of his. All of this was hers to keep and would be memories to be cherished for as long as she had memory. He was her first love and would be her only love because somehow she knew there could be no other.

*   *   *

Lillian thought the day would never conclude. She had great difficulty keeping her thoughts on the Sterling House tasks. She watched the pies comes from the ovens to cool for the delectable desserts after steak and roast dinners later in the evening. Vegetables simmered in pots to be served with the meats. Ham slices soaked in their own sugar cured juices waiting to be lightly seared just before being served with succulent sweet potatoes.

During the afternoon, sweet cakes disappear along with pots of steaming tea. Lillian actually missed seeing a few water spots on the silverware. Her obvious lack of attention to Sterling House details had most certainly not escaped her mother's intense scrutiny.

Abigale was very much aware of what was causing this behavior as well as what was going on between her daughter and this unwelcome intrusion into the Sterling House.

Unlike Charley Gaynor, she had listened at the door and had heard most of the conversation between her disrespectful daughter and this man who had returned to seduce her.

This angered Abigale. How dare this man come back to Denver and worse yet, seek the company of her daughter without gaining proper permission. Charley Gaynor was not the person to be asking. She was! And she would have refused.

As she had listened outside the door, Abigale had fought down the overwhelming urge to burst into the room where she would have caused a great scene when she ordered this 'Mexican' intruder to leave her home. She was shrewd enough to know this would have only caused anger with more rebellion from Lillian.

Abigale was also certain that no amount of talking would persuade her headstrong daughter to cease and desist seeing this man. There had to be another way and based partially on what she had heard, she thought she knew what needed to be done. To protect her daughter's honor, it must be done quickly.

She had stormed away from the door to calm her angry nerves by sipping a little laudanum while she pondered on her solution.

After her careful relaxation, Abigale penned a short invitation for the following morning. "Your presence for mid-morning tea is requested." was all it said and she signed her name. She carefully sealed the small note, wrote Paris Jacob . . . and then she paused. Abigale stared down at the paper in front of her. Try as she might, she could not recall his full and formal name. "Damn!" she muttered, a frown creased her forehead. *Something like mountain*, she thought. *Mount? Mont? Montana?*

"Montoya!" she said aloud, proud of herself for recalling that much of the ostentatiousness of his formal name. Oh, how just the thought of him irritated her and how she had hoped he would not return. But he had and she would deal with him along with his return.

Abigale finished the name on the outside of the folded note feeling secure in her plan to rid the Sterling House of this unwanted man.

Tucking the note into a small pocket of her dress, she carefully descended the stairway. She was still a bit light headed from the laudanum but would be patient for just the right moment to deliver the note to the one person who would deliver it for her.

As Abigale attended to the afternoon reservations for the coming evening, oversaw the table arrangements, ordered more freshly cut flowers, even though she knew Lillian disliked them, she kept a keen eye on her daughter.

Finally, Lillian excused herself to go upstairs to dress for the evening. It was obvious, in Abigale's mind, the dress would not be for the patrons of the Sterling House but rather for this man she would be dining with. Probably pale of ivory in color to set off Lillian's dark features with a low décolletage to reveal her charms.

With narrowed eyes, Abigale watched her daughter climb the stairs without saying a word. She did not try to stop her. Abigale had a plan which did not include having angry words with this willful young woman who was her daughter.

When she was sure Lillian was out of sight, she proceeded to the saloon doorway to get the attention of Charley Gaynor.

"Charley," she said very sweetly when he had excused himself from a conversation with several men at the end of the bar to join her.

"Yes, Abigale," he said.

"Would ya be so kind as ta see thet Mr." and she emphasized the word 'Mr.', "Montoya gits this lil' invitation. I would seek an audience with him."

Charley looked at her and then at the note in his hand. *What are you up to?* he thought, but said, "As you wish, Abigale. Would you like a glass of wine or," and he paused for a second, "perhaps a glass of sherry with me this afternoon?" he offered, only too aware of her weakness.

"Oh, Charley," she answered in a false, shy manner, "ya say the sweetest things. But ya know I never enter the saloon. Just please see the note is delivered." She smiled at him and Charley felt a cold chill.

"Of course," he said and watched her walk away. As he knew this woman, he knew there was no end to how far she would go when trying to achieve what she wanted. He strongly suspected that she wanted Paris Jacob LaRoche de la Montoya out of Denver and away from Lillian Anne Sterling.

Chapter
Eight

There was a strange chill in the Colorado morning air, a threat of rain and a hint of an early fall. There was even a stronger chill in the private dining room Abigale Francine Westmoreland Sterling had chosen to have her audience with Paris Jacob LaRoche de la Montoya.

Devoid of all jewelry and wearing one of her most somber dresses, she watched as he drank his tea, her thoughts precisely on what she wanted to say to him. She had rehearsed her side of this conversation being fully convinced she was within her rights, as Lillian's mother, to protect her daughter from this man.

She folded her napkin, placed it beside her cup, and let her hands rest in her lap where the envelope she would hand him was lying. "Mr. Montoya," she began, her voice cold and sharp as she came straight to the point, "I do not want yur presence in my daughter's life."

Paris leaned forward slightly, not sure he had heard her correctly. "I beg your pardon," he said.

Abigale cleared her throat, blinked her eyes and repeated, "I do not want yur presence in my daughter's life. I want ya ta leave Denver."

Paris stared at her, not sure what to say. He had heard her words but he was not sure he fully understood her. "May I ask what prompts this and is this Lillian's wish as well?"

"Yur not suitable fer her. Her wishes are not a consideration. She is far too young ta know her heart, her mind or what is properly right fer her."

"Oh," he replied sitting back in the chair. "What would you consider suitable?" he asked, beginning to feel anger take the place of the shock he had originally felt as this woman had caught him off guard with her abruptness.

With one hand, Abigale toyed with the teaspoon lying in its rest beside her cup. "Someone from a more, shall we say, presentable background." She stared straight at him, defiant with her words.

"I do not choose ta argue with you, Mr. Montoya or mince words." She ignored the spoon as she brought forth the envelope from her lap. "As her mother, I have my rights. I have my reasons. An'," she added with force, "I am prepared ta make it worth yur time ta leave her alone." She pushed the envelope across the table and waited, smug in her convictions.

Abigale was certain he would take the bank note and quietly leave. In her opinion, he was a ne'er-do-well, fortune seeking shyster. This intruder thought he had found some kind of mother lode with the Sterling family, but the vein had played out as far as she was concerned.

With uncertainty, he picked up the envelope, opened it and removed the content.

Paris Jacob Montoya stared down at the bank note in his hands. His mind focused on what he held in his hand. As the impact of its meaning became a reality, he found it incredulous this woman would try such a deceitful tactic regarding his staying or his leaving Denver.

This insult went beyond what he was capable of believing. As desperate as he was for money to salvage his home, and be of assistance to his family in California, he would not be compromised in such a manner. Let alone have his emotions bought off in such a tawdry fashion.

Without further thought, he slowly tore the $25,000 bank note in half. "It is not enough, Senora Sterling, to buy my emotions let alone control my life." he said with slow deliberation between each word as he turned a fiery dark anger in her direction. He had never felt such rage toward another human being in his entire life as he was feeling toward Abigale Sterling.

Abigale shrank back in her chair. The intense fire in his eyes suddenly frightened her. Abigale's hand flew to her throat. She clutched her lace trimmed handkerchief close to her lips.

She stood up, backing away from the table.

With that frightening look, and his angry refusal, this intrusive foreigner had taken a stand with her that no one else had ever so emphatically dared. He had told her "no." Paris Jacob Montoya was not going to acquiesce to her manipulations. This was an utter and complete threat to her control. Those brief words had struck her hard and she had difficulty believing this young, inexperienced man had refused her with such rage.

But it was more than the words he had said that frightened her. It was the manner in which he was glaring at her. For the first time in her life, she felt fear.

Paris waited another hard moment, stood up and spoke. "If you were a man, I would call you out on this great insult. But," he continued in a voice so low it was barely audible, "you are not. You are a woman and I will respect that. But, I will tell this. If you had all the gold that has come down from these mountains and all the money that has been spent for every head of cattle I have trailed into this city you would not have enough to change how I feel about Lillian."

Paris slowly shook his head and, with controlled restraint, said, "I love her, not your money or your mediocre affluency. I am from a family of great honor and old wealth. I find to be an insult to all I represent." He stared at her with only the snapping of his defiant eyes revealing his true infuriation with this woman.

"I beg yur pardon, how dare ya speak ta me in such a way!" Abigale flared, trying to bluster her way out of a situation she had created as she tried to regain control. She also felt at the moment he might do something to harm her. "You, sir, will leave my home immediately an' never come back!" she ordered, pointing a shaky finger toward the door.

Paris regarded her with utter contempt and disgust. He tore at the bank note until it was in very unrecognizable small pieces. He wondered how this cold, calculating crow of a woman could have spawned a child as beautiful as Lillian.

"Gladly, Senora Sterling," he said, controlling his words as he knew he must control the anger he felt toward her. He let the pieces of paper flutter from his hands to land on the carpet below.

He stopped at the door and glared back at the still motionless form of this woman who had become very small in his sight. If more was said, he knew he would, without restraint, lose control. Never in all life had he been so insulted as by this offer he had just torn into pieces as he wished to rip her shriveled heart into pieces.

As he descended the staircase, he hoped he would not encounter Lillian. There would be no way he could contain or hide the anger he was feeling. He desperatcly needed to talk to someone and the only person who might be able to explain this outrageous behavior would be Charley Gaynor.

"Mr. Charley is over at the Big House," Jonas told him and Paris Jacob Montoya left the Sterling House to find the answers he needed. This encounter certainly was not what he had expected.

*   *   *

Some of his anger had abated by the time he reached the Big House on Pennsylvania Street. He announced his arrival with the large brass knocker on the front door.

"Mr. Paris," Erwin said when he opened the door. "Is Mr. Charley expecting you?"

"No," he answered, "but it is rather important that I speak with him. Is he home?"

"Right this way, Mr. Paris. He is having coffee up on the balcony. I am sure he will want to see you."

"PJ, what brings out and about this early in the day?" Charley asked as Erwin showed Paris to the balcony. "Another cup for coffee," he said to Erwin. "You seem troubled my friend. Here, here, sit down." He indicated a chair across from the table where he sat.

Paris Jacob took the offered chair and then stared grimly into the far distance, not sure he should have came here either. "What is wrong at the Sterling House?" he asked not holding back. "Better yet, Abigale Sterling," he said, cutting right to the point of the anger he felt.

"Oh," Charley said, adjusting the blanket across his knees. "I take it you have had an encounter with the elder Mrs. Sterling."

"That is an understatement," Paris said and then thanked Erwin for the coffee which had been poured for him.

Charley added a measure of brandy to it. "Thank you, Erwin." he said and the young man left them alone. "So, what has happened?"

"There seems to be an extreme problem that has developed. Something just happened that Lillian must never find out about. I am not sure what to do."

Charley eyebrows arched upward. "What did Abigale do this time?" he asked.

"She offered me money to leave and never see Lillian again. It was a deplorable act from what I can only consider a depraved woman." He stopped talking as he could feel the anger rise like bile in his throat.

Charley adjusted his weight in the chair, poured more coffee from the urn and more brandy from the bottle into both cups. "Does not surprise me," he said. "Nothing the Mrs. Sterling does will ever surprise me. PJ, if it is still your intent to marry Lillian, and become a part of this Sterling family, just as Lillian would become a part of the Montoya family, then you must try to understand there have been many hardships her mother has faced. I loved my partner and my friend, Andrew Sterling, like the true brother I never had. But his love for another woman caused grief in the Sterling family, long before Lillian was born.

"It is a grief that will never be resolved." He studied Paris for a moment before continuing. *What to say?* he thought. The man deserved an explanation as to why he had been so shabbily treated.

"There was much that happened before I met Andrew Sterling on that crossing we made to get here back in 1860. He was running from something that threatened to destroy his home in Georgia. That unconscionable war between the states. Then there was the Indian woman he met and fell in love with here in the early days before his wife, Abigale, joined him. That involvement all but destroyed his life here as well."

"I know of the great war," Paris said, "I know many lives and property was lost on both sides before it ended. But," he added, "what about his being with an Indian woman here? Who was she? What happened to her? How does this affect me and my more than honorable intentions toward Lillian?"

Charley waited a moment appraising the warm and favorable blue sky above them. He remembered Pale Star and just how much Andrew had loved this young Arapaho woman who was from the Majesty which had once ruled the plains. But in answer, he continued referring to the Great War between the States. "Lives, land, property, but more importantly, a way of life we will probably never understand was destroyed by that hateful war of wars. It drove Andrew away from the South. They were both from that time. I do believe that was part of what stood between them. Old values that she favored in many ways, because it was all she knew. But, it was the lure of gold that brought him here to seek what he thought to be a better way. Lillian is a product of that and I do believe if she had not been born, they would not have stayed together."

"What about this Indian woman you mentioned?" Paris asked.

"Pale Star. Pale Star Rising. Beautiful young Arapaho girl that came into his life, because he was cold and alone out here. Who could have dreamed she would capture Andrew's love in every way," he said as he studied Paris for a moment. "Much as Lillian has captured yours."

He continued, with a darkness in his voice and a frown on his face. "Times were brutal and things happened that no man could have predicted or have changed. When Andrew found out that Abigale was on her way here from Georgia, he had to send Pale Star away because they were living at the Sterling House. Been together since before it was built. Andrew had a child with Pale Star. When she was forced to leave, she took that little boy with her."

Paris looked at him with disbelief.

"Yes, Paris, Lillian has a brother. An Indian half brother with blond hair like his fathers and yet dark like his mother, from the Indian side."

"My God," Paris said, "Lillian knows this?"

"They both do. Andrew would have probably kept this secret except for the fact that Pale Star was killed in a brutal attack on an Indian camp east of here out on the plains.

"Andrew was out of his mind not knowing what had happened to her or to his son. So, a trusted friend of ours went out there to find out. The woman was dead." Charley spared him the details.

"There wasn't much else he could do but bring the boy back here. That was when Abigale found out. If it had not been for that little blond haired boy, maybe the bitterness would not have twisted her quite so much."

"Where is this boy? He would be grown by now," Paris asked as he had not seen or been introduced to anyone like this at the Sterling House.

"Abigale was malicious and mean to that boy," Charley continued, recalling how she was always blaming him for things that got broken, keeping him in the back rooms as much as possible and hitting him or kicking at him with every chance she got.

"About a year before Abigale sent Lillian off to that fancy school, Buckland Kavanaugh, the mountain man who helped bring Andrew and myself out here, and the freed slave woman named Soolie who had taken a real shine to that baby, decided to leave here and go up to Montana.

"Guess they are still up there. No one has heard from them to the best of my knowledge. Abigale was delighted to see Buckland and the boy go. I don't think she ever got over the fact that Soolie, who was her slave back in Georgia, and I guess pretty much raised her, went with them. But, Soolie was in love with Buckland and a freed woman to do what she wanted. She could not abide seeing Abigale being mean to Charley Paul. So the three of them left."

"Charley Paul?" Paris questioned.

"Yes," Charley remembered from the night the baby was born. "Charley Paul Standing Horse Sterling. Charley for me, Paul from my father, Standing Horse for the horse that stands faithful and Sterling for the man who was his father.

"With all that has happened to her, I think you can understand why Abigale is not a well woman. She is in no condition to run the business. But, she has no where else to go. "I know that Lillian feels she must take care of her and the Sterling House."

Charley felt the truth had been told. "All of this, PJ, is what you are battling. Honor, duty and a woman twisted by bitterness. I was Andrew's business partner, however as things have changed, I only assist in the business affairs. I can do no more. I feel the best thing they could do would be to sell it all, but then where would they go and what would they do?"

Paris Jacob was silent as he pondered over what he had just been told. He drank his brandy laced coffee and watched the sun climb higher into the favorable blue sky. He had not been in Colorado long, but he was beginning to feel a love for its intense beauty.

"Thank you, Charley, for telling me of the Sterling family. Great sorrows from this family's past has brought them to where they are today. Just as my family's past has brought me to where I must stand.

"It is honor and pride that keeps us all. I feel I was in love with Lillian the first time I saw her. After being with her, just talking to her makes me know I want her as my wife, to bear my children despite the obstacles in our lives."

"Hard roads you are both on," Charley said.

Paris thought about it and then said, "The time is not right for either of us and I have no right to ask her to just wait for me, but that is what I am going to do with or without her mother's approval. That money would have saved my family from the financial disaster it faces, but it would not be an honorable acquisition."

Charley chuckled, feeling warmed by the sun, the coffee and the brandy. "Maybe should have just taken it, not told anyone, and then came back for Lillian when the time was right."

Paris rolled his eyes, shook his head and grinned. "A gambler's solution? But probably would have served the old crow right."

"So, what will you do?" Charley asked.

"I must go back to San Diego tomorrow or no later than the next day as my family waits to hear of my success with an investor."

"Have you been successful to find the cattle investors you are needing?" Charley asked, not wanting to pry into the man's personal business but curious.

Sadly Paris Jacob shook his head. "Seems there is not much future for the Spanish Corrientes in this country or for my family in California."

"I have a few thousand saved, if that would help?" he offered.

Paris was all but overwhelmed. "I greatly appreciate your offer, but I will say 'no'. I am extremely disillusioned myself and perhaps it will be for the best if my family no longer seeks a lifestyle based on cattle. So much has already been lost for us." Charley agreed by a nod of his head. He had offered what he could.

"There is something I must ask of you." Paris continued. "I know she has no father to protect her as one should. So, I ask of you, am I worthy of her?"

Charley studied the young Spaniard for a moment and then without hesitation said, "Yes, you are."

"Then I will ask to see her one more time before I leave, but not at the Sterling House. I want privacy to talk to her. I feel the very walls in that Sterling House will be listening if I try speaking with her there. I do not wish to encounter her mother again until my anger is completely gone."

"I understand," Charley said. "It will be no problem, I will bring her here this afternoon if desire. You will have the privacy you seek in my home for as long as require it."

"Yes," the man thankfully responded. "And the mother need not know?"

Charley grinned broadly. "The mother need not know."

Chapter Nine

Charley's Big House at 1340 Pennsylvania Street in Denver, Colorado, had witnessed many things since its cornerstone was laid. This house had sheltered a secret of the love Andrew had for an Indian woman, because her teepee had been stored in one of the outbuildings once Buckland had moved in after Pale Star had no choice but to leave. It had been the place Andrew had brought his family after the horror of the fire which had tried to destroy Denver in 1863.

It was a place of refuge after the horrendous flood of 1864, when dirty mud and debris had covered the main floors of the Sterling House.

Emma Frederson had died in this house and it had become a home for Jonas Gregory and baby Erwin who had grown to his own manhood after his mother, Emma, had died.

Charley Gaynor had never lavishly decorated or furnished his home, but it was comfortable and spacious with Jonas seeing to its overall upkeep and cleanliness.

As Erwin had matured, he had taken over this task and fussed over the house continually.

Erwin did not question when he was asked to prepare an afternoon tea. He was not truly surprised that Lillian Anne Sterling was receiving this gentleman caller at the Big House on such short notice. She had rejected many invitations from the local gentry and Erwin had his suspicions it was to spite her mother. Not blind to the relationship between Lillian and her mother, and knowing the Spaniard had returned, he was certain who the guest would be.

Erwin looked at his timepiece and then a mantle clock in the hallway as he once more checked the street out in front of the house to see if Charley had arrived with Miss Lillian. He felt he was in some way privileged to a secret, because of this meeting away from the Sterling House. As he inspected the tea service setting, Erwin wished it was one of the more opulent services from the Sterling House. He was pleased; however, with the pale rose china he had selected for the occasion.

Although quiet, shy and retiring, preferring the musical notes of the piano to the chatter of most people, he knew when to listen and when to observe what was going on around him. If he had his guess, this meeting had something to do with the fact he had seen Abigale Sterling eves dropping outside the front sitting room doors when the young couple had been visiting the day before. They were merely seeking some privacy with the Big House being a logical place to go.

Like so many others at the Sterling House, he made it a practice to stay out of the way of Abigale Sterling, who had probably crossed Senor Montoya in some way. Although still highly protective of Lillian, it was truly none of his affair. His business, at this day and time, was to make and serve the tea which he was going to do.

＊　　＊　　＊

Although a bit curious as to the suddenness of the invitation, Lillian did not hesitate for a moment to leave the Sterling House and go with her Uncle Charley to the Big House for a tea with Paris. She had not seen her mother watching the carriage as it left. Nor was she aware of the great apprehension which was causing her mother's heart to pound in her chest.

After Paris Montoya had left, Abigale had carefully gathered up every piece of the torn pieces of the bank note and hid them in her dress pocket. *What am I ta do,* she thought. Lillian would be in a rage if she knew of the bribery attempt to get the man to leave. Surely he would be honorable enough not to mention what she had tried to do. She was so nervous and weak in her knees she could barely climb the stairs to her room to find comfort and solace in a bit of laudanum and a glass of sherry while she burned those incriminating pieces of evidence.

*   *   *

All Lillian could think about was being with this man who was waiting for her. As afternoon shadows gathered over Denver, she was promptly ushered into the parlor of the Big House and the waiting arms of Paris Jacob Montoya.

"Lillian," Paris said, holding her close to him once the parlor room doors closed. He knew they were alone. "My beautiful Lillian." He held her away just to see into the face he had dreamed of so many nights and longed to see for equally as many days. "Paris, you make me blush just by the way you look at me," she said, not wavering in the least and loving the close feel of him. She wanted him to kiss her again and moved her face slightly closer.

"I want to kiss you over and over and never stop kissing you," he said, not missing her movement toward him. "I never want to let you go but, my sweet love, we must talk. There is so much that must be said."

Lillian frowned, but let him lead her to a chair beside the lace covered table set for tea.

"Will you pour the tea, please?" he asked following all the decorum he knew to be proper for this occasion, trying to be patient with himself completely realizing the issues of their lives must come before the issues of their hearts if the issues of their hearts were to survive.

"As you wish," she said, sensing his urgency to talk but doing as asked.

He stirred his tea, added the dollop of cream and the sugar he liked. "Do you love me, Lillian?" he asked, dropping all protocol barriers between them.

She studied her own thoughts before answering. "I am not sure what love is between a man and a woman. I know my heart longs to be with you. Belongs to you and has since the first moment I saw you. When you touch me, I feel as if I cannot stand. It seems as if nothing else matters. I want to open myself to you in every way a woman can." She faltered for words, but continued. "If this means I love you, then yes, I love you. But, Paris, I feel there is more, much more and only time can give us what we need."

"Time is a luxury we do not have. Not for me to court you properly. I must leave again, today. The latest, by tomorrow."

"I don't want you to go," she said with sadness in her voice.

"I don't wish to leave, but as I have told you, there is so much that has happened in the past year to my family in California. My parents grow old and weary with a lifestyle that I fear must change. I must see to their needs just as you must look after your mother here as well at the Sterling House. At this time, I cannot offer you a home such as you so richly deserve." He paused. "How can life be so complicated for both of us?" he asked.

It was difficult for Lillian to face this truth, yet knew it to be reality. As for her mother and the Sterling House, she had made a promise which would not be broken. She continued to memorize every detail of his face. The small mole on his right cheek, the sensuousness of his lips, the slightly arched dark eyebrows and always a hint of mischievousness in his warm dark colored eyes.

"You are right," she said. "The only home I have ever had is right here. All the years I thought I did not want to leave. Now that I want to, I cannot. My responsibility is here. I promised to take care of all of this when my father died. It can change but I don't know how."

"Our choices are quite limited as I cannot stay and you cannot leave. The Montoya family money here in America is gone. All I can ask at this time is that you find it in your heart to wait for me to resolve my home issues?" he asked, searching her face for answers.

Lillian's heart opened more as her mind accepted what he was saying.

"Do understand the promise ring?" he asked, reaching into his vest pocket. Her heart was pounding so hard she could hardly respond. "Yes," she said.

He held the ring in the palm of his hand and looked down at it as he said, "With this ring, I promise I will return. If you accept," he added, "you will promise to wait for that return."

Lillian picked up the silver ring, laid it in the palm of her hand and said, "Paris Jacob Montoya, with all my heart I promise I will wait for you."

He took the ring from her, held it up to the light and read the inscription. "No Tengo Mas Que D'arte." He slid the ring onto her finger, never letting his gaze leave her for a moment.

"What does it mean?" she asked, tears of complete happiness forming in her blue eyes.

"I have nothing to give you, but my heart," he answered, choked by his own emotions.

Chapter Ten

Aboard a transport ship, the French Frigate *Isere,* a magnificent work of art arrived in New York City. Once assembled from its 214 transport crates, the Statue of Liberty, this incredible gift from France to the United States, would come to stand for freedom, and a welcome, to all nations.

This copper over steel, 151 foot, one inch giant metal monolith with its unseeing eyes had no great love for the pedestal it stood on in the New York harbor, but those who saw it felt great love and saw hope.

About this same time in 1885, a train arrived in Denver to bring a man back to the city who also had strong ties to France, stronger ties to Spain with harsher, more demanding ties to a western civilization known as California.

Paris Jacob LaRoche de la Montoya had returned to once again find the woman he remembered through loving memory. Because it had been well over a year he felt he had no right to think she would be waiting for him. Yet as those who saw the Statue of Liberty for the first time, he too felt great love and had hope.

No letters had been sent as there was little he could have told her except to say he loved her and prayed she would honor her promise. He had watched the Montoya family money slowly dwindle because of the absolute and final loss of their cattle due to the intense droughts of

Southern California and the continuing Boundaries of Dispute issues which were a direct result of the Land Act of 1851.

This Land Act had caused the establishment of a commission of people in San Francisco whose charge was to pass judgment on all titles held under Spanish or Mexican grants. In the analysis and translation of it all, many lands had required forfeiture of all such title which could not be proven valid and legal. This had been costly and a lot of money had changed hands. The only ones to truly gain were the attorneys who may, or may not, have had the best interests of the landholder in mind.

This interest became quite apparent when the ownership of the land passed to the lawyers in lieu of extreme legal fees that could not be met after services had been rendered.

All that Paris Jacob had inwardly feared, yet refused to verbalize to his parents, had come to pass.

He was en route to New York City, where he would catch passage to Spain. His parents had sailed the month before from the San Francisco Harbor, while he finalized the disposition of what had once been their home in California.

He had to come back to see this woman who had stolen his very soul. There was still nothing he could offer her but his undying love and his hope was that she would still accept that.

After his anger with Abigale Sterling on his last visit, he did not want to just walk through the doors of the Sterling House and announce his return as some conquering warrior or hero as he felt no kinship to that status.

He had been formally presented and did not wish to go through the formality a second time. Under no circumstances did he wish to be confronted by that wretched woman who had tried to buy his favor away from her daughter.

He wanted to see Lillian. He had to know if what he felt in his heart was what she still felt in hers.

Had she waited?

He did not recall her as impetuous, but she was young, beautiful and probably had many suitors who might romantically sway her. All he knew was that before he went to Spain to attend to his parents, and their well being, he had to be with her at least one more time.

Paris Jacob had sent a telegram to Charley Gaynor announcing this return. Charley had gotten the message and was very happy to not only pick him up at Union Station but to be with his Spanish friend again.

It was late in the afternoon. The two men were on a front balcony of the Big House, overlooking a faraway downtown Denver and even farther away Rocky Mountains to the west.

Again, strong coffee tempered with rich brandy sat on a table between the two men as they gazed at the mountains and Paris began to relax after his long train ride from California.

Charley waited. He knew what the man wanted to ask, but he would let him do the asking in his own way. "The city has grown closer to me since your last visit," he said indicating the tall city buildings closer to where his home stood on Pennsylvania Street. "And the city officials keep changing the street names so fast, no one can keep up with all of it. No one remembers Golden Road anymore. It is now Colfax Avenue in honor of some politician."

"Seems there will always be those to honor in one way or another." Paris responded. "And," he added with a touch of sadness in his voice, "I suppose someday the buildings will completely block your magnificent view of the mountains."

"The houses and buildings are already far too close. It is progress and I cannot stop it. But, what of your home in San Diego?" Charley questioned. "By your arrival on the train, I see you are certainly without cattle."

Paris returned his large coffee cup to the table. He sighed heavily. "It is finished there. All of it is gone."

"Gone?" Charley said, not quite understanding. "What do mean finished and gone? Homes don't just disappear."

Paris' eyes narrowed a bit. "They do when the government gets involved, especially when it is not the government that gave the land in the first place," He was weary of thinking about what had happened. Charley had asked. He deserved an answer. "Before there was a complete United States, before there was a Colorado, and long before there was a Denver City, there was much land west of those big mountains we see in front of us. All of that land belonged to Spain and to Mexico. It was through that holding much land was made available to the Spanish and Mexican people. The land grants my grandfather and my father held title to."

He poured a small amount more of the bandy into his coffee and watched the dark liquids mingle. "This is how my family got its start with the Chinampo or Corriente cattle in California, brought here from Spain and imported from Mexico. Some for their hides, some for the tallow and some for the rodeos," he said, recalling better days. "Some very special in the breed were for the bull fighting in Mexico.

"We had fine seed stock to make the Longhorn breed and these bulls were taken to Northern Mexico and Tejas for such breeding. It was all complicated just as the ownership of the land we used and where we made our homes was complicated."

Charley frowned, took a big swallow of his coffee and let the liquid settle down his throat. The brandy helped, but he knew it was just a matter of time until he would require something stronger to help him tolerate the pain he was constantly feeling. He coughed, cleared his throat and asked, "How can the ownership of land be complicated? Either you own it or you don't," he said. He cast his eyes from one side of his property to the other as he took in the full scope of it. "All of this was measured out and sold to me."

"All men do not measure in the same way," Paris said. "California is different than what you have here. You have no dispute with your neighbors. Is that not true?"

"Only that they are too close to me and far too many of them," Charley said.

"The lines divide your property from theirs and they do not come like thieves in the night to take a part of yours."

"No. It was surveyed and staked out and sold as a whole piece of property."

"And," Paris continued, "no one comes to take a piece of the Sterling House as it was surveyed, staked out and is owned by the Sterling family with no boundaries of dispute. No Limites de Disputas. Do you understand about the land grants and how they were given?"

"No," Charley said, thinking about it for a moment, "I don't think I really do. I just know of them."

"Men were honorable when the grants were made with no actual legal surveys made to set boundaries for the land grants. Instead, it was common practice for a vaquero to take a 50 yard long reata, drive a spike into the ground and ride to the end of the reata. They would drive another spike and repeat this until the size of a parcel of land was determined.

"Rocks were piled at the intervals to mark boundaries. This process could cover many miles in one day. This is how the land was claimed. No one disputed. No one said anything. You lived on what was yours to live on and according to the Spanish rule it was correct to do so."

"The Montoya family had one of these 'reata measured' pieces of land?" Charley asked not fully understanding the logic of it but he also found surveying to be a bit baffling as well.

"Yes, we did. We ranged our cattle far and wide because much of it was California desert and drought areas. They were acres hard to live on and harder yet to control.

"The taking ways of the white immigrants actually started before California became a state after the war between Mexico and the United States. The squatters who would come and build their little shacks, trying to live any way they could claiming they owned the land because we had no recognized United States boundaries and no fences to keep them out.

"Many said that because Mexico had lost the war, we had no rights. Then the gold was found and people by the thousands ran over every inch of our land with no regard."

"That was a long time ago. That gold rush was in '49, more than 30 years ago. How could that be affecting you now?" Charley asked.

Paris shook his head, picked up his cup and finished his coffee. "Since before the time of my birth, my father has fought the legal battle to hold our land. The United States government set up a commission to resolve land issues. They confirmed much that could be retained by the original owner, but the attorney fees and the huge costs to produce original proof of ownership from records in Monterrey, Mexico proved to be costly. Unlike many others who borrowed money, with extreme interest rates to cover the cost of such proceedings, my father relied on our cattle to fund the attorneys."

"So, what is the problem? What has happened to your cattle? You had a fair decent investment with the herds you helped trail here." Charley asked adjusting his glasses which had slipped to the bridge of his nose. "And your hacienda?" he added.

Still feeling the sharp pain of loss, Paris Jacob let his steps take him to the railing where he faced west into the setting sun. Turning back toward his host, he said, "The sun has taken all the water from the earth. There has been no rain. No grass can grow and there has been no more money to buy what we need.

"The land is eroded and drifts away with nothing to stop it. Many cattle, not only ours but from other rancheros as well, have perished and cannot be replaced. There are those who will take our land when we can no longer pay the taxes. They will wait for the rains to come back.

"Even those who have proven their ownership of the land are reduced to poverty and work for new owners who do not take to our traditional ways."

Paris averted his eyes before he continued. "Although my father is a strong man, this has broken his spirit. My mother has become quite ill from all of this and wishes to return to Spain before foreclosure forces them to leave. The decision has been made to sell what was left and return to Cordoba. They are gone, the land is sold and I must go to Spain to help them."

Charley hesitated before he spoke, "There is no other way?"

Paris shook his head. He continued staring toward the west, not seeing the mountains before him but a clouded memory of a home in California that could no longer be his. "I am not so sad for myself but for the loss suffered by my father and that of my mother. This is the only true home she has ever had even though her birth place and place of her early childhood was in France. They lived for a short time in Cordoba before coming to California. The home in Cordoba has been cared for by my father's brothers.

They have no place to go but back to Spain and I must go with them to see to their needs. I am their only son."

"A large responsibility for an only child," Charley said, sensing the honor in this man, but also sensing the intense sadness as well.

"There is another only child who has taken on a great responsibility," Paris said.

"How is she? How is the Sterling House?" There was no further need to discuss his problem. The solution was set and he had to follow the road back to Spain.

"Times are hard here, too, but she is well and has learned the affairs of her father. She manages the Sterling House with the same iron will of her father." He paused, "Without your asking, PJ," Charley said putting the unspoken issue before him, "she waits for you." Charley saw Paris Jacob give what could only be called a sigh of relief.

"As I have waited for her and thought of no other." He continued, "but, there is the problem of her mother. She was not in favor of me the last time I was here if recall."

"I remember."

Paris remained standing near the balcony railing. "You once said I was the man for Lillian. Do you still feel that way?" He turned to face Charley wanting to reconfirm his support. "Senora Sterling said I was not from a presentable background. I had little to offer Lillian. I have less now. All I know is that I want her as my wife."

Charley finished his coffee and hid the pain of his standing by a flash of his smile. "I will bring her here in the morning and you must tell her these things. Explain things to her. PJ, I believe she will wait for you.

"My home is your home for as long as require a place of comfort and shelter. She has not said much but her heart is with yours from what I know. There is nothing in her life except for the Sterling House.

"Now, my friend, on that note, I am going to retire. Night air, old bones and too much rich brandy."

"Good night, mi amigo and thank you," Paris replied seeing the difficulty the man had in getting up from the chair. He sensed there might be more than age playing a part in what ailed him.

Charley left Paris Jacob standing on the balcony, staring into the far distance with much on his mind and more in his heart. Charley could have told him much more, but it was enough for him to know that Lillian Anne Sterling had waited for him.

Chapter Eleven

Lillian had been awake since before sunrise enjoying the quiet of the house. Her thoughts felt solid in some areas, jumbled and disturbed in others. The Sterling House was doing reasonably well. It had; however, taken hard determination to keep it that way plus hours of tedious concentration on the business of running a saloon and place of fine dining. She did not know what she would have done without Charley, Jonas and Erwin and how each, in his own way, contributed to her understanding the business as they helped her learn and hold it all together.

Her mother fought her on many turns, but it had been Abigale's insistence about continuing the use of Soolie's old recipes that brought many steady patrons back day after day and week after week. Many still remembered the black woman and the mountain man who had taken her away. Lillian remembered them too but in a much different way. With great control Charley quietly approached her in the kitchen area where she was enjoying her coffee.

"You are here early today." she remarked.

"Yes, Baby Lily." he replied and then handed her the note he carried.

Lillian frowned a little as she took the note from him but before she could speak, he said, "I will send the carriage for you later." He then quickly walked away but not before adding, "I am so happy for you."

Strange, she thought as she watched him go before she opened the note.

Come to the Big House. Paris waits for you.

Instantly her hands began to shake as Lillian reread the note to make sure she was reading it correctly. All she could seem to focus on were the words, "Paris waits for you." Questions swirled through her head. *Was it true? Was he back? Why was he not at the Sterling House? Why was he at the Big House?* Her mind went to a thousand places as the reality of the note became a reality to her mind. Paris Jacob Montoya had returned and had asked for her.

She sat there staring at the piece of paper in her hand and then the ring she still wore on her finger. She recalled her mother's nasty, bitter, blistering words when she had seen the ring and asked what it was and where she had gotten it.

"Promise!" Abigale spit the word like an ill mannered lout expelling something distasteful from his mouth. "I seriously doubt thet man knows of keepin' any kind a proper promise. Besides," she said, "he had absolutely no right an' certainly no permission to present ya with such a distasteful, improper piece a jewelry."

Lillian quickly pushed those horrible words from her mind. Paris Jacob LaRoche de la Montoya had returned. At the moment, that was all that was important to her. She started to rise but then sat back down. *How am I to do this?*

It had been so long since she had seen him. It was possible her mother had softened in her opinion of him and Lillian felt she should seek some family permission before just running off to see this man. *Protocol,* she thought, *always proper, proper protocol.*

Not knowing exactly why, she wanted her mother's approval.

*   *   *

Lillian sat with her mother and Charley Gaynor in one of the private dining rooms with fresh coffee and sweet cakes before them. Nothing had been touched.

As she nervously looked from Abigale to Charley, she was not sure this had been the right decision. Maybe she should have just gone to the Big House without seeking approval.

"I do not approve of this!" Abigale angrily said when she read the note as she threw it away from her hand as something dirty.

Charley Gaynor removed a toothpick from his mouth, studied it for a moment and then spoke, "I know I am not exactly blood kin to the Sterling family, but I am the closest thing to a male representative that Lillian has.

" Senor Montoya came to see me after his last visit here at the Sterling House." He stopped. With no expression, he stared directly at Abigale, "Seems he was seeking advice on a certain matter and on the proper courtship of Lillian."

Abigale swallowed hard. She had been caught off guard. It was only too apparent he knew of her bribery attempt. Was he going to use this knowledge as a weapon against her very existence? Her relationship with her daughter?

"The man is honorable," Charley continued. "Has a reputable background and is from a very old and respectable Spanish family from California. He came to me, man to man, and asked permission to court Miss Lillian and I said yes."

"Thank you, Uncle Charley," Lillian breathed.

Abigale stood up and leaned heavily on her cane. She held back her rage and the words she truly wanted to say. Instead, with great restraint, she said, "If'n yur father was still alive, none a this would be allowed. Because he is gone, God rest his soul, I see my words carry no weight.

110

But I will tell ya this! You will come to despise the day ya consummate anything with thet man." She glared at Charley and quietly left the presence of her rebellious daughter and this man who was usurping her parental authority with his knowledge of her bribery attempt. He had held his silence on the matter for all this time waiting for just the right moment to assert his authority over hers.

For some reason, he had not spoken up regarding what she was certain he knew. At this moment, she did not truly want to know why. It was bad enough he knew. All she wanted to do was go to her room to seek the liquid relief that awaited her in that privacy. They could do whatever they chose as she no longer had any control anywhere in the Sterling House.

*　　*　　*

Lillian turned the ring on her finger and still thought there was something that had happened without her knowledge. Charley knew, but was not talking.

She would put nothing past her mother as she knew only too well where Abigale's manipulations could lead. Although brief, the innuendo had been there of some occurrence the last time Paris had been in Denver. Perhaps it was best she not know whatever it was they all, apparently including Paris, had kept secret.

Lillian did not have time to ponder on what had been said some time in the past. She was eager beyond belief, but took great care to dress, groom her dark hair, slipping a ribbon in place to hold her curls, selecting an appropriate hat to keep the wind from disturbing her curls while she made the carriage ride to the Big House. As a final touch, she dropped a moderate drop of her favorite New Orleans, French Quarter, Bourbon Francais Parfum at the base of her throat.

Would it be the same? Would she feel the same? He had promised to return and he had. She had promised to wait and she had.

It was not Charley who came with the carriage but rather Erwin. She felt certain her Uncle Charley would chaperone once she arrived.

"I am so happy he has returned, Miss Lillian," Erwin said as he drove her toward Pennsylvania Street and the Big House. He knew she had waited faithfully for this day and now it was here. He had great feelings for this woman and all she had endured each day of her life especially since her return from her eastern schooling. Just by listening and watching, he had observed how the running of the Sterling House had consumed her; but Erwin knew it was a necessary consumption if she was to preserve a lifestyle favorable to them all.

As they rode along, Lillian tried to concentrate on his few words as well as her demeanor. Anything but the nervousness that threatened to make her swoon.

As usual, Erwin remained mostly silent with her not knowing what to say unless she initiated the conversation. Glancing sideways, he saw her beautiful profile and understood why men wished her favor.

He had also seen other men, some young, but usually older, whom Mrs. Sterling and her staunch supporter, Mrs. Hortence Wilson, considered eligible suitors. They were interviewed at private teas, accepted or rejected by these two would be matriarchs who presumed to hold authority over the family. These carefully interviewed, would be suitors were instructed to come calling at specified times with flowers or candy in hand. Lillian had, in her most gracious way, rebuked them all. Erwin knew she waited and for whom she waited. "I am glad you waited for Senor Montoya's return," he cautiously said.

Lillian regarded the shy young man who was always there, always following along as he silently protected her for as far back as she could remember.

"Erwin, you are like a brother to me. Have I ever told you how much I truly do appreciate your thoughts and your constant care. I, too, am glad I waited." She turned her head away, but not before she saw him smile as he urged the horse faster to their destination and her destiny.

*   *   *

Erwin felt it a great honor to escort Lillian to the gazebo on the south side of the Big House, where the sun was warm, yet they could be secluded from the street. He looked back one time with great admiration for these two people who, without words, just embraced one another. He hurried away to steep the morning tea for them.

"Lillian, my beautiful Lillian," Paris said, barely able to let her go long enough for her to catch her breath. "You waited for me."

"Sir, how do know that?" she asked, playing with his emotions for the moment.

"By the way you came to me and stand here in my arms."

With no reserve, she very boldly kissed him. Paris Jacob was immensely pleased with her boldness. It was as if the months from their last meeting to this time vanished from between them and she held no reservc.

They sat down and quietly waited, recalling each intimate detail from memories they both had held within their hearts.

She took off her hat and laid it on a small table. The facets of her jeweled hat pins glittered in the sun's rays that filtered through the latticework of the gazebo.

Lillian spoke first. "I wish you had written," was all she said.

Paris stood up and walked a little away from her to calm his explosive passion. He wanted nothing more than to run his hands through the glossiness of her silken locks. "I have no excuse," he

113

replied, righting his mind to the moment. "Only the reasoning that each letter I tried to write to you was filled with nothing but the doom of my family in California."

"Paris, tell me what has happened and why it has taken so long," she questioned with genuine concern in her voice.

He heard this, yet waited a moment before replying.

How to begin, he thought.

"I did not want to involve you with my family's desperation. Perhaps I should have, but there was nothing you could do. I wanted to spare you the worry, but I see where I should have at least reassured you that I was well." He returned to his seat beside her.

"Each time I have been here has been more desperate than the time before." He sighed heavily. "No matter what I could do, I could not save what was left. The last of the cattle are gone, sold off with many dead from the drought.

"Without them, my family could not survive in California. Also, those who would take the land were standing outside the gates, waiting for this to happen. My fears came to pass, but before the vultures could claim the dead carcass, the hacienda and its land had been sold. The papers that would prove my family's ownership of the land never came from Monterrey. With the cattle gone and no proof, there was no other choice."

"Your family, Paris, what of them? Where are they if not in California?"

"On their way to Cordoba, Spain, our homeland. That is where I must go to help and care for them."

Lillian refused to speak, fearing what she might say would sound like so much babble. *Had she heard him correctly?* "You are leaving to go to Spain?" she asked, slowly, letting her words trail out.

Unable to bear the hurt in her magnificent blue eyes on the edge of tears, Paris looked down at the wide flooring of the gazebo and watched a small bug find its way to a dark, cool place under the flooring. "Yes. I have no choice. They are old and they need me to get them settled and see to the family affairs in Spain." He desperately wanted her to understand.

"Then why did you come back here?" she asked as one tear escaped.

He caught it on the tip of his finger and said, "Because I love you, I need you and I want you."

Lillian stumbled for words as she tried to keep her composure. It was then she noticed Erwin standing a little way away from the gazebo.

"Yes, Erwin." she said aware of his presence, knowing he would not interrupt but wait to be addressed. She needed the moment but knew what her answer would be. Although he had not heard their words, Erwin strongly sensed the extreme emotion between them. "Tea is served in the main parlor," he said.

"Thank you, Erwin," she said and returned her attention to Paris.

"I, too, need, love and want you." she said.

"This is not a time for tears, but a time to understand. Let's have tea and let the answers present themselves." She would not feel distress nor would she cry. He loved her and he was here with her. In her heart nothing else mattered but the moments they could share.

After they sat down in the parlor, Erwin poured the tea and then said, "Mr. Charley said to tell you he would be out for the day and that I was to return to the Sterling House and leave the horse and carriage out in the carriage house for your disposal."

"Thank you, Erwin," Lillian said thankful as she realized they would have complete privacy for the day. She did not wish to share these moments with anyone. Nor, in her opinion, did she require a chaperone.

Without words Erwin left, quietly closing the doors behind him. They needed their time and their privacy. The room was quiet as Paris and Lillian sipped their tea. They were both lost in thoughts they were not sure how to share.

"Your teas are always the finest," he said finishing his tea and setting the cup aside.

"Do wish more?" she asked, maintaining decorum as she watched every move he made.

Paris shook his head. *What do I say to her?* He thought. "The Sterling House survives well?" he asked faltering for words.

"It has taken hard work each day to learn the saloon and restaurant business. I have degrees of success. Uncle Charley, Jonas and Erwin have been staunchly supportive. We survive."

"And your mother?"

How was she to answer? Lillian walked to a bay window. "Mother is not well," she said, staring off at a newly planted maple tree. "She thinks I don't know, but I do. She drinks and takes medicine to stay calm." She paused. "No matter what, I must take care of her and my home. It is all she has. It is all we have." She turned to face him. "But it does not mean I don't love you with all my heart and wish you to be here with me. Yet," she said quietly, "I will not beg you to stay, because you are honor bound to go."

He crossed the room to her and held her close to him gently covering her face, her closed eyes, her neck and her lips with small kisses.

"I tried," she said, tears threatening her words, "to understand the why of all of this. My father dying when he did along with all that became mine to care for. The legacy he left me and the mother who, regardless of herself, needs me.

"Then there was you, the memory of you and the promise you made to me. Now are you here and telling me you must leave. I am trying to understand it all, Paris, but it is difficult."

It was hard for him to be logical when holding her so close. He could smell the intoxicating perfume she wore, but it was more than the underlying musk of the scented water. It was her, the woman he smelled and the woman he wanted.

"No matter where I must go to honor those who gave me my life, it is you I wish to honor. It is you, Lillian, I want to marry and take for my own."

"How can do this if must leave me again?" she implored of him.

Paris sadly shut his eyes and said, "I don't know, except to once again promise I will come back to you."

She pulled a little away from him, strongly feeling her emotions, but studying her thoughts before she spoke. "Shall I come to you one time as the woman want me to be?"

"No," he answered, "As the wife I want you to be." He held out his hand to her and Lillian was flooded with emotion which was beyond all expectations as she saw the gold band he was offering her. "In my heart, we are married and have been since the beginning. With this ring will you accept with all my heart what I can offer and what I yet cannot give you?"

She took the ring in her hand and felt the warmth of the gold, but more so the warmth of the love it represented from this man to her. She looked up at him and her eyes told him the answer as they radiated complete love for him. Her lips formed the word 'yes,' but before she could say it, his sensuous lips found hers.

He knew. She knew. They both knew. This was what they wanted.

He took the ring from her trembling fingers and placed it on her finger next to the promise ring he had given her. "A promise fulfilled and a commitment made as with this ring I thee wed," he said.

"Paris," she said, "with all my heart I say I will be yours and yours alone until time is no more."

Slowly Lillian reached to unfasten the chain from her neck. The chain that supported the ivory snowflake. She placed it in the palm of his hand and folded his fingers over it.

"A long time ago, this small piece of ivory came into the Sterling family. It symbolized love. First of all the love a friend had for a friend. Then the love a man had for a woman he could not have. Then it came to me at his death. I will give it to you as a symbol of love from me to you as with this ivory I thee wed."

Paris opened his hand and looked down at the piece of ivory he held and knew it had great value to her as he had never seen her without it. He hung it around his neck proud to have this token from her.

He waited and watched as she walked away, slowly turned to welcome him with her eyes. She slowly, unpinned her hair and let her dark curls fall to her shoulders. "Can we go upstairs to a bedroom that was once mine?" she asked letting her blue eyes find every emotion Paris felt. She slowly moved toward the door.

* * *

At first they were like innocents exploring, touching, feeling, letting bare skin touch bare skin and lips find places of arousal with no shyness between them.

Paris kissed her bare nipples. Lillian was delighted when they stood erect and proud under his lips. She ran her hands over his bare chest and marveled at the coppery color of his nipples which also stood hard when she touched them. She kissed them and felt her own blood race stronger as fires burned she had never felt before.

His encouragement for her to touch him led her to places she had never experienced before. Places of arousal when her fingers lightly touched the soft skin of his penis which immediately became enlarged in her hand.

"Oh!" she said, pleased by the result of this touch. Out of extreme curiosity, she kissed that soft skin and knew he was more aroused by the intense intake of his breath. In her uncertainty and embarrassment at what she had just done, she turned her back to him. Paris covered her body with his and began kissing her neck and shoulders, covering her back and hips with his kisses, turning her over and letting his lips touch the mound of where her womanhood would soon be.

She could feel the hardness of his body against hers.

It was their time. A time to lift the veils of innocence. He did it gently, as gently as he could, saying "I don't want to hurt you. I never want to hurt you."

He too cried as she cried out when he entered her body in the only way a man can possess a woman the first time.

Not once, never once, did she try to push him away because of fear or pain when she lost her innocent youth to became a woman with him.

The union had been there all along. Now it was complete.

They both slept.

*   *   *

Paris Jacob slowly opened his eyes and surveyed the unfamiliar room. In a corner was a rocking horse and he could see an old trunk with several dolls sitting around it with one very beautiful, large doll on its top. Lying on the doll's lap he thought he saw what appeared to be a silver railroad spike. *Impossible,* he thought. *Just a child's toy.*

In the room were many things reminiscent of a childhood which had once belonged to the woman who lie sleeping in his arms. This was the woman he wanted and had claimed as the precious treasure she was to him.

His wife, his heart connection and the woman he would love forever. He moved a dark strand of hair from her forehead and marveled at the porcelain like quality of her skin, the darkness of her hair, the arch of her eyebrows and the dark lashes that were closed over the bluest eyes he had ever seen. He had thought he had made love before as he had touched other young women in his quest for manhood, but had never felt the complete satisfaction he knew to be possible when the spiritual heart was also given. Lillian moved in her sleep and woke up. Without opening her eyes, she reached for him to hold him close to her. She could feel the heat from his body, the pulse of his heart and love within the circle of his embrace.

"I love you," she whispered as her lips sought his. "Will it be the same again?" she asked in her innocence.

"No," Paris replied. "It will only get better, my love," he said, stroking her cheek and kissing her forehead as he smoothed back her hair.

"How do know?" she asked.

"A man knows these things," he answered.

"And what must a woman know after the first time?"

"That there can never be another first time."

"Then I want a second and a third and a forth and . . ."

Paris laughed. "We may have to rest a little between each time."

They passed the day, eating light snacks of sweet cakes that someone had thoughtfully left in the warmer oven, drinking strong tea, sleeping, talking about a future that someday would be theirs to have and making love. The place was perfect. The day was perfect. They were perfect together.

As the sun was beginning to touch the tops of the mountains to the west, Lillian slowly dressed. "Our day here must end, my husband," she said as she twisted her hair into a crown and fastened it down, again threading the ribbon through her relaxed curls.

Paris understood her words to be true. When this day ended, their time, this special day, would be a memory for them both. Pulling her into his arms one more time, he said as he touched the ivory snowflake that hung around his neck. "I will honor my wife and the day will come when I will return."

"And I will honor you, my husband, until that day."

Paris Jacob LaRoche de la Montoya drove Lillian Anne Sterling to the Sterling House. Once again to leave her there as he left to go to Spain and the uncertainty that awaited him there.

Chapter
Twelve

Long shadows from the mountains were reaching for the western edges of Denver when Lillian quietly entered the back door of the Sterling House's kitchen. She hoped she would not encounter her mother.

The cooks were busy, barely taking notice of her when she came through the door and the serving ladies were carrying food out into the lower dining area and to the upper rooms concentrating on each tray to make sure nothing was left amiss.

At first, Lillian thought she had slipped past her mother but she only made it as far as the second floor when there was no escaping her mother's wrathful and watchful eye.

"Where have ya been?" Abigale demanded.

"At the Big House," she said, quickly seeing if anyone was watching or listening as her mother was not quiet with her question. Lillian continued her ascent of the stairs with her mother right behind her.

"What have ya been doin'?" she demanded. "As if'n I do not know," she quickly added.

Lillian entered her room and tried to close the door, but her mother was too quick for her. She followed her daughter into the room, slamming the door behind her. Lillian sat down in front of her mirror and began unpinning her hair. "Mother, please just go away. I wish to be alone."

"I do not care what ya want. Look at you. Disheveled, like ya have come from one bed an' are lookin' fer another."

Lillian instantly understood this mother/daughter talk was not going to be pleasant. "Only one part of what you say is true," she said with restraint.

Abigale stopped, taken aback by her daughter, but it did not stop her verbal assault. "Ya have been with thet man, have you not?" she accused. "Ya have!" she repeated, anger causing her voice to shrill.

"Mother, please keep your voice down and that man has a name. It is Paris Jacob Montoya. And, yes," Lillian said through a tightened jaw, "I have been with him all day long. Plus we were completely without chaperone. So let your mind go where it will," she snapped not wanting to prolong the inevitable.

"Young lady, an' I doubt if'n ya are anymore, I do not have ta allow my mind ta go anywhere. All I have ta do is look at ya an' see where ya are an immoral, tainted an' ruined woman."

Lillian gave a short laugh. "Tainted?" she questioned. "I have not been contaminated or morally corrupted."

"Ya allowed thet man ta strip ya of yur decency, did you not?"

Lillian ignored her.

"Ya did!" her mother shrieked at her.

Lillian stood up to her complete height and said, "I made love to Paris Jacob because I love him. There was nothing indecent or immoral about anything we did."

Her mother sank into a chair, fighting tears. "Ya have ruined yur life, Lillian. No decent man will ever have ya after ya have sullied yurself with the likes of thet . . . thet . . . thet . . . inferior person," she said for lack of better words. "Now I suppose ya are pregnant with some vile lil' half-breed growin' inside of you, because of yur actions an' there will be another illegitimate bastard added into this family."

Lillian, shocked and horrified, could hardly believe the bitterness in those words. She slowly shook her head from side to side to try and clear her thinking. "You are sick," she slowly said. "How can you say such dreadful things to me? I am your child. You are my mother."

"Oh so true, Lillian," her mother replied. "But, what ya have done is filthy, nasty an' disgustin'."

Lillian frowned in complete disbelief in what she was hearing. In defiance, she said, "I hope I am carrying his child." She held her head up proudly, glaring at her mother. "I hope I am pregnant." Wordlessly, her blue eyes full of emotion, she opened the door.

Lillian turned the full intensity of her blue eyed stare toward her mother. "I don't believe you have ever loved anyone your whole entire miserable life. I want you to leave my room or must I have to leave to get away from you? I no longer wish to hear your sick, twisted words." Lillian stood there, sullen and angry.

Leaning heavily on her cane, Abigale walked toward the open door. "Oh, I will leave yur room. But, let me tell ya, I am not the one who is sick. Yur the one who, without benefit of marriage, gave up yur virginity ta thet man of low life an' character. An' fer yur information," she added, "I tried ta love yur father, but he would not let me. "An' I have tried ta love you but you have turned me away, too." She stepped through the doorway, stopped and looked down at her daughter's hand. "An' do not think I missed thet cheap piece a gold 'round yur finger. Yur not married. Not ta thet man an' ya never will be. Thet piece a trash will tarnish, just as yur tarnished by what ya have done." Without another word, Abigale stormed out of the room and out of her daughter's presence.

Lillian closed the door behind her and locked it.

Undressing, she laid down, naked, across her bed and let the silent tears flow. She had tried for years to understand her mother's brutal ways, but the words she had just listened to were unforgivable in their depth of cruelty. Her mother knew nothing of loving, being loved or giving love. Abigale knew nothing of Paris Jacob Montoya. How could she speak so disparagingly of him?

Lillian sobbed deeply, stopped her tears and closed her eye, letting her mind drift back to the events of the afternoon and how loved and protected she had felt while lying in his arms.

She touched her lips with the tips of her fingers and let her finger trace a line to the hollow of her throat, remembering Paris' lips as they had done the same thing. She let her hands rest on her breasts and could still feel the gentleness of his hands as they had caressed her body. Placing her hands on her stomach, she could feel the flatness of it and could not help but wonder if a small child would grow there swelling her body as it grew inside of her. It would be a compelling statement of her love for Paris—a child between them.

Logic began to rule her emotions. Lillian wisely knew it would not be a good thing to happen in her life at this time. Gently touching the mound of her dark pubic hair, she intensely recalled the pressure it had taken from his body to reach the womanhood that lie beneath her innocence and she was glad it had all happened just the way it had. Smiling, Lillian slowly turned the two rings that she wore on her left hand ring finger. One was a promise of a heart given and the other, the plain gold band, was a commitment from a heart that would stay. *You are wrong*, she thought of her mother's stinging, spiteful comments. *These rings will never tarnish, just as my love for Paris will never tarnish.* It was as her father had told her. She knew love when she had found it. There could never be another.

Lillian pulled a coverlet up over herself, closed her eyes and fell asleep holding her left hand over her heart. This was one night the Sterling House could do without her. She would hold fast to her memories, each and every precious one of them she shared with Paris

Jacob. Nothing her mother could say or ever do would take that from her.

*   *   *

The days passed. A week extended into a month. Bloating, cramps and menstrual stain let her know she was not pregnant. Lillian deliberately refused to tell her mother that her time of the month was with her and there would be no child born into the Sterling family. Legitimate or otherwise.

They spoke primarily about the business of the Sterling House, but exchanged no pleasantries. Lillian loved her mother, but had no doubt she would never trust her with any of her personal feelings ever again.

The one good thing that happened was that the barrage of interviewed, scrutinized, eligible, sanctimonious, staunch, stiff upper lipped and approved suitors her mother and Mrs. Wilson had paraded through the Sterling House—stopped.

Abigale had realized it was a fruitless endeavor. She was also wise to not promote more talk or discussion regarding Paris Jacob LaRoche de la Montoya. Abigale was convinced that her daughter was completely wasting her life waiting for this fortune hunter to return.

Lillian had built a strong defiance into her thinking to prove her mother wrong. She was determined to wait for Paris' return as she had promised. This waiting would be with or without her mother's blessing.

*   *   *

Denver, and the continual building of it, evolved around the three-story brick structure situated at 1901 and Larimer Street. Abigale rarely, if ever, left the comforts of the Sterling House. Charley would invite her to come to the Big House for afternoon teas, but she refused stating modestly she had everything she needed at the Sterling House and that is where she wished to stay.

On the other hand, Lillian enjoyed an occasional Sunday afternoon away from the constant surveillance of where she worked and lived. She would gladly allow Erwin to drive her to the Big House where she could visit with her uncle who seemed to tire so easily. Her drive was not complete before a turn around town and along the ever busy streets around Larimer.

She marveled at the constant growth and knew that the boundaries were far beyond where and what her mind could accept. The better businesses, she observed, were moving away from the original heartbeat in and around the confluence of the South Platte River and the spindly little Cherry Creek, where she, Charley Paul and Erwin had played when they were young.

She also recalled the floods of the past and had listened to many stories of survival. Had they not just survived another of those raging torrents back in July with minimal water and mud damage? Most of the heavy damage from this flood had occurred to the south and west of them.

Yet each time the water levels rose, there was a threat. Cherry Creek seemed to run a little cleaner most of the time, as it was a smaller, faster moving stream. The South Platte, on the other hand, was sluggish and slow being so polluted most folks would not go near it, let alone consider wading in its vile waters.

It was trashy and nasty, infested with vermin of all kinds. Even after the flood waters receded, piles of debris clung to the normal stream banks. It would take another flood to clean out so much trash.

Health issues were a concern, but Lillian was more concerned with the safety of the Sterling House and those who called it their home. More and more incorrigibles, the homeless, bums and bummers seemed to surround them on the streets and in the alleyways.

She was so concerned, despite the fact that Jonas lived on the premises, that she constantly encouraged these undesirables to move along. She had acquired a single shot derringer pistol which was not too far from her at any given time. Her Uncle Charley had taught her how to shoot and said it was a practiced matter of "aiming at the tree and not hitting the mule." She felt better with her little friend with the big voice close at hand. She was concerned about many things, but what most concerned her was that the affluent, those who spent great amounts of money on self-indulgences, frequented the Sterling House less and less often.

There were; however, many loyal patrons and Lillian knew and recognized many of the men who came to the saloon for an afternoon of relaxation and drinking. Some came to gamble through a deck of Monte with Charley, when he was there, some sought quiet poker games within their own gentlemanly groupings or to challenge the faro and blackjack dealers with games of "21." All of these operated under the carefully trained and watchful eyes of Jonas Gregory who saw to the collection of fees for the use of Sterling House tables for gaming.

Strangers, shady in their appearance, would stop by late at night. They did not seem to be there to enjoy the drinking, gambling or the eating.

Lillian would see them as they appraised everything from the drinks poured, the nude painting behind the bar, the dealers of faro and blackjack to even her own personage. They would speak with Charley, sometimes Jonas, and then leave as abruptly as they had appeared.

Within a few days, Lillian had noticed that some of the local law enforcement officers would stop by, have a drink, usually with Charley, and he always paid the saloon bill for these men.

Lillian had also seen Charley hand them small envelopes When she asked, he had told her it was a small payment for insuring the games could continue without threat of the gaming tables being removed from the saloon.

"Uncle Charley, that is bribery," she said as they sat sipping tea at the Big House. Charley began whittling a new toothpick, and said, "No, baby girl. It is survival." She understood it only too well and knew that Charley paid these payoffs and bribes from his own winnings. It was not right, but this was an area she could not enter as the business of the saloon and the gambling was under the control of the men in her life. Also. apparently under the control of some unseen threat that required money to keep under control. She completely trusted Charley Gaynor, Jonas Gregory and Erwin Frederson to attend to these matters. They apparently did, as the saloon doors stayed open and the gaming continued.

Chapter Thirteen

Jonas Gregory was a quiet man. From the beginning out on the crossing from Missouri to Colorado, he had been greatly appreciative to all he had come to consider as his family.

Of his past there was little to nothing to tell and less he cared to remember. They had respected that and allowed him his privacy.

At first, he reasoned if no one knew who his father was, no one could send him back, which had been his greatest fear. As the years had passed, that fear had died just as he felt certain so had his past. On the crossing he had found his greatest joy being given responsibility to care for the livestock, the wagon and the supplies.

He knew he had been blessed by a strange, but good, fortune from the time he had escaped the evil brutality of his father to the place he finally chose to call his home. It was all a far cry from the hot, humid Ozark Mountains of Southern Missouri, where his life had begun and where it had almost ended at the hands of his loutish father.

Not raised with a conscious awareness of religion, or a God of creation, he only knew he had been looked on with favor to have been put into the care of Buckland Kavanaugh back in Missouri when all others had turned him away.

Then there had been Andrew and Charley, who had provided another home when the Fredersons had lost it all due to the uncontrollable acts of Mother Nature and the unconscionable acts of a woman who had been starved for love to the point she would accept illicit sex from strangers as a substitute. That cruel substitute ultimately took her life and left him with a child to raise, because Elias Frederson had deserted all of them. The Sterling House and Charley Gaynor's Big House had become his homes. And, he loved both his homes and the men who had provided them. Andrew's untimely death had stunned and shocked him, but there had been no question as to his moving to the Sterling House to help and to protect the Sterling ladies.

Quietly giving care to Emma Frederson, baby Erwin, the Sterling House, the saloon, and the Sterling ladies had given him a strong sense of purpose in life, security and of well being.

Yet on this hot summer day, as he sat in the Sterling House kitchen watching the two young Oriental sisters, Ming Su and Ling Su, he was questioning his logic, reasoning and sanity.

Not wishing to marry, but being a normal man with moderate sexual appetites, he had sought and found quiet delights with some of the soiled doves that resided just across the alleyway from the Sterling House. Just as the entire Sterling household, he was not ignorant of the fact that the strongest part of the row of the Scarlet Sisterhood ran from roughly 19th and Holladay, or Market Street as it was known to newcomers, to about 21st Street. This street ran parallel to Larimer, so the ladies' lascivious and raucous behavior could be heard at all hours of the night. These sounds and wild sexual abandonment would send Abigale Sterling into a rage as she swore demons had possessed these women who caused them to open their legs in such a manner. Their willingness to accept money for such behavior was beyond her comprehension.

If Abigale saw any of the ladies in the alleyway between the Sterling House and the row parlors, she would turn a calloused eye away from them, refusing to speak to these women. They were usually scantily clad and seemed to have little to no morals as to the state of their undress as they carelessly displayed their charms. All of this was more than she could abide, but could not find a way to eradicate them, or their means of livelihood, from the street behind the Sterling House.

No one, but Abigale, seemed to pay much attention to this immoral conduct just steps from their backdoor. About all she could do was hope and pray this lascivious behavior would not in some way taint the quality of the Sterling House.

Jonas had met some of the nocturnal shades of the neighborhood in this alleyway while emptying trash. Through the girls, he had met several of the Madams of Denver's brothel trade. These notorious names, birth given or aliases, belonged to Jennie Rogers, Mattie Silks, Amy Bassett, Mary Leary, Lizzie Preston and Kate Fulton who seemed to have a constant and running feud with Mattie Silks. It was over someone named Cort Thompson, who was apparently married to Mattie Silks. Jonas had never met the man, noted to be a foot racer, as he always seemed to be away on business. It was even rumored there had been a duel, of varying intensity depending on who one listened to, over this man between the two woman.

Jonas did not know the sordid details for sure, had never asked, because he felt this was Mrs. Silks' private business and he had never met Kate Fulton. Only the name was familiar. It was all just a part of the riotous and bawdy affairs of what was deemed by some to be the wickedest street in the west no matter what its current name might be. Jonas did not view the row in that way. As he had come to know some of the ladies, he did not perceive them to be wicked or immoral. When he was not working at the Sterling House, he would slip across the alley, where he would spend some time in the parlors, tidying up and doing little favors for the girls who always seemed to have something broken that he could fix.

He adored Mattie with her blonde curls, baby doll face and opulent figure, but was in awe of the six foot tall, statuesque Jennie Rogers, who always wore emerald earrings and owned the largest, most lavish parlor house on the row diagonally across the alley from the Sterling House.

In this parlor, and others like it, were many delights for the masculine eye as Denver's gentry, and any who sought these nocturnal pleasures, would find. Their feet would tread on the plushest carpets, their bodies reclining on velvety furnishings. Their eyes saw gigantic potted plants, gold and diamond dust mirrors along with erotic statues and nude paintings.

Their thirsty lips touched thin china and delicate crystal as they were served exotic drinks and fed enticing foods by those who would, for a larger price, tempt them with lascivious sexual pleasures. This was meant for those with bravado and money enough to seek the charms of the bordellos of Denver's most notorious red light district. Jonas Gregory's willingness to care for the ladies of the night and their personal requirements had earned him favors from the girls in the parlor houses.

What had gotten him into the situation he was facing had not been his dalliances with the ladies of the row, but more so his unusual friendship with Mattie Silks. When she was not busy with the affairs of her parlor, and when he was not busy at the Sterling House, they would occasionally sit in her parlor house's kitchen, drinking coffee and talking.

He had found her to be, in many ways, a decent and intelligent woman who had chosen a lifestyle and way of life which provided a precarious, but strong living for her. She had told him she had never been one of the girls, but had started as a madam in Illinois and considered herself to be a high class business woman. She had also told him that she, unlike her competitors, never hired the innocents to work for her.

"Ladies come to me for the same reasons that I hire them," she had said one morning over coffee, while the ladies of the house slept off their debauchery of the night before. "There is money in it for all of us. But only the willing," She had winked at him. It was this decent streak of morality in this most unusual woman from the trade of the Cyprians that had involved Jonas in the moral future of two young, Chinese girls.

"Jonas, I need your help," Mattie said. "These two lovelies ran away from over at Lizzie's place where they have been since that horrible riot on Hop Alley." She nodded in the direction of the two, young Oriental girls who sat quietly on a mat beside the back door. "Seems the older they have gotten, the more scared they are of the men folk over there. Some of Lizzie's ladies told them my place would be safer for them.

"You recall I told you I never recruit the innocents and I believe these two to be that. Can you maybe find them some work at the Sterling House. Hopefully a better place to stay at night than here where I can't watch every minute what might come their way?" Mattie Silks motioned for the two girls to stand. "They might not be of much value with their own kind. Probably why they got left behind in the riot. I would hate to see them disappear into the slave markets that take their kind. From what I have seen and know a lot younger than these two are."

*   *   *

Not sure what to do, Jonas had agreed to help. Now he sat in the Sterling House kitchen, worried, because of what he had gotten himself into. "I remember that riot an' how bad it was for the Chinese that night," Jonas said. "Do ya recall it too?" he asked.

"Yes," Charley said, "I do recall that Chinese riot. "Been maybe seven or eight years ago," he said. "Over in Hop Alley. Does not surprise me these two got left behind in all the confusion that night," he said, taking in the Orientals where they quietly stood near the back door acting as if they might bolt and run at any moment.

"What riot?" Lillian asked, walking into the room and hearing only part of the conversation. "And who are these lovely young ladies?"

"Miss Lillian, meet Ling Su an' Ming Su," Jonas said.

Hearing their names mentioned and seeing what appeared to be a great lady enter the room, both girls bowed deeply from the waist.

"How elegant," Lillian said walking to them. "Which is Ming Su?"

The taller of the girls answered with a voice like wind gently touching crystals on a chandelier, "I am Ming Su, missy."

"Both of you, please be seated. Uncle Charley, where are your manners?" she playfully chided him. Both girls looked to Jonas, who nodded and then helped get chairs for them. Both girls sat down, still remaining very quiet.

Lillian also sat down and then repeated, "What riot?"

"Lillian, you are aware of the section of town just a little north of us over on Blake where the Chinese live?" Charley asked.

"Oh, yes," she replied, recalling how she had been absolutely forbidden by both her mother and father to ever go into that section of the city. At a very young age she had been made aware there were true and extremely dangerous dens of iniquity where the Chinese lived. Most of the danger seemed to be due to the usage of a drug known as opium. She knew little to nothing about opium or its usage. It was always talked about in hushed whispers when spoken about at all.

These dens seemed to be concentrated in Hop Alley. Although curious, this had been one area she had cautiously listened to her parents about and obeyed them. The Chinese men she saw lounging about on the street over near Blake, in what could only be called a dazed stupor, did frighten her. Yet, seeing these two young Chinese ladies did not frighten her in the least.

Charley continued, "While you were away at school, there was an argument that broke out between some Chinese men and some white men in one of the local saloons over on Wazee Street. The men tried to get away, but were caught and beaten by the whites.

"People just seemed to be hell bent, pardon the expression, Lillian, to rid this part of the city of what they called the "Yellow Plague." This was the excuse they were waiting for. They torched and burned where these people lived and the riot ensued. It may not have been a healthy place, the way they were stacked up and piled up on top if one another, but these were their homes. A lot of Chinese businesses were burned that night as well. A couple of people even lost their lives."

Lillian looked at him in disbelief. "All of this truly happened?" she questioned.

"Yes," Charley assured her. "The Chinese laundries, along with other respectable businesses are gone where honest people were trying to make a decent living. Seems these folks were good enough to work on connecting our country as railroad workers, do our grunt work, carry slop and do laundry but not fit, according to some, to live with us."

"People were runnin' wild everywhere," Jonas added. "Not only was there riotin' an' burnin' but a lot of lootin' went on that night too. Before daylight there were a lot of displaced an' homeless people. Many Chinese ran for their lives as they scattered ta who knows where. Seems these two, who were just lil' girls back then, were found huddled in a doorway an' were taken ta Lizzie Preston's house where they have stayed ever since."

"Who is Lizzie Preston?" Lillian wanted to know.

Jonas turned toward Charley, who smiled and turned his face away. Jonas felt his face begin to flush as he tried to answer. "Well, uh . . . she is . . . uh . . ."

"A business woman of a lady's work," Charley said, rescuing Jonas without revealing that Lizzie Preston was one of the Row's notorious madams with a bevy of beautiful, painted doves.

"Oh," Lillian said coolly as she watched Jonas, who was looking everywhere but at her. She understood the nature of the business being spoken of but did not wish to pursue its pursuits. "I believe I understand the delicate nature of what are saying." she expressed. "I further surmise now these young ladies are of age, this 'ladies work' is not what they wish to pursue." She judged them to be in their early teens.

"Another lady friend of Mrs. Preston, Mrs. Silks, did ask if I could find something more suitable than the place of business where they were stayin'. They have no true home ta go ta at night. If great care is not given, they could be in serious trouble if left where they are." He said discreetly. "I thought ta bring them here." Jonas looked hopefully at Lillian and then back at Charley. "I realize I ask a lot."

"Are they good at cleaning?" Charley asked.

"Yes," Jonas replied. "That is what they have been doin'."

"The Big House could use a good cleaning. Just haven't felt up to it lately. With Erwin here most of the time, a lot gets left undone. For the time being, they could stay in one of the extra rooms," Charley offered. "They will be safe in my home and with winter coming on so strong this year, it will be the best place for them." *Safe, warm and dry*, he thought recalling the blonde woman who had been found frozen to death just two winters before and how he had personally witnessed this frozen body being taken off the street. Many froze to death during the winter months on what had become and was becoming even worse, Denver's interior decaying streets. He for one, did not want to see this happen to these two young women just as he did want to see them fall into, or be taken into, the prostitution parlors and cribs as a way of survival.

Lillian looked at the men and smiled, her business mind looking ahead. "If I have any say in their future, I would like to start training them to work here as well where they are." He." She had not been fooled by their round robin talk. It was fairly obvious someone had thought these girls too young and too valuable to face the perils of prostitution. She knew what the businesses were on the street bordering where the Sterling House. If this Mrs. Silks and Jonas felt these young ladies deserved a better life than what awaited them in the brothels of Denver, then she, too, would help.

This arrangement could possibly help one more issue facing the Sterling House—good, reliable, dependable help. If training her own help was the way to produce reliable workers, then train them she would. Maybe then they would stay. Not steal food, liquor and silverware, leaving countless messes and then run off with no word as to a return. Jonas walked over to where Ming Su and Ling Su sat and talked in hushed tones to them.

"Oh yes, Mr. Jonas, sir," Ming Su said, whose eyes darted first at Charley and then at Lillian. "We work hard both houses. Long hours. You see. Ming Su and Ling Su young and strong."

"Who is going to tell your mother about this addition?" Charley asked Lillian. "I will discuss it with her and then, Uncle Charley, like so many other issues, I will have to tell her how it will be."

"Charley, if it is all right, I will take the girls over ta the Big House an' get them settled," Jonas said, "I cannot thank ya both enough."

"Think nothing of it. Little enough to do to help a friend."

Jonas started to say more, but changed his mind as he ushered the girls out the door.

Charley waved them on and then turned back to Lillian. "Not meaning to interfere, but your mother does concern me. She will not take well to these Celestials."

"No, probably not," she agreed. "Uncle Charley," she continued, "my mother concerns me as well. I cannot reason with her on any level." Lillian recalled many arguments about the business, about Paris and how she felt about the man. She put the memory away, brought her attention back to her uncle trying to keep her mind on the discussion between them.

"She may have at one time understood the needs of this business, the kitchen, the serving of fine foods. She still has a fine eye for elegance but, unfortunately, it may be an elegance of a time passing. Times have changed and our world around us is rapidly changing as well. She is not. Tea?" she offered.

"No," he replied. "Coffee." He reached for his brandy flask. "Seems to help me feel better."

Lillian waited for a moment as another dark cloud set more heavily in her mind. Although he hid it well, her Uncle Charley was not well. She walked to the stove and brought back two cups of coffee. "You don't mind if I join you, do you?" she asked, pushing her cup toward him as he laced his coffee with the dark brandy. "Mother is not the only one to drink."

"A drop or two, baby girl." he said, studying her for a moment. "Are you aware how much your mother drinks?" he cautiously asked.

"No, not for sure. I know she is tipsy by nightfall just about every night. There is nothing I can do. She will not listen to me. Far too many angry words are between us. I do not believe there will ever be a meeting of our minds let alone a healing of our hearts." She sipped her coffee and wrinkled her nose a bit. How could anyone spoil their coffee in such a way? It tasted terrible with the brandy in it.

Charley was amused seeing the displeasure on her face. "It is definitely an acquired taste. You don't have to drink it if don't like it."

Lillian pushed the cup away went back over to the stove to put water on for tea. "Mother seems to have acquired the taste." she said and then to face him as she boldly asked, "Have you been to the doctor to find out why you are so tired all the time?" She did not wish to talk about her mother, as it was a moot point. Life was harsh and life was coarse, but it took a forgiving heart to make it and keep it manageable. This was something that in her mother's lifetime of grief and bitterness, she had lost. That was if she had ever had a forgiving heart.

Charley peered into the dark mixture of coffee and brandy in his cup, picked it up and cautiously sipped the hot liquid. "No, I just get tired a lot more than I used to. My age, Lillian. I am getting to be an old man and old men get tired."

She returned to the table, put her arms around his shoulders and held him close to her for a moment. "You must take care of yourself," she said. "Sometimes I feel I have so little left with no one to talk to about how I feel or what I should do." She stepped back, studying him as she tried to read his thoughts. "I sometimes see it all slipping away and feel at the mercy of Denver City as our business dims. What more can I do except wait?"

He also knew that, as Denver had continued its outward and upward sprawl with newer homes and more appealing businesses, the Sterling House seemed to shrink. He, too, had walked the streets that once had been so favorable to them all. Now, it seemed, bits of blight were being left behind and the old part of the city was decaying from the inside out. Just as his body was and he knew that, too. She needed words of encouragement and comfort, but what could they be that would help her?

Lillian poured the hot water and began steeping her tea. He observed how proudly she held her shoulders, the straightness of her back and the cascade of dark hair down her back. Other men had seen this great beauty that was hers. She rebuked them all, usually with a dark look from those incredibly blue eyes. In his opinion, she was doing all she could and, he also knew for whom she waited. There was no missing the double rings she wore.

Charley replied, "There has been a lot of life lived here within these four walls, but so much of it has not been a life of your living. But this house rules how you are living your life."

She returned to the table with the teapot and a fresh cup for the tea, keeping her thoughts private. He was right but what could she do about it?

"You and the Sterling House will continue to survive, because like your father, you are of the finest sterling quality. It all worked for him. It will continue to work for you. You have learned and applied yourself well in the face of business adversities. And, Lillian," he said very quietly. "The man you wait for is worth waiting for. He will be back."

Lillian fought down her tears. She wondered if there would ever be a time for them but decided to let the conversation drop.

They sat quietly. He sipping coffee that had grown cold but the brandy made it palatable for him and she sipping her hot tea. Each lost in collective thoughts and private ones as well.

Chapter Fourteen

Winter swirled across Colorado, leaving blankets of snow to cover the Rocky Mountains. Denver shuddered and paused as the little queen city alternately froze and thawed, thawed and froze. The ice cracked and popped in the shallow frozen Cherry Creek and chunks of ice floated in the slow moving South Platte River.

The air hung heavy from the constant dark smoke pouring from many chimneys where bituminous coal and knotty cords of pine were burned in fireplaces and potbelly stoves.

In the White Ash Coal Mine, west of town, coal miners worked endless shifts to cut away and dig out the blackish brown chunks of prehistoric vegetation remains, which, over eons, had been compressed to produced the coal seams that were being taken from the earth one chunk at a time.

One of the byproducts of this amazing source of heat was the black smoke that made the winter air appear dingy until the winds from the mountains would push it far out to the eastern plains.

Unfortunately for the homeowner or businessman who used coal as a source of heat, the second byproduct was the ashy and dirty cinders that remained when all that was burnable had burned. This did; however, create an industry for cinder and ash removers. On a daily basis, the cinder wagons would roll through the city collecting the waste product from the coal to deposit it outside of the city in ever widening cinder beds. These beds were regularly crushed down in preparation for new buildings as the city continued to spread. This was all a part of the 'paving of the way'.

Lillian was not concerned with the current cinder beds or the future ones, either. She was glad the coal bins were full of the tarry chunks. Not certain where it all came from but happy to hear the crash and rumble as the coal was delivered each week to be dropped down the chute into the basement. It meant they would all be warm for another week, even if the burning of the coal produced the soot that blackened the buildings, the dark smoke that hung in the air and cinders that had to be removed from the alleyway behind the Sterling House. It was all a part of the winter days that stretched out before them.

It was late in the morning, later than usual for Erwin to arrive at the Sterling House. When he did, Charley was not with him and he was quite anxious to find Lillian. "Miss Lillian," he said, as he pulled off his mittens and stood near one of the stoves that was nicely banked with coal to hold and produce the welcome heat. "I don't mean to alarm you, but maybe you should come to the Big House. Mr. Charley seems to be very sick," he said rubbing his hands together more from being nervous than from being cold.

Lillian looked up from her ledger, alarmed by his words. She grew even more concerned when she saw how worried he seemed to be. "Erwin, what is wrong? What has happened?"

She was very aware her uncle was not feeling well. He tired easily and went home earlier and earlier. Rarely, if ever as of late, did he spend an evening dealing Monte. However, he was yet not come in with Erwin on a daily basis.

"Sick with a fever and chills, plus he cannot stand up, let alone walk," he responded, his voice becoming quick and urgent.

Without hesitation, she said, "I'll take the carriage. Go tell my mother where I have gone. Find Jonas, tell him to take charge here and then fetch Doctor Safford. Bring him immediately to the Big House."

"It is getting colder outside," Erwin said. "Won't you wait. Let me take you, so you can stay warm?"

She sensed he was probably right, but wanted to get to the Big House as quickly as possible. "I will be just fine, Erwin." she said. "I will dress warmly and take a warming brick for my feet."

His face was very somber as he went to find Jonas and deliver the information to the elder Mrs. Sterling. Erwin was very alarmed and felt time was of the essence to also find and bring the doctor.

*　　*　　*

Once again, the black bag containing the magic elixirs sat on a table in the Big House on Pennsylvania Street as Doctor Safford prodded, poked, thumped and listened to an ailing body. He knew that Charley Gaynor had a strange, but solid, connection to the Sterling Family and had been Andrew Sterling's best friend and partner until Andrew's death. He liked the Sterling family and came immediately when they called.

"How long, Charley? How long have had this?" Doctor Safford asked of him.

"What part of it?" Charley asked in return. "This not being able to stand just started last night," he answered, wincing from the pressure of the doctor's hands on his legs. "The stiffness in my joints has been coming on for years. I just thought it was arthritis."

Doctor Safford frowned as he continued running his hands along Charley's leg and arm bones. "Can you turn over?" he asked.

Charley complied and the doctor felt along his shoulders, neck and back bone. With great effort, Charley turned back over and covered up when the doctor finished. "The stiff joints and swelling is arthritis, isn't it?" he asked with hopeful anticipation in his voice. Arthritis was normal for a man of his age; but Charley also sensed what he was feeling and how he was feeling was somehow not normal.

"Not exactly, Charley," Doctor Safford said. "I'm afraid it's a lot more complicated than that. Do want Miss Sterling and Erwin to hear my diagnosis, because at this point of your tumors, you are going to have to have someone take care of you."

Charley swallowed hard as he heard the word "tumors." He laid back harder against the pillows and closed his eyes. "They are my family. Yes, let them come in here." His fears were growing, as he had suspected for a long time there was something more seriously wrong with him than just arthritic joints.

Tumors! His mind screamed at him. Although he did not know exactly what tumors were, he knew this could not be good.

Erwin stood at the foot of the bed and Lillian sat in a chair close to the head of the bed, holding Charley's hand. She felt a knot growing in her stomach, because she knew this was not going to be the common cold or even the more deadly influenza that sickened people unto their dying if not given proper care.

Doctor Safford took off his glasses, wiped them on a white cloth he pulled from a vest pocket, put them back on and returned the cloth to its pocket. "Yes, Charley, you have arthritis," he began. "People who get old get arthritis and rheumatism from exposure to the wet and the cold. Gout from drinking and eating too much.

"But there is something more with what you have. I feel hard lumps along your leg, arm and neck bones and spinal column. When I push on these lumps, your pain increases. Am I right?" he asked, knowing what the answer would be as he had seen the reaction his prodding had produced.

Charley nodded in agreement, fully aware that lying down caused him moderate pain, but the more intense pain was in his legs.

"What are these lumps?" Lillian asked.

"Without cutting one of them away and examining it, I cannot be sure, but I believe they are bone tumors. Charley, there is not an easy way to tell you this, but I am convinced you have something called osteosarcoma."

There is was. Another medical term from Doctor Safford, the same doctor who had pronounced a death sentence on Andrew Sterling with another strange word.

"Just what is this 'osteosar . . .' whatever you called it?" Charley asked. "In plain English, doc, what does this mean? What does it mean for me?"

"Osteosarcoma," the doctor repeated. "Tumors. If these tumors are malignant, it means cancer," Doctor Safford said, bluntly. "There is a lot of research on this disease but little to no cure except to possibly cut away the tumors to keep them from enlarging and spreading and hope for the best."

Lillian felt Charley's grip tighten as he listened to these words which held little to no promise for a return to good health.

"Is this contagious?" Charley asked, suddenly trying to pull his hand away from Lillian's.

"I know of no cases of contagiousness." the doctor replied.

"Just what is this cancer?" Lillian asked. She held firm to her uncle's hand, refusing to let it go.

"In layman's terms, it is a deadly infectious growth of unhealthy body cells that destroy the good cells that make up the body. They build the sarcoma, a tumor. One leads to another and another and another until there is complete destruction of whatever they have attached to."

"What about a cure for this?" Charley asked.

"As I said, there is no real cure, except to cut away the tumors. I would recommend you try this as soon as possible beginning with the legs."

Erwin looked from Charley to Lillian and back to Charley. Close to tears, he had to back away. He had witnessed Andrew dying of some horrible disease no one could seem to cure. Again, he found himself trying to listen to words of death again so close to the heart of his family.

Charley face was grim as he harshly asked, "If I let you do this cutting on me, how long do give me to live?"

Doctor Safford's answer was gravely honest. "There is no way to tell. There are a lot of these tumors in your body from what I felt and probably more that I could not."

"What if you don't cut?" Charley asked.

Doctor Safford let out a sigh. How he wished he knew more. Alas, wishing did not make it so, just as it did it make his job any easier when complicated advice was all he could give.

"Months, weeks. Again it is difficult to say. There is so much the medical profession does not understand about tumors and how they spread. Many of them are cancerous and there is no cure. A lot depends on you and your strength of will to live. All I know is that the tumors will not go away on their on. They will continue to spread."

"With or without the cutting?" Lillian managed to say in a very low tone.

Doctor Safford could only nod.

Charley said, "No!" He closed his eyes as he painfully made up his mind. He opened his eyes, fixed his vision on the doctor and said emphatically, "There will be no cutting. All I ask is that you keep me out of pain. Can you do that?"

"For the most part. I can give you opiates and morphine to ease the discomforts. Herbs to calm the stomach. We need to keep your fever down and you need complete bed rest."

"I already take laudanum," Charley muttered grimly.

"Double it," the doctor said. "If you are a praying man, Charley, I suggest you pray." He put on his coat, looked at Lillian and sadly shook his head. "Just as with your father, I wish there was more I could do. Many things are beyond my medical knowledge. Maybe if you were back East somewhere, another doctor might do better, but . . ." and again, he shook his head, "I doubt if you could make the trip, Charley. I'll show myself out." he said and quietly left the room. There was nothing more he could do.

Lillian crossed the room to stare outside. "It is starting to snow," she said, watching the small flakes swirl outside the window. "We will need to bring more wood in and bank the big stoves downstairs. I will remain here the rest of the afternoon as well as tonight."

"I will see to the wood and the big stoves." Erwin said.

Lillian closed the heavy drapes to keep out the cold. She came back to her chair beside the bed. "Well, Uncle Charley, this is a fine set of conditions you have put upon yourself," she said, holding her emotions under as much control as she could muster.

"Didn't ask for it, Baby Girl," he said, "but then we just don't know what will be our demise when we start this life. Who would have thought it would be a knife blade that would cause your father's dying or a bullet that would end Simon Pails' miserable existence." He reached for his flask of brandy and swilled down a considerable amount before he closed the container.

Lillian cautiously watched him, but said nothing.

"I always kind of imagined it would be a jealous husband who would put me out of his way or a more than disgruntled Monte player who thought me to cheat him in some way."

With great tenderness Lillian took his hand in hers. "That jealous husband still might find you, but I doubt the other as I am held to believe you have never cheated at cards. You may have done many things in your life, Uncle Charley, but cheating at cards is certainly not one of them."

"I appreciate your respect and your concern," he said. "You must listen to me. I will not be a problem for you or for anyone. The Sterling House needs your fulltime attention. Not a sick and dying man."

"Nonsense," she said. "You are not dying yet. As for The Sterling House, it is stealing my life from me just as surely as these tumors, if we are to believe what Doctor Safford says, are stealing the life from you.

"You said you would not have them cut away but I can remove myself from the Sterling House when it suits me. Uncle Charley," she said, her eyes brimming with tears as the holding of emotion was slowly leaving her control. "It suits me to be here with you. Who else will care for you but me?"

He reached out with one hand and brushed the tears from her cheeks. "Seems you are taking care of a lot for one so young," he said, dropping his hand and looking up at the ceiling. "I am an old man who can only thank you and wonder who will take care of you, Baby Girl?"

"There is one who cares," she said.

"But have not heard from him, have you?" he asked, sympathetic to her emotional state yet knowing there had been no word as he too had received none.

"No," she said, "I am so afraid something has happened. I know Spain is a long way from here but a letter would certainly put my fears to rest. If it would not be so improper and I had the means, I would go to Cordoba and find him. But . . ." she let her voice trail away. "it would not be proper and I obviously have no means to do so."

"All I know, Lillian, is that he loves you," Charley said. Again he reached for his flask and also the bottle of laudanum.

"Are you sure you should do that?" she asked indicating the brown bottle.

"I am tired and I need to sleep," was his answer. "He loves you, Baby Girl and he . . . will . . . be . . . back."

Lillian took both the bottle and the flask from him. She placed them on the table within his reach. She kissed him lightly on the forehead. "If you wish these things, then these things you shall have and anything else you want. I will always respect your wishes."

"Wait . . . wait . . . for . . ." Charley slowly began fading into his drugged sleep.

"Yes, Uncle Charley," she quietly said as she pulled the covers securely up over him. "I will wait for Paris Jacob and I will take care of you."

Lillian had new circumstances to consider, and decisions about her uncle's care to be made, and made quickly. From the way Charley's illness was taking him and what Doctor Safford had said, she doubted if he would be on his feet soon, if ever.

As Lillian walked down the hallway to the stairs, she rationalized it would be next to impossible for her to take complete care of him. Nurses could be retained but she was also quite sure he would not allow strangers to come into the house to give that care. She knew she could count on Erwin and Jonas as well as Ming Su and Ling Su. Between them all, they would manage this.

"Tea ready, Missy Lillian," Ming Su said and Ling Su poured one cup. "Please, both of you, join me," Lillian said and wearily sat down. "Where is Erwin?" she asked noticing that he was not in the kitchen, nor had she seen him anywhere else in the house.

"He go back to Sterling House before snow get too much." Ming Su answered. Both girls sat down and kept their eyes downcast toward their cups of steaming tea.

Lillian walked to the back door. She shivered as she saw the snow falling harder and the wind pushing it in all different directions at the same time. She took note that the wood boxes were filled to overflowing and the coal buckets were also piled high.

She pulled her shawl tighter to her shoulders and joined the girls at the small kitchen table. "Ming Su and Ling Su," she said, "I am aware it is against your custom, but would be so kind as to look at me when we talk? It is not disrespectful to me, I assure you."

They looked up and she marveled at their perfectly slanted eyelids and how dark their eyes were. These beautiful girls were like the porcelain dolls she had upstairs in her old bedroom with their flawless skin and not a strand of hair out of place. They were gentle and delicate; probably deserving an even better life than the one they had. Still, this was far better than their likely fates just one street over from the Sterling House.

"As I am sure you have seen," she began, "my Uncle Charley is very sick. The doctor says he will die from what is wrong with him."

"No white doctor cure?" Ming Su asked, alarm in her gentle voice.

"No," Lillian answered, "no white doctor cure."

Ling Su, the very quiet sister, kept her vision averted. Lillian saw her stifle a sob.

"What we do, Missy?" Ming Su asked.

Lillian saw the genuine concern in those beautiful dark eyes. "He will require a lot of care, and very special care, as he may never walk again. I could hire nurses to come but I think he would be happier with all of us caring for him instead of strangers. He must be fed and make sure he takes what medicines the doctor wants him to take. He must be bathed and kept very clean. Erwin will do most of that as it would not be proper for young ladies as yourself to do the washing of his body."

Ming Su cleared her throat. Then, with a sudden burst of boldness, said, "We see man before at the old house we live in, but not something we want to see again. So we thank you for saying Erwin do that part for us. But, Missy Lillian, we do all the rest. We care for him because he is honorable man. Man with honor who give us good, decent home."

Lillian reached across the table to take Ming Su's hand in her own. "Thank you," she said, "and thank you, too, Ling Su. I am confident you will do all you can to see to his comforts and his care. He is sleeping now, but with this storm coming, he will need an extra blanket before morning as we all will."

"You stay night, too?" Ming Su asked.

"Yes. I must be near my uncle. I also fear the storm is too strong for me to safely travel back to the Sterling House. Besides, Erwin took the carriage and I do not expect him back until this storm is finished. We will keep the fires burning, to stay warm as we wait it out."

She knew there would be many hours of vigilance and waiting for more than this storm to pass. Her father's death, Paris Jacob leaving her and now this. Her uncle was dying and although she was strong willed and had taken complete charge of the Sterling House, as well as her life and livelihood, she had no power to change her loved ones leaving her.

"Is there plenty of food in the house? Do remember how to make the Sterling House soups?"

"Oh, yes, Missy," Ming Su assured her.

"Prepare soup and make sweetbreads. Keep the coffee made and we will take care of Mr. Charley until this storm passes."

Lillian stood up and the girls rose with her. "I am going up to my old room and prepare it for tonight."

"We help?' Ming Su offered.

"No," she responded. With a different sadness, she realized this would be the first time she would be back in the room where her young innocence had lovingly been changed into womanhood. The place and time were locked forever in her mind when she had committed herself to love a man that, for whatever the reasons, could not stay with her, or apparently come back for her.

As she slowly climbed the stairs, she once again challenged herself to never fail her family, keep her commitment to Paris and the love she had for him, and never forget the qualities that were hers by her Sterling birthright.

*   *   *

Two days passed before Erwin returned, bringing Jonas Gregory with him. Erwin immediately set about refilling the wood boxes and coal buckets before he went to Charley's room to sit with him.

"This has been about the coldest I can recall its ever being here," Jonas said, gratefully accepting the hot coffee offered by Ming Su. "We have not gotten too much snow at the Sterling House but it has been bitter, bitter cold. We could not get out, Lillian. It was just too cold. We were worried about all of ya over here but I knew ya would be just fine here. This is a strong house an' I knew the provisions were here."

"I knew it was extremely cold." Lillian responded. "We kept the fires stoked, kettle of soup going, tea steeping and coffee brewing. All we could do was wait. It was not wise to venture out."

"I am glad your common sense kept you here. The worst part of the blizzard has been east of us. Reports that are comin' in, from out on the plains east of us, are sayin' the snow drifts are impossible ta get through. Those who have gotten through for shelter here in the city are sayin' thousands of head of cattle have died."

"What?" she questioned, hardly believing what she had just heard. "What has happened out there? What do mean the cattle are dead?"

"Thank you, Ming Su," Jonas said when she refilled his coffee. He was so thankful that both she and her sister, who was busy stirring the kettle of rich smelling soup bubbling away on the stove, were safe in the Big House.

He blew across the hot liquid before answering. "I am not really sure. Don't know much about what has happened yet, but they are sayin' cattle have dropped by the thousands in the big herds because of this extreme cold, no shelters an' massive snow drifts. They froze where they stood. The cattlemen an' ranchers will have ta wait until spring thaw ta find out how bad their losses will be."

Lillian sadly shook her head, imagining how terrible this had to be for those who were suffering this loss. She thought for a moment and then another realty came into her thinking. "Jonas, do you have any idea what this will do to the price of beef?' she asked.

Jonas just shook his head. "Perhaps we won't be servin' as many steaks," he replied playing with the edge of his cup. He knew that when the supply was cut off from the demand, the demand would increase but without proper funding, the increase could not always be paid.

Lillian took her cup to the wash sink and saw past the frost covered kitchen window to a dreary world outside where she knew it was bitterly cold. They were in a safe, warm and dry shelter. Lillian knew there was nothing that could be done about frozen cattle somewhere out on the Great Plains. If the price of beef rose, it would rise for all who wanted a good piece of beef. She turned back and faced Jonas. "How is my mother faring during all of this and of course, how is the Sterling House holding up?"

"Haven't been open for a couple of days. No one was out an' about until today. Cook did not show up an' only one of the servin' girls. I let her ready the dinin' room an' upper rooms so we can open tomorrow."

Lillian carefully listened to what he was saying. Being closed, even for just one day, was not good. However, there was logic of not being open if no one was out and about. "And my mother?" she repeated.

"Your mother is your mother. She is well an' safe at the Sterling House," he said. He would not be disrespectful, but cared little for the woman, avoiding her when he could. "Doctor Safford did stop by just as we were leavin' an' told me to tell you that he will be by in the mornin' to see how Charley is doin' an' bring more medicine. Lillian," he questioned, "this is serious isn't it?"

Lillian shook her head yes. "The laudanum helps him sleep and he insists on brandy in his coffee. I won't refuse him and I don't want anyone else to either. He tends to his private needs. How I don't know as he is in a lot of pain from those tumors. Ming Su and Ling Su are good with all of this and especially with him. But soon, very soon, I believe we will need to have a man here at all times to help with his personal needs as this is something I do not want the girls tending too. It is one thing for them to take the chamber mug to the privy but quite another for them to attend him privately."

"Erwin an' I will share the responsibility for his personal needs an' I thank you for not askin' them ta do somethin' . . ." and he faltered for

155

words, "privately questionable. But, Lillian," he said, "what are these tumor things? The doctor tried to explain but I still don't understand."

Lillian shook her head, weary of trying to understand it herself. "I am still not sure. Something that goes wrong in the body and these growths appear taking over and killing off what is good in the body."

Jonas just looked at her. He wanted to understand, but all of this was beyond them or their understanding of such things.

While Lillian and Jonas talked, Ming Su and Ling Su had prepared trays to be taken to Charley and were going toward the doorway.

"Is that for Mr. Charley?" he asked.

"Yes, Mr. Jonas," Ming Su said.

"Lillian, I will go with them an' sit with him for awhile. Erwin will take ya back ta the Sterling House when you are ready, but I wouldn't wait too late as the temperature will start fallin' again early."

"Yes, Jonas," she said. "I suppose I should be getting back."

He gave her a reassuring hug. "I will stay here with him. You are not ta worry. I just want you ta know we will all take care of him."

Lillian struggled with her emotions. Jonas Gregory did not need to see her cry.

*   *   *

"Jonas," Charley said as he tried to sit up in the bed. Ling Su set her tray down and gently assisted his efforts. "These two girls are a true Godsend." He was thankful they were there being so willing to help. He looked toward the trays she and her sister had brought into the room. "Smells good."

"Soup, Mr. Charley," Ming Su said. "Good soup from Sterling House."

"I am so glad you brought these young ladies into our lives, Jonas. They have made a big difference in my life. Thank you, Ming Su and you too, Ling Su."

In response both girls bowed slightly and silently left the room.

"They are quiet and clean and take care of this house as if it were their own," Charley said, spooning the soup and smiling with satisfaction.

"They had good teachers in the houses they were in," Jonas said, taking a chair near the bed. "Those same teachers were about teachin' other things these girls did not need ta learn, at least not in those houses over on Market."

Charley thoughts were inwardly happy as he recalled another house he had frequented on many occasions. He wondered what had ever happened to Ada Lamont. He peeked under the second, lesser, napkin on his plate and picked up a small piece of wood. Holding it up, he said, "See this? They know I like to whittle my own toothpicks and always provide a little piece of wood for me."

Jonas smiled as he reflected on how many times he had seen this man do exactly that, whittle a toothpick to keep his teeth clean. He ran his tongue over his own teeth and realized he had not taken such good care.

"Jonas, will you remove the tray?" Charley asked, pushing the half eaten soup away. "If I eat too much, I get sick to my stomach."

Jonas did as asked and sat back down. "I want ta thank you, Charley," he said.

"For what?"

"For all ya have done for me since those days at the boardin' house back in Missouri, even before we came across, everything that happened on the crossin' an' right up ta your acceptin' Ming Su an' Ling Su. I ain't never had many friends an' no family ta recall. But you an' Andrew, an' of course, always Mr. Buck, all accepted me an' gave me a chance. A man couldn't ask for more."

Charley narrowed his vision toward the end of the little toothpick he had whittled and decided it would suffice. Working on his teeth, he said between picks, "Perhaps we saw the man you would someday become if but given the chance to get there. None of us ever asked of your business before you came into our lives, but we noticed the remains of the bruises. You weren't always that careful."

Jonas studied the floor before he responded and decided to tell the truth. "I lied," he said. "I was only in my fifteenth year that summer but I had to keep runnin'. Keep goin'. Get away from Missouri an' the man that was my paw." Jonas realized it was time he told someone and who better than this charitable man who had helped him in so many ways.

"When he was liquored up, my paw would beat me. From as far back as I could remember, that was all I knew. He claimed I was responsible for the death of my maw, 135 with her dyin' when I was born. I guess he reckoned that would make it better somehow. "I think that I kinda knew the day would come when it would be him or me. I left because I did not want ta have ta kill him. It was a bad time, Charley, bad for me an' that is why ya all became so important to me. Ya was the family I never had. An'," he continued, "the only family I ever want especially after I saw what Miss Emma went through givin' birth ta Erwin an' how sick she was. I vowed I would never take a wife an' have her bear me children."

"I see," Charley said. " You were brave, Jonas, and strong of mind to do what you did back then. I hate to think of all the things that could have happened to you, but didn't because you came our way. In a way, you are like the son I never had and never will have." He closed his eyes. For a moment, was lost in his own sad memories. "Would you pour me some coffee?" he asked, reaching for his brandy flask.

As Jonas poured the coffee, he asked, "What about you? All I know is that you are from a place known as New York an' are the best gambler I ever knew." He carefully filled the cup only part way recalling what Lillian had said about the alcohol addition.

"Oh, I am not the best," Charley said as he poured a good measure of brandy into his coffee. "I learned from the best and that was my father. Where he learned the cards, I never knew, but he was good. Better than good.

"He never missed. When I was young, I watched him, memorizing every move, every turn. When I was old enough, he took me with him. I was playing grown up men and dealing cards by the time I was maybe 12 years old. I won, because I knew how. "It was at about that time my mother just up and left. Said it was more than her heart could take and she somehow knew she could not change him or me.

"My father said there was another man, one who could give her the home life she so desperately wanted and did not have with him. I don't remember really missing her all that much as the cards took over. I probably wasn't the son she needed, either." He drank half of the coffee down and then refilled the cup with more brandy.

Jonas didn't say anything. If the brandy helped, then let him drink it. It was obvious he was not going anywhere.

"The day came when I became too much of a threat to the old man. We argued violently about the cards and where we would deal. He wanted it all, so I let him have it. "I had a dream. It was to seek my fortune in the gold fields. He said I would fail on my own. How was I to know I would meet such a man as Andrew Sterling or that the Sterling House would happen. Plus all of this." He gestured around the room, indicating his home. "Maybe this is the home my father should have given my mother. Maybe I was making up for something I missed."

"Or something ya had taken away from you," Jonas said also remembering Emma Frederson.

"You might say that."

"Why did ya build such a big house all the way out here away from the Sterling House?"

"Seemed the thing to do at the time. Guess I wanted something to call my own away from what Andrew was providing for his family. You and Erwin will have it, as there is no one else."

"What about Lillian?" Jonas asked

"She has the Sterling House. That is her home. It's where she needs to be and that is where she will stay. Since this illness has happened, I have thought about it and this is a legacy I can leave to you and Erwin. Live in it, sell it, do as you will."

Charley leaned back on the pillows and closed his eyes. "I don't think I have failed in my life, but I am tired of living it," he said.

He opened his eyes that were becoming a bit glassy from the brandy. "If there is but one thing in your life truly wish to do, Jonas, go and do it. You more or less raised Erwin. Now it seems have those two Celestials in your care. They might want to see their homeland someday. You would be the one to take them to China. Maybe should just plan on that." Charley's smile was faint as the cup slid from his hand.

Jonas caught it before the contents spilled on the bedding and pulled the blankets higher to cover the man's body. Charley's eyes were closed, his breathing was shallow. His color was cold grey ash and his cheeks were sunken. Whatever these tumors were, they were claiming this man and claiming him fast.

Erwin came into the room with an armload of pine slabs and stoked the fire in the fireplace. He walked over to the bed and looked down at Charley Gaynor. He could not find words he could say to him or to anyone for that matter. His heart was filled with love for this man who had been like a quiet father for him, always there, always steadfast.

He wanted words of comfort, but could find none. He was just too shy. Charley Gaynor was their friend and their friend was dying. *What more can I do?* he thought, *but see to all their needs and keep the fires burning.*

Chapter
Fifteen

The major storm passed. The snow melted and the cold drifted away. Over the weeks that followed the revelation of Charley's illness, Lillian alternated her days between the Sterling House and the Big House. Charley always told her she need not stay so close beside him if she was needed at the restaurant.

"Mother is quite capable," she answered him and continued her vigil, encouraging him to talk about the days of the crossing and the early days of the Sterling House. She delighted in the story of how her father and Uncle had seen the plats of land the first time. The thought of the rotted pickled eggs still made her laugh and how the only thing they thought to be salvageable was the nude painting.

"Don't know why your mother objected so keenly to that painting," Charley said.

"She is quite Victorian in her thinking," Lillian answered.

"What about your thinking?" Charley asked.

"As you very well know, not so much."

They both laughed, knowing exactly what the other meant.

*   *   *

When the weather cleared more, Abigale dutifully paid her respects. She sat very primly on the edge of one of the brocade tapestry chairs in Charley's bedroom as she sipped the tea, properly served to her by Ming Su. "There is so much talk about these two young girls being here the way they are," she said.

"Really?" Charley said, unable to rise from his pillows. "And just what do people say they are doing out here, except taking care of an old man who is dying?" He looked at her and his smile dimmed. He could not hold it especially not for Abigale Sterling.

"We all know what the Orientals are capable of," she replied, not wavering.

Charley gratefully accepted a generous amount of laudanum from Ling Su's ministering hands and welcomed the coolness of those hands on his forehead as she smoothed back his hair.

"They have comforting ways," he managed. He just wanted Abigale to leave his room. Ling Su moistened a towel and cooled his face with it, never taking her eyes off the harsh woman who sat so stiffly in the chair sipping the tea but not tasting it.

"Ya should have told me," she said.

"Told you what, Abigale?" he asked leery of where she might be trying to take the conversation.

"What Andrew was doin' all the time before I got here." she said nonchalantly all the while her mind churned with wanting to hear the story from the man who had been closest to her wayward husband before her arrival.

"He was my friend and I honored him. I still do. It was not my place to speak out of turn about affairs that were not mine to speak of and they still are not," he said firmly.

"Humph!" she said. "How many others were there? Those savage Indian women he seemed ta prefer ta a civilized white woman."

Charley could not stand to listen to her anymore and turned his attention toward the light coming from the open, draperied window. *How different things might have been if this woman had never existed in Andrew's life. But then, there would never have been the beautiful woman, Lillian Anne, if this woman had not existed.*

He marveled at how Lillian could be the incredible woman she was with a mother as cold, shrewish and calculating as Abigale Sterling was. "I guess we will never know," he said and sank back into his pillows and bedding. "The laudanum is working." he said deliberately stumbling over his words. "I feel very tired."

"Yes," Abigale said. "How completely convenient."

*   *   *

Doctor Safford made regular visits, prescribing more and more of the opiates combined with more and more laudanum. He knew the tumors were spreading and were rampant inside the body of what at one time had been a very healthy and virile man.

The medical man was professional in Charley's presence. He held out hope and promise to the family but wearily shook his head as he drove away from the handsome house on Pennsylvania Street. Charley Gaynor was not the only grimly ill dying person he was attending. Literally hundreds of his patients suffered from the Great White Plague, more medically described as tuberculosis. These sick people were scattered all about the great city and there was little to no hope for them either.

There was no cure for this strange lung disease. Just as there was no cure for the sorrow he felt as a doctor who seemed to be failing in his duty to his patients. Nothing he could do except retire, which he fully planned on doing as soon as he pronounced the final words for Charley Gaynor. He hoped for the man's sake those words would not be too far away as he was in more pain than the laudanum and strong opiates could relieve.

*   *   *

When Charley Gaynor died, the ice had stopped cracking and popping in Cherry Creek and the stream was lively from the melting snows and spring rains. The South Platte had lost its ice flows and returned to its polluted state, with water running strong from bank to bank trying to wash away the putrefying refuse that constantly threatened to choke its flow. The air over Denver was cleaner and the long shifts at the White Ash Coal Mine had been reduced as the demand for coal slowed.

Charley Gaynor was buried beside Andrew Wesley Sterling and, as befitted who the man was, he was wearing his finest silk brocade vest with his gold watch and chain, along with three diamond stick pins holding his cravat in place. Lying beside him was an unbroken Monte deck. Because Lillian knew the stories, she had placed the canvass pouch of pebbles from the crossing close to his right hand and included the matching shot glass, the mate to the one buried with her father. At the last moment, Ling Su placed a small box filled with small pieces of wood into his coffin. Ming Su put a small carving knife under his hand.

As with Andrew, many came to pay their respects. Those who saw him lying in state prior to the funeral commented on how handsome they all remembered his being through all the years he had dealt the cards and how tragic his sickness had been to rob him of so much.

The processional to Riverside Cemetery had been long and difficult, since the ground was muddy in spots from the last rain, but birds had sung in the trees and the leaves were fresh and newly green. Nearby, the Platte River ran full to its banks and the sky was a brilliant blue overhead.

Words were spoken for Charley Gaynor by the same reverend who had attended to Andrew's eulogy. At the final "amen" he solemnly walked away from the closed coffin with his Bible under his arm and an accepted donation in his pocket for words delivered for the peace of mind of those in attendance.

Finally, only Lillian, Abigale, Jonas and Erwin, along with Ming Su and Ling Su, remained at the graveside. It had been a long four months for all of them, watching this man wither and die from something no one could see or stop. It was better this way, but Lillian already missed him terribly. He, like her father, could never be replaced at the Sterling House or in her heart. She took notice of her mother.

"Mother, are you crying?"

From behind her gloved hand, Abigale said, "Thet is what one is supposed ta do at a funeral. Or have ya forgotten everything ya learned at thet fancy school thet cost me so much money."

"I have forgotten nothing, Mother," she said. Her mother had not shed one tear when her father had died. With sad dignity, Lillian turned and walked away.

*   *   *

Charley Gaynor's will had been blunt and to the point. He left his worldly holdings, equally, to Jonas and Erwin. Lillian knew there was a strong partnership between her father and her Uncle Charley, but in all her searching through documents and papers in various strongboxes and the safe in the office, she had found nothing to substantiate his being a part owner in the Sterling House. She was satisfied it had been a verbal agreement between the two men and she was satisfied the bond was broken at both their deaths.

Jonas and Erwin had discussed with her what to do with the property and house.

"Do you wish to live there, Erwin as Jonas primarily lives here," Lillian asked.

Erwin waited for Jonas to say something but, as usual, he was soberly quiet. "The Big House has been my home for as long as I can remember," Erwin finally replied. "We played there, Lillian. You and me and Charley Paul. I took all those piano lessons there, but now," he said, his heart heavy, "I don't know where to go or what to do. There is also Ming Su and Ling Su to be considered. They should have a future too. Somewhere." He let his voice trail off.

The three of them sat in the front sitting room on the third story of the Sterling House. Lillian was certain her mother was probably listening just outside the big double doors, but she wisely ignored her suspicion. Tea and sweet cakes had been served none of which had been touched.

Lillian picked up a cake and then placed it back on its silver tray. She picked up her teacup and realized the tea was cold. She set the cup down. They were depending on her for answers she clearly did not have. Needing a moment to collect her thoughts, she walked to a front window where she stared down at the street. A cable car clattered by, stopped and let passengers off. It then rattled on to its next predicted stop. The car had no choice but at least it knew where it was going.

"No matter how cleverly concealed," she said slowly, " this is a lawless town. Ruled by outside the law from within the law. There have been lynchings, legal hangings and murders within blocks of where we call our home. We face this each and every day. I have learned to face all adversity with the support of my family." She turned to face them where they seemed to anticipate her words of wisdom about their future.

She waited while Erwin dumped their cold tea in a standing porcelain basin and refreshed the cups.

Lillian continued, "People have become rich from the gold my father came here to find, and found, but not in those ravines and mountains to the west of us. He and my Uncle Charley found it here in this Sterling House. Many find silver in much the same way, but it is not my future to dig in the ground for such riches.

"I must supervise as I see to the bottom of flour barrels and empty whiskey bottles to secure the future of the Sterling House. I have learned well from you, Jonas, and you, too, Erwin. I pray it is enough for us to continue.

"Jonas, you live here at the Sterling House. This is your home." She faced Erwin directly. "This is also your home, Erwin. You are like a brother to me and I love you deeply. Both of you must make the decisions about your own lives and where you live. You are my family, all I have ever known. I will support you in your decisions; however, I cannot tell you what to do." She waited.

Jonas drank his tea and bit into a sweet cake. "I remember these from the very beginnin' when Soolie made them. When I first came here when Erwin was just a lil' boy."

Erwin nodded, his memory in agreement.

Jonas continued, "We cannot live in both places. I think I speak for Erwin when I say this. Let us sell the house on Pennsylvania an' its contents. I believe there is room for Erwin ta move in here as well as Ming Su an' Ling Su, if ya will have them.

"They are good an' they will work hard ta secure where they live. The money from the sale can be split equally between Erwin an' myself. I will give half of my proceeds ta you, Lillian, ta help in whatever way needed.

"The Celestial sisters will work for little ta no pay for a good home an' safe place ta live. In the long run it will save ya money an' it will make ya money. I cannot speak for Erwin, but we need ta get this family all under one roof." He sat back in his chair and was quiet.

Lillian looked at Erwin. "I agree," he said without hesitation and they waited for Lillian's response.

She scrutinized the traffic on Larimer Street as she thought on the logic of what they were saying. This is how her Paw Paw would have wanted it and how her Uncle Charley would have seen it. She turned to face them. "We should seal this agreement with something stronger than tea, but I fear I have nothing else to drink here in this setting." She picked up her cup and held it out to them.

Jonas and Erwin both rose, walked to her and they touched the rims of their tea cups to hers. It was a bargain well struck.

*　　*　　*

Within a matter of a few weeks, a contractual agreement for the amount of $4,000 had been made between Jonas Gregory, Erwin Frederson and a young couple by the names of Isaac and Mary Large, who had recently made a considerable fortune from their silver holdings in the mountains of Colorado.

The furniture was sold at auction and Charley's Pennsylvania Big House was torn down to make room for the architectural dream of William Lang, a developer who saw in its place a three-story Colorado rhyolite lava stone structure with red sand stone trim. Erwin moved into the opposite end of the second story of the Sterling House from where Jonas slept and quickly converted that dining room to his sleeping quarters. Lillian was delighted to see it converted to this new use, because only on very rare occasions was that back dining area was used for dining purposes.

As he had stated, Jonas gave Lillian half of the money from his proceeds and began using half of his earnings to pay off the men who still came to the Sterling House to collect payment for the privilege of allowing the gambling to continue.

Lillian was aware of this, but said nothing. She did not like what she suspected was true, but knew asking Jonas about it would only embarrass the man. Bribes and payoffs were unsavory issues she still left between the men.

As much as her mother had loudly disapproved of the two sisters, Ming Su and Ling Su, coming to work at the Sterling House, their culinary expertise, once they learned Soolie's recipes, far surpassed any others in the kitchen, as did their cleanliness.

With Charley Gaynor's home sold and Jonas and Erwin both living at the Sterling House, it had also made perfect sense to have the Celestial sisters live there as well. This created on onsite house staff with little to no outside help required.

Abigale; however, did not see it that way. She had been listening at the door that day when the plans were made to sell the Big House and have them all move into the Sterling House. She had remained quiet during the sale of the property and Erwin's move. However, she became quite verbal when Ming Su and Ling Su arrived to take up residence.

"I know exactly where they came from an' thet is where their kind belongs," Abigale had said. "An' I will not have thet kind of goin's on here under the very roof of the Sterling House."

"I will send them away, if that is what ya want me ta do" Jonas had said to Lillian. The argument had erupted while the girls stood in the kitchen, their belongings in small tote bags waiting to be told where to go and what to do. "But, I will go with them, if they go," he added with solemn determination.

Lillian glared at her mother, who was still frowning. She looked at Jonas who was patiently waiting for an answer. She considered the two delicate young girls who stood silently awaiting their fate.

Lillian cleared her throat before she spoke. "They will be moving into my old nursery room and will continue working in the kitchen as well as tend to serving," she said, "unless, mother, you wish to cook, serve, polish silver and wash dishes?

"This was part of the agreement when the Big House was sold and it is to all our benefit to have Jonas with us. Ming Su and Ling Su will be welcome here as long as they, and you Jonas, wish to call the Sterling House home."

Abigale glared at her daughter. "No one asked me if'n I would agree ta this," she harshly muttered and she shot a look of utter contempt in the direction of the sisters before she stormed from the room to seek a glass of comfort.

It was apparent she had no voice and it was obvious she had no say. She certainly had no ruling when it came to her very own home, the Sterling House. She was not blind to the deterioration of the neighborhoods surrounding 'their' portion of Larimer Street. It had become quite obvious to her that the Sterling House was rapidly becoming nothing more than a hotel for the homeless.

First Jonas, then Erwin an' now these two . . . two . . . Celestial street waifs who will probably cut our throats while we sleep, she thought as she locked her bedroom door and once again barricaded herself into the dim world of her creation where there was no one to disagree with her.

Abigale undressed, utilized her porcelain chamber mug, put on one of her most elegant Victorian dressing gowns, drank a measure of laudanum and then began sipping sherry.

There was so little for her to do. Her daughter and those Orientals saw to that. There was no one to talk to since Hortence Wilson had taken to her sickbed with some ailment which she had presumably succumbed to as there had been no answer to the last message sent to the household where she lived. There was no where to go and it was clear her opinions were not valued when it came to major decisions regarding the Sterling House.

She took off her spectacles and then squinted at the blurred image that stared back at her in the mirror. It was sad she had come so far to mean so little to anyone. Abigale finished her generous glass of sherry, turned out the light and went to bed to seek the sleep of one who depended on alcohol and drugs to escape the pain of continued living. She had no tears as they too had dried up along with her life.

Chapter Sixteen

She held it in her hand. She could not believe it, but she held it in her hand. A letter packet all the way from Cordoba, Spain. It was bedraggled, it was torn. It was smudged. It was water stained.

Yet she held it in her hand!

"Kinda hard ta know where this packet was supposed ta go. 'pears like it has been around the world a few times over." The young messenger said when he handed the letter packet to her. "They didn't seem ta know over ta the post office, but I knew." he said, puffing up his chest with pride and a bit of dignity. "I told 'em I knowed the Sterling House."

"Oh," Lillian said, hardly able to control her trembling hands, "just how did you have that distinct honor?"

"My ma an' my pa dun brought me here on my birthday, Ma'am. Thet's how I knew this elegant place," he said proudly trying to peek around her to see into the dining area.

"Let me bring a coin for your trouble," Lillian offered wanting the young man to leave so she could open this packet that was so long overdue.

"Oh, no Ma'am," he said. "If it would be no trouble though, I would like to sit an' have tea an' a sweet cake, an' I can pay."

Lillian smiled. "Most certainly," she said. "Ming Su," she called out.

"Yes, Missy Lillian."

"Whatever this young man wants is my pleasure for him to have."

The young messenger looked down at his scuffed, worn shoes and then meekly followed the Oriental girl to a front window table where he cautiously sat down.

He watched Lillian Anne Sterling, the most beautiful woman he had ever seen, climb the spiral staircase to places he could only imagine.

Gazing out the front window to the bustling Larimer Street, he sat up a bit straighter. His appraisal of the silver service set on the table before him made him realize he still did not know which utensil to use anymore so than he had on his birthday.

*   *   *

Lillian maintained her composure until she reached her room. Once safely inside, she leaned heavily against the door. Closing her eyes, she trembled clutching the soiled packet to her heart to she fought back the tears of mingled joy and relief.

She opened her eyes and, through a bleary mist of tears, read what she could clearly read of the return address.

Spain!

She walked across the room and placed the packet on a table near the window. She stared at it, still not believing what she was seeing. It was stamped and smeared and so smudged with the grime of many hands. It was obvious it had been many places by the stamp marks all over it. The addresses, both send to and coming from, were barely discernable. She traced her finger across the ink stained return address that read Casa . . . toya, with the next two lines completely missing and then there was . . . doba Spain. The only readable words in the send address was L . . . Sterling . . . Larimer and Den . . . rado. The rest was so stained it was obliterated.

Lillian was amazed the packet had reached her. *How long had this taken?*

She thought she could read one of the stamps as "Australia" or possibly "Austria" and the date "1887" and yet another that read what might be part of the words "Africa" and several others that were stamped over stamps. They were so smudged it was all impossible to decipher.

Turning the packet over, she saw where it had been re-closed with sealing wax what seemed like several times over. She very carefully broke through the layers of wax to the first one and could see where it once had been the letter "M." She opened the page as if breaking the original seal for the first time.

The inside of the letter packet had fared no better than the outside. It was obvious the moisture had seeped to the inside, doing its damage and she could only read parts of what was written, especially where the letter packet had been creased and folded.

At the top of the page was a crest that could only be that of Casa de la Montoya. Beneath that, she made out the date to be 1886 and the words "Lillian, my love," and then the ink blurred until she got to a place where it was clear he had become quite ill on the sea voyage to Spain, a fever of some kind. She could not read the rest of it.

Then there was something about a recovery somewhere else in Spain other than Cordoba, but the name of the city was smeared beyond readability. She could also make out, if she read it correctly, his mother had died and there was unrest in his country. Beyond that, the words were gone. A smear of dark ink with only portions of a letter or two visible until she got to the very bottom of the page.

Wait for me. I promise I will return. Paris

Lillian held the letter sheet up to the light, but nothing more could be discerned. She laid the letter back down on table and walked to the window to stare out at a world she did not want and a place she did want to be. All of it rushed in and she cried letting her emotions take over as she let the tears flow. She sank to the floor and sobbed her sorrow to a room where only she knew how she felt and where she was safe to feel like a woman.

Once the tears ran their course, she struggled to her feet and washed her face in cold water from the porcelain pitcher at her wash basin. Lillian looked at her reflection in the mirror and then back at the letter lying on the table.

Wait for me. I promise I will return. Paris

It had taken two years to get this precious piece of paper to her. How long would it take for him to return? She looked back into the mirror and dark blue, sad eyes stared back at her.

If it takes forever, I will wait for you, she vowed. *Here in this place where you left me, Paris Jacob LaRoche de la Montoya, you will find me.*

Chapter
Seventeen

For the haughty little princess of the plains, the next two years passed quickly. One more time, Cherry Creek flowed out of its banks and the South Platte River flooded. This put many low lying areas under brackish water for days. The Sterling House weathered the flood waters, cleaned the mud from Her skirts and stood solid.

This was not; however, the case with some structures located closer to these unpredictable waterways where the buildings languished under the stagnant waters for days. These hellish waters receded or evaporated leaving layers of foul smelling mud resulting in complete structural devastation.

One of the greatest losses to Denver's elite society, along with those who visited the city, had been Bartholomew's beautiful five-acre lush Olympic Resort Gardens located where Larimer Street challenged the Platte River. Too much flooding only added to the complete demise of this once gracious area where in the early 1870s, an entrepreneur with a different dream had created a zoo, a beer garden and flower lined walkways, as well as carriage drives.

The animals were long gone, the grounds deserted and the smell of fresh lemonade no longer pervaded the air. By the late 1880s, the area reeked from the stench of neglect.

This was nothing new for those who understood Denver and continued to meet the challenges of living there. Those who lived close by ignored the city ordinances which strictly forbade swimming or bathing in the Platte. This included the waifs, strays and homeless bummers whose numbers were growing as they drifted more and more into the lower end of Larimer Street to find habitation.

Denverites, for the most part, turned their faces away from the dying little river which had once been a proud 300 feet wide, running up to 12 feet deep in the summer. The South Platte River had become an eyesore, a breeding ground for vermin, pestilence and disease as it continued to be a costly aggravation when the floods came. During the earlier years, in an effort to keep Denver and its inhabitants connected, many bridges had been built to cross this river that challenged the core of the city. Just as many bridges had been torn away from their abutments when the South Platte flooded. The Denver City Cable Railway solved the issue when they built the city's first viaduct across the Platte. This structure climbed to an awesome three stories high, crossed the railroad tracks and the eyesore river far below, descending into northwest Denver's predominately Jewish neighborhood.

This eased the traffic problems over and across the railroad tracks to say nothing of the disgusting, polluted waters of the Platte. The transfer of traffic across the viaduct decreased the commerce for the small business owners of lower Larimer Street. As they slowly lost their businesses they were left with no choice except to move on. These deserted buildings became shoddy rat invested warehouses and make shift homes for the homeless.

New growth sprawled further and further from the original confluence of Cherry Creek and the South Fork of the Platte River as the hills continued to be leveled, terminating prairie grasslands as it drained life from the land. Newer foundations were laid and roadbeds spread in all directions.

The old time residents of Denver proper were a breed apart from the upstart newcomers who considered themselves to be truly civilized. Denver had surrounded itself with the elitists and smart set that saw it advantageous to frequent establishments where only the well heeled would, and could, be seen.

In reality, there was little to no difference in the eye of the casual observer. The tourists, and those who came to visit the little city, were welcomed by the entrepreneurs and businesses of every cultural standing.

From the bummers begging drinks on street corners up to and including the newly opened David May's May Shoe and Clothing store at 15th and Larimer, all seemed to prosper in one way or the other from these enthralled visitors. This prospering continued to enhance those who had been firmly entrenched from the beginning at the confluence of Cherry Creek and the South Platte River.

A brass band parade celebrated the opening of the elaborate May Store. David May, the owner, was delighted when the store's inventory sold out in a few weeks and he had to completely reinvent his merchandise. Although its location was not ideal, being only a few blocks from the stagnating lower end of Larimer, the May Company was well on its way to becoming a most prosperous clothing stores.

However, there was no brass band for the bummers of Larimer Street whose numbers increased daily. They were content with a cheap bottle of wine and an alley, or deserted building, to burrow into when the night swept over the city.

The scarlet sisterhood, advertised their pleasures under the new street lights which illuminated their popular street as well as all the streets in the downtown area. These lascivious ladies would call from open windows and doorways to any passerby extolling their various sexual favors which were available for a price. Whatever one wanted, wherever they wanted it, it could be found, for a price, in this city lusting for life.

Denver was a boom town for many and a bust town for many more. Silver was far more in demand than its predecessor—gold. Just as the fledgling little sister cities of Auraria and Denver City had been the funneling hourglass for the gold seekers of old, providing all the accouterments necessary for the digging of the gold, it now provided the same for those who would seek a fortune in silver. The over zealous, enthusiastic boomers of the day would rush off to exotic sounding places such as Silver Plume, the Roaring Fork River Valley, Telluride, Silver Cliff and far away Aspen to chase a silver dream.

Reality said, if they were lucky enough to survive the harsh rigors of the Rocky Mountains, they would be back in Denver when the dream became the nightmare and their silver bubble burst. The staunch and solid entrepreneurs profited from all sides of this more than lucrative business. They provided for those seeking the dream, capitalized on those whose silver coffers were full by obliging them with further enhancements as they continued to add more ostentatious blocks of buildings. This ultimately provided one more street corner where one more bummer, who had lost it all, could beg.

Along with the bawdy to the gaudy, from street vendors hawking food to opulent drinking and dining, the Sterling House continued to stand on its own. It was a fine, delicate balance that Lillian oversaw and managed to maintained.

The Monte games had diminished, private poker games increased, card cheats were not allowed and Jonas kept a watchful eye on the saloon where whiskey, bourbon and beer was still served. Soolie's old recipes for pies, pastries, sweet breads and cakes continued to compliment fine meals in the restaurant. The old patrons kept most of the money flowing, sometimes merely trickling, but continuing to come into the Sterling House.

It had been over six years since Lillian's father had died. She had grown quite adept at perpetuating the business of the Sterling House. Much more so than when she had first returned from school and life had been thrust into her face.

Charley and Jonas ordered the liquor for the saloon. She had little to no choice but to trust their judgment as to the quality of what was served. She sensed it was not quite the quality her Paw Paw had provided. It had also been her observance, though, it didn't seem to make a difference as men continued to drink the strong whiskies, beer and wine. However, the elaborate bar glasses that once contained rich cognacs, imported liqueurs, and strong brandies sat on a saloon back shelf collecting dust. Moderate amounts of the finer quality liquors were served in the private dining rooms but most of those patrons preferred wines and champagnes. The only genteel alcohol being ordered in any quantity was the nutty flavored Spanish sherry her mother secreted away and consumed on a regular basis. It kept her quiet most of the time so Lillian did not object. Although Lillian had childhood memories of going to Barthomomew's Park where she had enjoyed the natural history museum along with the garden's grandeur, her mind were not on the decay of the lower end of Larimer Street. On this particular late evening, her thoughts were also not on the blight that slowly encroached toward the Sterling House. She sat in the office work room, where she studied over figures, counted money and struggled in her mind as to how to keep the creditors paid, and find a little surplus.

She required little time for herself as the Sterling House had become her life. Other than her very guarded memories of Paris Jacob Montoya, she thought of little else. As she stared down at the black ink figures staring silently back up at her, she let her thoughts go to the four remaining dining rooms on the second level. They were in desperate need of new wall coverings. Lillian felt the heavy velvet drapes also needed to be replaced. She wanted to replace the drapery with an Irish lace window covering and light velvet drape to allow more light into the rooms. Abigale had argued that privacy and intimacy could not be maintained. She also argued that the darker, rich colors of the old wallpaper would continue the traditions she had begun for the Sterling House.

"I only want to advance the Sterling House with good taste, lighter shades, less pattern and better workmanship according to designs by William Morris." Lillian said as they had argued the issue of room renovations.

"An' who is this William Morris?" her mother had flared at her.

"A learned man who has studied such matters and suggests we all come out of the dark ages with window treatments and room design if we are to continue attracting patronage."

"Are ya sayin' I am livin' in some dark age?" Abigale stormed.

"No, I am not. The Sterling House needs to keep up with the times. We must have changes if we are to survive. There is competition being built all around us. Some offering more than we could possibly hope to offer. The Windsor Hotel is only a block away and the size of it is overwhelming. Mother, they have everything there. We can only offer quiet elegance with more refined class.

"We can no longer rely on just reputation. People passing by on the street must be able to see that the second floor of the Sterling House is for finer dining. That can only be accomplished if the drapes are drawn open during the dining hour. If those who dine wish intimacy, the drapes can be drawn closed."

"We are not the Windsor. We were not built ta be the Windsor or the Albany or the Alford or a host of others in this city," her mother said, hotly defending the Sterling House, "but ya do what ya think is right. Ya always do."

Lillian shook her head to clear the memory of that argument. It was but one of many when it came to the management of the Sterling House. It was very difficult to compete with the menus of so many beautiful dining rooms all around the small establishment which had its humble beginnings in 1861 at what had been Larimer and J Street. It seemed the newly named 19th and Larimer was being dwarfed by its rivals as the riches from the gold and silver being found in the mountains to the West poured into the city. The ostentatiousness produced by these riches was obvious in the enormity of the buildings being constructed where once a one or two-story small business was adequate for the needs of the few. Now the needs were many as were those who were needful. Adding to the complication were the tent cities that were springing up all around Denver to house the infirm who continued to come to Colorado for the magical cure.

The magical cure, Lillian thought, *for those wheezing, coughing, phlegm choked invalids who can not breathe from forms of lung consumption with the worst being that Great White Plague, tuberculosis.*

There were doctors and there were nurses in the sanatoriums for the chronically ill. In Lillian's opinion, there was no magic in the purity of Colorado's air which was being contaminated by the presence of those who were ill from these maladies. A new disparaging term followed the sickly, as most people considered them to be 'lungers' and to be avoided. Those who could not afford to stay in the sanatoriums, pay the doctors or nurses for their services, were slowly filtering into the oldest parts of Denver, seeking shelter where they could in some of the older dilapidated buildings. These were rapidly becoming low rent boarding houses and missions with soup kitchens.

As serious as this invasion of the sick was, it was not Lillian's immediate concern. The Sterling House was and she had no intension of its becoming either a boarding house, a mission or a soup kitchen. She had the front entry ways for the restaurant and saloon swept and scrubbed daily to remove the filth collecting on their very doorstep. Many thought nothing of hacking, gagging, coughing up and eliminating this poison from their lungs onto the streets of Denver. She did not want it tracked into the Sterling House.

There was a light knock on the door. "Yes." she answered.

"Missy Sterling," said Ming Su, the older of the Celestials who always worked somewhere in the Sterling House, no matter what the hour. "I beg pardon but old man at back door want to see you."

"Who is it, Ming Su? Is it a regular?"

"No, Missy, he not say. I never see this man before."

"Did you offer food?" Lillian wearily questioned, thinking this to be one more bum at the door begging for food.

"Oh, yes, Missy, like all, but this man who smell like old leather and strong tobacco, say no to food. He ask for old Mr. Andrew Sterling, and I tell him, old Mister die. Then he ask for Miss Lillian. He say Boss Girl come now."

Ming Su waited for Lillian to instruct her about what to tell the man at the back door. She was instead greatly surprised when Lillian rushed past her down the stairs toward the kitchen's back door. Ming Su quickly followed, curious as to who or what could cause such a reaction.

Not seeing anyone at first, and throwing all caution aside, Lillian stepped out on the platform and peered into the darkness. "Grand Paw Paw?" she called out. There could be only one person, other than her father, who would call her 'Boss Girl'.

She stood perfectly still as the old man who had waited in the alley stepped forward. Slowly he climbed the steps to stand in front of her.

"Grand Paw Paw!" she cried, tears forming in her eyes as she immediately put her arms around Buckland LeRoy Kavanaugh.

"Boss Girl," he replied, and she felt him weaken in her arms.

"You must come in out of the cold." she encouraged, taking him by the arm and pulling him into the kitchen area toward the heat of the stove. "Ling Su, Ming Su," she called out. "Quickly, coffee and hot soup." She pulled out a chair by the small kitchen table. She could scarcely believe her eyes. "Where have you been and is Sool Sool with you and my Charley Paul?" she asked, expecting to see them come into the kitchen at any moment.

"Only me, Boss Girl. Only me," he replied, removing his hooded Capote blanket coat and shaking off the cold before he sat down. He reached for the cup of coffee Ming Su had set down on the table in front of him.

"Soup come," she said and walked away, but not before carefully scrutinizing this strange old man Lillian seemed to be crying over. These Occidentals were a strange group of people and not easily understood. She walked away to check on the soup.

Buckland wiped his eyes as he watched Ming Su leave. *Interesting*, he thought, letting his tired mind recall another interesting young woman he had seen in this house so many years before. Dismissing the memory, he began filling his pipe from his very old, sweat and tobacco stained gadamour.

As Lillian watched his unsteady hands, she recognized this man's familiar action as she also remembered the same weather leather tobacco pouch. Childhood memories and a thousand questions flooded through her but she waited for him to exhale the pungent smoke.

He lit his pipe and inhaled unsteadily, exhaling with a small wheeze. "I buried Soolie up in the Bitterroot after the fever took her from me," he said. "Better than a year ago as I recall. She was tendin' ta a young Cheyenne family all down with the fever an' she come down with it herself." He stopped and seemed to be seeing an image from another time and place. "She died in my arms." he added, and turned away, the memory still as raw as the night it had happened.

Lillian blinked hard as she stared down at the table, letting the news of Soolie's death rest in her mind. "She always was a caring, decent woman," she said. She held back her own tears.

"Finest woman I ever knew," Buckland said. He sucked in his breath, cleared his thinking and continued. "Charley Paul left with some young warriors out of our camp. Heard he was runnin' with some bad Cheyenne somewhere up north in Canada." He looked back at Lillian and his eyes narrowed a bit. "He never did quite fit, no matter what me an' Soolie did fer him. His torment bein' from two worlds caused him ta do bad things sometimes. Weren't no fault, Boss Girl. Maybe someday there will be a place fer his kind."

Ling Su shyly brought the soup to the table and gave this strange old man the same curious scrutiny as her sister had given him. She wrinkled her nose at the unfamiliar leather smell of him and quietly backed away. Whoever he was, Missy Lillian had not taken her eyes off him since he had sat down. She waited with her sister in the corner of the room beside the large cook stove to see if more soup would be needed.

"Ten years, Grand Paw Paw. Ten years since I saw you last," Lillian said, watching him as he spooned the soup. "And you say Soolie is gone," she said, frowning and closer to tears.

"Buried in some place I have never heard of so far away from here. I know you loved her so much. This is a great sadness for you. And, my brother is gone away to places unknown." She looked down and then back into the face of this man she had loved second only to her father.

There was no easy way to tell him. "Paw Paw is gone too?"

Buck let the spoon fall into the soup. "All I know is what the young Oriental said when I asked fer him. What happened?" He asked, grievous to know.

186

"He was killed by some madman who held a grudge for him from many years ago. He was stabbed the night of my homecoming from school. It was the most terrible night of my life," she said, still remembering the flash of that knife. "Uncle Charley shot the man dead, but it was too late. Paw Paw died after the stabbing from some infection the doctor could not stop."

Buckland's eyes were dark with despair at hearing this news. On his journey all the way back to the Sterling House, he had thought of nothing much except to see the people he cared about the most. He could still see that curly blond hair and the intense blue eyes of the boy that had become a man.

Buck recalled another time when they had all reacted quickly and violently when another grudge had been created. A grudge that had cost an innocent young Indian woman her life and a gruesome, but just end to the man who had killed her. "The weight of a grudge can kill a man's good judgment." he said. "I am sad ta hear of yur loss. He was a man I was proud ta call my friend. Where is Charley Gaynor, Jonas an' the red haired boy he brought here?"

"Erwin. The boy's name is Erwin Frederson and he lives here at the Sterling House. Most nights plays the piano and assists me with keeping the doors open. Jonas moved in to help us after Paw Paw was killed. He tends bar and takes care of the saloon especially since . . ." She stopped, choked by her own emotions.

This is so difficult, she thought. "Since Uncle Charley was taken from us too, Grand Paw Paw. He was so weak toward the end and was bed ridden over at the Big House."

"What do ya mean, bed ridden? What ailed him?" Buck questioned, finding it hard to believe what he was hearing. He pushed the soup away, his appetite completely gone.

"A thing called cancer that grows tumors in the body. Deadly things that won't heal." She tried to recall the doctor's words as she continued. "He saw the doctor a lot and took a compound of opium, sherry wine and herbs that the doctor prescribed." She stopped talking and let it all settle between them. Death was never an easy thing. They had just talked about too many people they both loved that were dead and gone.

"I never heard of such a thing," Buckland said, drinking his coffee and trying to take in all she was telling him How could it be possible he would have outlived both Andrew and Charley? He was too late.

Lillian cleared her throat. "Both Jonas and Erwin will be so glad to see you," she said, smiling at him in an effort to lift both their spirits.

"An' I will be glad ta see them too. It has been too long," he agreed. He swallowed the last of the coffee, and his emotions, as he stared down into the empty cup. "You have taken over the Sterling House haven't you?" he asked.

She nodded her head. "I had no choice," she said taking note of how old he had become and then realized she had never known how old he really was.

"An' yur mother?" he questioned, returning Lillian to the present.

"Upstairs in her room."

"Can we leave her there?" Buckland said, a slight smile playing with the great wrinkles beside his mouth.

The people he had loved were gone. He could not bring them back, any more so than he could bring his Soolie back. But this beautiful woman who was across the table from him was very much alive. He could see by the cut of her, she was a tribute to her kinfolk.

Lillian nodded, recalling the animosity that always seemed to run between them. "Oh. I believe she can stay right where she is tonight." She smiled in return. Lillian reached across the table and took his hands in hers, not missing how calloused and how gnarled they were. "Grand Paw Paw, how old are you?"

"Nigh onto 70, I suppose. Maybe a bit more. I don't recall exactly when I was born, but I reckin it's been about thet many years," he said, holding her hand up to the light. "What is this? Are ya married?" he questioned seeing the gold band on her finger and the silver one right beside it.

"In my heart, Grand Paw Paw, yes, I am. He is so wonderful and I love this man very much."

"Well, Boss Girl, git him out here so I can meet the man who stole yur heart away from me."

Lillian quietly excused Ling Su and Ming Su. She could take care of her Grand Paw Paw. She brought the coffee pot to replenish both their cups. "He is not here," she said and sat back down. "Why is nothing easy in this family which seems to be so littered with such disorder?" she managed, a tinge of anger in her voice.

"His name is Paris Jacob Montoya and I met him the night that horrible man stabbed Paw Paw. He helped all of us that night and then respectfully stayed away until a proper time for us to meet could be well be arranged. He is a cultured gentleman. We both knew from that first moment we were meant for each other. But," she said sadly, "to be together has not been allowed."

"What do ya mean, not allowed? Folks allow what they want."

"There was the death of Paw Paw and my grieving."

"Understandable," Buckland said.

"From the beginning, mother objected. Why I have never truly understood. I saw him as a man with class, honor and respectability. She just said he was unfit. That I was being foolish to give my heart away so easily."

"Does not surprise me. Knowin' how yur mother felt about men folk. But I still see those rings on your finger. Where is this man?"

"In Spain, somewhere, with his family. The Montoya family had holdings in California that were in great dispute when California became a part of the United States. Their cattle died due to extreme drought and there was not enough money to fight the courts to prove the land was theirs granted by the old Spanish Land Grants which the United States Government did not honor. Rather than lose it all, the hacienda and all the land was sold. Paris took his mother and father back to Cordoba Spain where the Montoya family had its origin to begin their lives again in a more favorable land."

"Why didn't ya go with him?" Buck asked.

Lillian bit at her lower lip. "I made a promise to Paw Paw and that was to take care of my mother and the Sterling House. He felt he had betrayed her so much, not giving her what she deserved. He loved her but he loved Pale Star more and she knew that too."

"Ya knew 'bout thet?" Buck asked, a little surprised, but then, not really. Charley Paul had known that Lillian was his sister. It made sense she would know he was her brother but by a different mother. It explained the mean spirit Abigale had toward the boy.

"I knew most of it long before Paw Paw told me the entire story when he was dying. Charley Paul and I had figured it when we were just children. I knew his mother was not my mother and that my mother was not his mother but we knew Paw Paw was Paw Paw to us both." It was complicated.

Lillian continued. "I believe he felt a strange kind of guilt in some way, but he loved Pale Star. The last words he spoke to me was her name." It grieved her to recall the moment. Her sigh was heavy before she continued. "I saw to everything he wanted and was with him to the end. The Sterling House became mine and the care of mother became my responsibility. I cannot break my promise."

"An' this Montoya could not stay with you?"

"No," she answered. "Because of his honor to his family."

"So you an' this Montoya got married in secret an' he goes off ta Spain an' you stay here?" Buckland said trying to fit all pieces together.

"Well . . . yes, more or less," she answered, not sure how to answer. Buckland scratched his stubbly beard, ran his hand through his thinning hair. "Boss Girl, Soolie an' I never stood before no preacher man, but she was mine an' I was hers. Only the power above could take her away from me. I never knew a heart could be so connected as I was ta thet woman. If an' your Spaniard are the same way with each other, no paper will make it better an' ya have my blessin'."

Lillian smiled pleased with the blessing from this old man who sat across the table from her. "Thank you," she said. "Paw Paw would have understood. There seems to be no one else as I take care of everything here while I wait for his return as he asked and as I promised." She looked away and closed her eyes as first one tear and then another escaped her blue eyes.

"Boss Girl, look at me."

She raised her dark, blue eyed gaze to the face of this man who had lived a lifetime far beyond her understanding.

"If ya have yur heart an' mind set ta wait fer this man then honor the promise ya made. Yur Paw Paw would expect none less from ya an' neither would I. If he is the man ya say he is, he will return when the time is right. The Sterling House is a good place ta wait an' then ya honor yur Paw Paw as well."

Lillian understood only too well why this man of the mountains had meant so much to her father, her Uncle Charley. Also why Soolie had loved him enough to leave with him. He might be illiterate, by some standards, poorly dressed by other standards, and have done things perhaps he should not have done, yet this man had more common sense than most anyone she had ever known. There were no words she could give him at this moment. Only a warm, sincere feeling from her heart.

"Miss Lillian, there is somethin' I need ta ask, though," he said pulling back to his own thoughts. "I ain't never been one ta ask favors an' I won't ask quarter from you, neither," he paused and looked straight into who she was. "I once came here what seems like a lifetime ago. Yur poppa an' Charley Gaynor gave me a home, one I was respectful of an' worked ta keep. The years have had their way with me, but I can still lend a hand. There is no place left fer me ta go anymore."

Lillian Anne went to where he sat. She put her arms around his shoulders, cradling his head against her chest, stopping the tears that constantly wanted to flood into her life when she least wanted them.

Buckland could hear and feel her heartbeat. For the first time since Soolie had walked on without him, he felt comfort.

"Grand Paw Paw, the Sterling House has always been your home and it always will be. She kissed him on the forehead and stepped back. "You don't have to work another day of your life unless you truly want to. If you do, I am sure there will be plenty to do just as there always was."

He saw so much of her father in those intense blue eyes and yet the beauty of Abigale in her face. He knew the being of this woman was all Lillian Anne Sterling, who had been given a strange and yet strong hand to be played at a very early age. Other than his mother, there had been only two other women he had ever loved. The little girl he had seen grow into this beautiful woman was the second.

*   *   *

Three days later, at the age of 73, Buckland LeRoy Kavanaugh died.

Lillian had him buried wearing his worn leathers with the beaded gadamour around his neck and his little pipe resting comfortably under his hand. His final resting place was next to her father in a space which should have been reserved for her mother, who had refused to see Buckland on his deathbed, let alone go to Riverside for his funeral. She had claimed a frailty staying home to rest with her frailty and drink her sherry.

Some might have raised a serious family complaint to these arrangements. As Lillian stood in front of the grave sites of Andrew Wesley Sterling, her father, Charley Gaynor, the only uncle she had ever had, and the final resting place of Buckland LeRoy Kavanaugh the only grandfather she had ever known, she knew in her heart that these three men deserved to rest in peace together.

Chapter
Eighteen

Abigale had sat at a front window table of the Sterling House for most of the afternoon. Ming Su had served her tea and little sweet cakes. Abigale had begrudgingly accepted the service. She did not like these slant eyed, dark haired little women who worked in the kitchen of the Sterling House. Plus she was appalled they publicly served the guests. There seemed to be no one else to hire off the streets and no one to be entrusted to provide the services the Sterling House still provided.

She could find no fault with the impeccable way they served, but she was distrustful of their sing-song little voices and the way they always looked down, as if they had done something wrong, which they probably had.

It had taken her several years, but she had finally learned the difference between Ling Su and Ming Su. At the moment, she was watching Ling Su clean another table. Ming Su said something to her in passing. Abigale could have sworn there was a furtive glance in her direction, but she could not prove it. Like many other distasteful items and issues in the Sterling House, Abigale had finally come to accept their presence as they seemed to have no plans she knew of to be leaving in the near future.

Abigale redirected her attention toward the street, and dismissed the two Oriental women from her mind. It had been over 30 years, maybe even 35, since she and Soolie made that perilous crossing by stagecoach to come here.

Although young and beautiful, she had quickly learned she was also extremely naïve about the ways of what was, in her opinion, a barren wasteland with people of no values trying to inhabit it, build on it and control it. Their controls had been severely tested in every way imaginable, from the greedy flames of many fires trying to burn them out, to the flood waters trying to wash them away. This was to say nothing of the blizzards that would bury them under immense layers of snow. As calloused as she had become, she still remembered with great dread the reports from that horrible blizzard of '88 when so many school children had perished in Nebraska from an unexpected storm. She had listened to Jonas relay the grim stories, in the days that followed, about so many who had tried to reach their homes who had frozen to death. Many had suffocated to death in the blinding, icy, dust like snow with winds so ferocious that voices could not be heard more than a few feet away.

During that January, from Canada to Texas, it was reported many temperatures dropped to 40 degrees below zero in some places. As she recalled, Denver had not received the blinding fury of the snow from that blizzard, but their balmy, light wrap, no fire in the fireplace day had dropped to below zero in a matter of hours.

Abigale blinked her eyes and forced the mental image of those frozen bodies from her mind. She could not be responsible for those who would choose to live in such desolate places where adequate protection could not be provided. Denver might be uncivilized, but at least it offered buildings with protection from the elements.

Her attention was drawn down along the wide baseboard in time to see a small beetle bug seek a crevice where it disappeared from her sight. Abigale was rudely reminded insect infestations and vermin of all kinds shared the buildings with them. Like everyone, she knew how to step on the bugs when she could and swat the pesky flying insects when they came too close to her. Being from the South, she had learned at an early age how to eradicate the crawling, flying torments. Her memory did not recall them being quite so prolific as they were here on Larimer Street so close to the little Cherry Creek and Platte River. She was very much aware this prolific intrusion was coming from Cherry Creek and the Platte River, both so polluted from the runoff of humanity that the smell was overwhelming. These two waterways were a breeding ground for all kinds of pestilence. This human created disgrace was overtaking them and when the wind came from just the right direction, she could smell the decay of it. Abigale leaned forward to better view busy Larimer Street. It was paved now with a new hard substance called asphalt. For the most part, her never ending battle with the dirt, dust, and mud when it rained or when the snows melted, was finally over.

What caught and held her attention though, was one more of the newest and most unusual contraptions the mind could ever imagine. Another horseless carriage had belched, sparked and rumbled past the Sterling House scaring every horse that was snubbed to the hitching rails along the street as this contraption made its way to some destination down the road.

Larimer Street had always had more than its share of horses, buggies, carriages, livestock and wagons all going in different directions as destinations dictated. This had become over complicated and cluttered with electric and steam powered vehicles, cable and trolley cars. This unsightly contraption had been invented by those who seemed to thing the world needed to move faster and faster. Many thought this automobile would make that possible.

Abigale highly doubted this as these new, hideous, ugly things, that were constantly beeping and beeping, beeping and honking to get folks out of their way would not last long as they were just too noisy and far too unreliable.

It was termed to be the horseless age, but she saw it as the senseless age. Progression that was nothing more than another form of pestilence to pollute the very air they breathed as if it was not bad enough already.

Men with means wanted to go faster and faster as they built taller and bigger structures all around them. Every foot of available space for as far as one could see was being taken up and built on no matter what the shape of the lot.

The most peculiar, to Abigale's way of thinking, was the triangular Brown Palace Hotel right in the center of old Denver. She recalled when cows had grazed on that oddly shaped, unfavorable piece of land.

Then along came another schemer/dreamer named Henry Brown. Not only had he homesteaded a large tract of land south of Colfax, eventually selling it off where many palatial homes now stood, but he bought up the odd shaped parcel and built, what Abigale considered, a red stone monstrosity. This "ship of the desert" as some referred to it, had risen out of the heart of Denver City's worn and tired old buildings as it filled once more piece of land.

On one of her infrequent outings, Abigale had allowed herself to be driven past this oddly shaped red building which did remind her of a gigantic sailing ship. She had been told that inside, there was an atrium lobby with balconies that rose to over eight floors high with an overlook to the great elegance below.

"God lives up thet high," she had said. "I do not choose to meet Him in some outlandish, overly built hotel."

Abigale Westmoreland Sterling was one of the very few who had absolutely no desire to see the interior with its imported onyx and marble inlays or lavish furnishings. She leaned back recalling another building erected a lot closer to the Sterling House than the Brown Palace. She had listened to and heard the intense hammering and sawing that had came from diagonally across the alley behind the Sterling House. When she had questioned Jonas about the all the noise, he had at first, been evasive. After her persistence he finally told her "a new house" was going up on Market Street. "Another house of ill repute?" she had more sharply questioned. Jonas became even more solemn, excused himself from her presence and walked away.

After the sawing and hammering had subsided to be replaced by the strains of a piano being played late at night, and raucous laughter emanating from that direction, her worst fears had been realized. The old building had been replaced by a new one all right.

A more splendid brothel known as the House of Mirrors. She shuddered to think where those mirrors might be placed.

Abigale was even more appalled when the rumors of how the notorious Jennie Rogers, the owner and madam of this famed house of ill repute, had secured her money to build this house.

It had been over an afternoon tea when one of the ladies had confided, as rumor would have it, bribery money from a prominent Denver banker had financed construction. The banker, as the same rumor revealed, was having an illicit affair with one of the 'ladies of the common streets'. As all of this was becoming public, his wife suddenly, quite mysteriously disappeared. When questioned, the banker claimed she was merely back east visiting family.

Allegedly one of Jennie's noted clients had stolen some Indian bones from a burial scaffold and buried them in the banker's backyard, threatening exposure of murder of the banker's missing wife if the bones were revealed.

Reportedly, enough bribe money was paid so the bones would never come to light to prove or disprove the claim. The wife never returned and the banker soon left as well. However, he had apparently been the source for the money that had financed this newest house of dark pleasures on Market Street.

Dark pleasures or not, The House of Mirrors was a tribute to elegance with its crystal chandeliers, golden harp, grand piano and oriental rugs extending up the stairs and into the halls to the private rooms where sexual delights awaited those who could pay the price. Abigale felt it was disgusting and it was immoral. To her complete chagrin, it all resided across the alley from the Sterling House.

Abigale wanted to leave, but had no inkling of where she could go to remove herself from such disgraceful behavior. Georgia and Westmoreland came to her mind. She just as quickly dismissed those distressing thoughts as that land, and that lifestyle, was forever gone. Pulled away by the hideous winds of war and man's insatiable greed for power and control.

These bodacious houses of ill repute were obviously one more form of man's insatiable greed for another kind of power, especially over women. They provided sex and sexual pleasures, in which Abigale found no pleasure what-so-ever. Just as the South had fallen, so would the nefarious Mrs. Rogers and all her kind.

Abigale looked back over her shoulder and watched her daughter take reservations as she greeted early afternoon diners. She truly was an elegant, beautiful and intelligent woman who had assumed control of their lives, making the best for them in a world that was changing all around them.

Abigale always had privilege to the books and knew the cost of licensing the Sterling House as a saloon. The High License Act had raised the saloon business license to well over $1,000 and the liquor license assessment was over $5,000.

If the high cost to stay in business was not enough, it seemed they were constantly visited by either the police who served more ordinance papers limiting when they could serve their drinks or it was unsavory men who came late at night and collected money from Jonas so they could stay in business of serving drinks.

Women could no longer drink in the saloon. And unless lunch was served in the saloon on Sunday, they could not serve strong drink on that day at all. How Lillian kept up with all that seemed to plague them was beyond Abigale's reasoning.

Abigale had never felt safe in Denver, with its filth, diseases, violence and wild people left free to roam the streets. Now it seemed they were slowly being driven out of business by laws and ordinances beyond their control. She felt it could be different if Lillian had taken to any of the various suitors who had tried to charm their way into her life as they would have brought financial support to the Sterling House. Lillian graciously refused them all as she continued to wear those double rings of disgust from a man who for all intent and purpose had disappeared.

Good riddance, Abigale thought as she resumed her viewing of Larimer Street. Perhaps it was all for the best her daughter not become involved with anyone. Who was to know what kind of background and breeding was being spawned from the streets of Denver.

There were enough changes all around them. Abigale knew no one and nothing could truly be trusted. It was not only the asphalt that had changed Larimer. Although the paving had been good, not all changes were for the better. She saw where bums and obviously migratory people littered the walkways. At night, she could hear those ruffians along with street orphans rummaging in the alley for whatever trash they felt had value. All the upper class businesses had slowly moved over to Curtis Street. "The Great White Way," as it was called because of all the electric lights that seemed to illuminate the way at all hours of the night while Larimer Street seemed to be growing dimmer and darker.

"More tea, Missy Sterling?" Ming Su asked, approaching the woman where she sat lost in her reverie.

"No!" Abigale, answered, sharply clipping the word. "Tell my daughter ta come over here."

Ming Su bowed her head slightly in Abigale's direction. She had been told it was their way of showing politeness, but she saw it as their way of not speaking what was on their minds.

"Go!" she demanded and watched Ming Su cross the room where she waited ever so politely while Lillian finished with a reservation.

She whispered to Lillian, who looked in her mother's direction.

Lillian closed the reservation book, crossed the room and took a seat across from her waiting mother.

"Mother," she said. "Was there something you wanted?"

"The reservations. Do they go well?"

"Not nearly enough of them," Lillian answered.

"Did ya ever think the reason might be because of where we are?"

"What?" Lillian said, wondering just where this conversation might be going. "Well, land sakes," Abigale said, arrogance spicing her words, "a person of refinement dare not walk out on the street in front of our building, because of all the riffraff thet seems ta be takin' over Larimer Street. I think thet every out of work silver miner is roamin' Larimer jist waitin' fer silver ta come back into fashion lookin' fer handouts until it does."

"Mother," Lillian patiently said, "silver, or gold neither for that matter, is not something of fashion. Our government has seen fit to base our money on gold and not silver. There have been many financial disasters with many men losing all they have or will ever have. For many there is no work with scant little for them to do except to return to our streets from the mountains hoping to survive here."

Lillian was very much aware of what the demonetization of silver and the government forced issue of the gold standard had done to their economy. Colorado may have started as a territory based on the lure of gold, but its status as the Silver State had been seriously damaged to a critical level of gloom and depression after the silver panic of 1893, when great men of wealth became paupers practically overnight.

Lillian had heard that even the Large family, who had bought her Uncle Charley's old place over on Pennsylvania Street where they had built their ostentatious home, had lost their silver fortune.

They had sold out to some newcomers by the name of Brown from Leadville who had apparently made a fortune from their Little Jonny Mine. It was said Mr. J.J. Brown was well heeled, however, his garish wife, Margaret, could never be accepted in Denver's polite society. Was it any wonder? She had been heard yodeling from the second floor of their home as well as having two stone lions placed in front of the house as a silent guard. Someone had said, she had been heard to laughingly say that if a virgin walked past, those lions would roar. It was even rumored Mrs. Brown allowed some of the local Ute Indians to have coffee in her kitchen with a breakfast of biscuits and bacon dipped in sugar. Lillian had never met this Brown woman, but if this was her behavior, she was not demonstrating proper decorum by anyone's standards.

"Are ya listenin' ta me?" her mother impatiently snapped.

"Of course I am," Lillian responded with some guilt as she had let her mind wander as her mother had been prattling about well known issues.

"Well, I want ya to jist look across thet street an' tell me what ya see."

"Yes, mother. It is the same as it was yesterday and the day before."

"Oh, no, Lillian. It is not the same an' never will be again. The Orientals an' the Mexicans have taken over. Ya can smell those horrible greasy tortilla bread things thet the Mexicans make all the way up here when the wind blows from where they are takin' over jist one block from here. One block, Lillian. I could never abide those brown skinned heathen from south a the border an' most recently we have those yellow skinned freaks a nature right in our front door. An' this is ta say nothing of those dreadful houses . . ." she shuddered at the thought of what she said next, " . . . of female moral an' sexual decay thet exist right behind us on Market Street. It is lil' wonder we have lost our good standin'. We need ta move the Sterling House away from this filthy debris thet is sweepin' over us."

Abigale stopped and cut her eyes in the direction of Ling Su, who was working nearby sweeping the carpet. She hoped the little yellow wretch had heard every word.

Lillian's thoughts were sad toward her mother as she wearily shook her head. How many times had she heard these dissertations regarding other races of people? Plus she was only too aware of the houses from 19th and Market Street north and east for several blocks. She was also very much aware of the clientele frequenting and supporting the businesses of these women on the fringes of what was considered to be a respectable society. She knew it would not avail to speak back on this subject of racial differences, but her words tumbled into the air. "You thought mighty finely of the Negro people and not so long ago."

"Things were different then. 'They' could be controlled," her mother retorted.

"You did not control Soolie so very well, did you?" Lillian's blue eyed gaze was steady as she delivered this statement. She was so weary of this baiting her mother had done for so many years. As her mother aged, it was becoming worse. Lillian had realized some time back, that she could not stop it, but she could close down the conversations usually by walking away.

Abigale started to say something, but let the words die in her throat as she swallowed hard. Instead of her first thoughts to defend her actions around Soolie, she said, "Yur as defiant as yur father an' equally as rude ta me."

"All in fair measure, mother. All in fair measure."

Lillian rose to her feet. She looked down at her mother, still admiring her beauty and grace, but disdaining her negative projected thoughts about life and people. "We are not moving the Sterling House anywhere. We have no measurable funds to accomplish that endeavor. I have told you just how precarious our finances are. You have access to the books and can read the sums as easily as I can."

"Ya could always dismiss Ming/Ling or whatever their names are."

Lillian quietly, deliberately said, "Please excuse me as I have calculations and ledger work to attend to while I take care of what is left of the Sterling House." She quietly walked away. Further words were futile, and Lillian did not need her mother's frustrations to filter into the difficulty of her day.

Abigale fought back angry retorts, one piling on top of another, as she watched her daughter's abrupt departure. Again, she had been summarily dismissed. She gripped her cane firmly, rose, crossed the room and painfully made her way up the stairs to her solitary room. Perhaps a touch of sherry would soothe her mind. She also recalled the brown bottle of laudanum and knew a touch of that would calm her nerves and ease the pains of the body and the mind.

Abigale knew she had let the years walk away from her. While growing up and living in the heartland of the South, on the magnificent Westmoreland Plantation, she had blindly and foolishly loved a childhood sweetheart. Being raised the way she was had given her many advantages as a budding young woman of the South should have had. Had she not done the absolutely proper expected thing by wedding herself to one of Georgia's prominent plantation sons? *I should have become the grand mistress at Westmoreland an' possibly Ironwood plantation as well,* she thought letting the bitterness boil over in her mind.

Even though sex, and 'wifely duty' were not comfortable parts of her role as a woman and she feared the mysteries of birthing, she would have dutifully born the sons and daughters to carry on the traditions which had filled her world.

Trying to be the 'dutiful' wife, she had been uprooted from her genteel world and viciously thrust into a common land where her life had been reduced to nothingless by the actions of others.

Undressing herself, Abigale put on one of her luxurious dressing gowns of brocade satins and slid her tired feet into soft velvet slippers. Taking out her hair combs, she sat down before the mirror and began brushing her long hair. *How many times had Soolie had done this?* she wondered. It was a pleasurable memory as far back as her memory would let her go.

Where has it all gone? Soolie would probably still be alive if she had not taken off with that dreadful man of no worth. *He is dead too,* she thought. *No one will miss the likes a him.*

Abigale stared into the mirror at the hardened, bitter face that stared back at her. She could not help but notice that her dark hair was dull and streaked with dismal grey. Her eyes no longer sparkled. Possibly for the first time in her life, she saw who she truly was.

A miserable excuse for a woman who, because of her own fears, bull headed stubbornness and anger, had allowed all that had meant anything to her to slip away piece, person and thing at a time.

She laid down the brush, reached for her bottle of sherry and poured a generous portion into a rose colored crystal glass. She first sipped, then gulped the amber liquid, feeling the alcohol burn down her throat into the chest. It felt so good. She refilled her glass taking note of the laudanum bottle in the drawer next to where she kept her sherry. *A small sip*, she thought. *Just a lil' ta calm my nerves.*

She thought about the mystery of love and how for her, it would forever precisely that. A mystery. Baffling, confusing and something she would never understand. There had been something akin to love when she had married Andrew. Although she had not known it at the time, she had lost him the day he rode away from Westmoreland Plantation so many years ago.

She let more laudanum slip down her throat and then rinsed the taste of it away with more sherry.

Her brother, her mother and her father were all lost to greed, rage and a violence of man against man that she had never understood either. The place where she had grown into a young woman of Southern refinement, a lady of grace and elegance. Only to have it all lost to the ravages of her life in a place she had never loved with people who merely tolerated her.

They all loved thet Indian woman. Why could they not love me jist a lil' bit, too, she thought, sipping first the laudanum and then gulping the sherry again. She was beginning to feel calmly relaxed, superior in her thoughts even though a bit light headed and dizzy.

Abigale let her mind stop wandering and wondering as she focused on both the brown bottles sitting in front of her. It had all come to this. Sips of laudanum and glasses of sherry to elevate her mind while dulling her senses.

A small silver jewelry box glinted in the light and caught her attention. Abigale reached for it recalling only too well its contents. The only remains of her true Southern home.

Anne Francine Westmoreland's wedding ring and Albert Roger Westmoreland's watch chain.

She slipped the ring on her little finger and held it to the light as she admired the gleam of gold from the band. "I love you, momma," she mumbled as she picked up the gold watch chain and let it fall into her palm where she closed her fingers over it.

She started to stand up but had to sit back down as she was very unsteady on her feet. Her hairbrush fell to the floor. She reached for it, but realized she could not steady herself well enough to pick it up from the floor where it had fallen.

"I jist want ta go ta sleep," she said to her blurry image in the mirror. She picked up one of the bottles and steadied herself with her cane long enough to make it to the bed. Tipping up the bottle, she drank again and then realized it was the laudanum—not the sherry. *Who cares? I want all of this ta go away,* her befuddled mind screamed at her. Abigale reclined on the bed, her hair fanned out around her aging still beautiful, face. She let the bottle fall to the floor and the remainder of its contents gurgled out of the bottle making a strangely shaped reddish brown stained pattern on the beautiful carpet. Abigale Westmorland Sterling did not see it. Just as she no longer cared about the beauty or elegance that had been her room, and her home, in the Sterling House.

Her heart had stopped. Her days of torment were over.

*   *   *

It was a quiet funeral with only Lillian, Jonas, Erwin, and strangely enough Ming Su and Ling Su, standing in silent attendance. One more strange minister, this time provided by Olinger's Mortuary one of the newest in Denver, delivered a fitting eulogy. Lillian looked toward the cottonwoods. She recalled another time when there had seemed to be a ghostly image under those trees, a figment of her imagination. This time, she saw only frail yellow leaves fluttering slowly toward a receptive earth while she listened to the sound of an unfamiliar voice drone on about the virtues of heaven. That brought her attention back to the people who stood around the open hole in the ground. There were no tears, not even her own. She wondered, *had anyone ever really known Abigale Westmoreland Sterling?*

Lillian had loved her mother and, in her own ways, had forgiven her for all the insults and hateful things she had said through all the years. Perhaps she should have told her. Perhaps not. Somehow, she knew it would not have mattered.

The bitterness had been there for far too long and no words of comfort from her would have eased her mother's mental discomforts. Abigale Westmoreland Sterling was at rest and her torments, real or imaginary, could no longer hurt her.

*   *   *

Some months later, on a cold wintry day, for reasons unclear even to her, Lillian came to visit Riverside Cemetery.

She stood in front of the graves. Her father's and his two best friends. How were they to know? How were any of them to know?

Buckland LeRoy Kavanaugh ~ A Man of Trust ~ Died Age 70 ~ 1888

Andrew Wesley Sterling ~ A Man Of Sterling Quality ~ 1841 ~ 1882

Charley Gaynor ~ 1887 ~ Partner and Friend ~ A Good Life Shortened

Lillian turned to the far right where her mother's final resting place was. At the time of necessity, it had not occurred to her how strange this burial layout was. Yet, as she stared down at the four cemetery mounds with their perfect marble markers, there was a touch of irony in what she saw.

Her father rested between the two men he had loved and admired the most during all the years when trust and true loyalty had meant the most. Her mother would lie for all eternity beside the man she had despised the most and blamed for far too much. Buckland LeRoy Kavanaugh.

Abigale Westmoreland Sterling ~ 1842 ~ 1896 ~ An Interloper

How fitting it truly all was! Lillian walked back to the road where Erwin waited with the carriage. She had been blessed by what all of these people had given her each in their own way.

Erwin said nothing to her on the ride back to the Sterling House. He was most respectful of the moods of this beautiful woman he cherished in so many ways. With the death of her mother, she had no one left except for Jonas and himself. She was truly alone with her Sterling House but he knew she was determined to hold it as her own.

It was her legacy, her home and about all she had ever had. He also knew she loved that foreign man with the strange name and dark eyes. He too was gone and had not been back to the Sterling House for several years. Erwin knew she wore that double set of rings and waited for the man to return that had given them to her. That was all he knew. They never spoke of it.

Chapter Nineteen

She had never forgotten her training or let her learning succumb to a lazy mind. Her decorum was accurate and purely precise. She knew a tea napkin from a dinner linen; a salt spoon from a teaspoon from a soup spoon and a butter knife from a bread knife. She also did not forget just how deplorable it was to pick up crumbs from a plate or sop one's gravy. How proper it was to sit erectly on the edge of a chair, allowing only the point of one's delicate kid leather slippers to peek from under the hem of he garment, be it a morning frock, afternoon day dress or evening gown. She remained mindful that, from one to two inches of space was all that could possibly be allowed between the feet while properly seated and to never gap or cross the knees.

All these upper refinement, properly applied ladylike qualities were imbedded in her mind. Her mother had seen to all of these teachings, and so much more, which had become second nature to her at the school where not one 'inaccuracy of personality' was left unattended or unchanged.

Lillian was aware it was nothing more than a keen mind set and when she allowed it, her deliberate willfulness could get in the way of such refinements. As it was today and at this precise moment, when that willfulness marked her thoughts and Lillian deliberately set her feet a good two feet apart letting her knees gap under her skirt as she relaxed her tense posture. She sighed. *Oh the freedoms of not being so precisely a lady!* She dismissed the thoughts. Far more important issues in her life than knowing which spoon or fork to use or which napkin was required to wipe imaginary smudges held her attention.

If her financial situation was not dramatically altered soon, she would be considering herself fortunate to have just a plate with edible crumbs, and even more fortunate to have gravy to mix with the crumbs.

The Sterling House was broke!

Raising her teacup to her lips, she let her gaze drop to the dark, sweetened liquid in the cup before she set it back down in its matching saucer. "Jonas, Erwin," she began, "mere words of thankfulness cannot convey to both of you all that I feel about your devotion and loyalty to me, the Sterling House and the life you both have here.

"I have no one to talk to but the two of you. I must tell you there are serious financial problems threatening to collapse the walls of the Sterling House. I may have no choice but to close the doors and retreat into financial oblivion. Jonas, you have skillfully continued to manage the saloon in the face of all adversities which have diminished it."

"Thank you, Miss Lillian," Jonas replied and quietly waited for her to continue.

"And you, Erwin, my special friend, have balanced the ledgers with me as you have a keen mind for figures. You kept the staff in perfect working order while I tried to maintain and oversee all of it. All the while playing the piano as you have done for so many years providing perfect and quality entertainment." She smiled at him and Erwin blushed under that smile. It was something he had never been able to control and probably never would.

Lillian moved to the window to view the street below, as she had done so many times before when thoughts were not always kind to her mind. "We have a beautiful home here and an incredible business carefully put into place by my father and by my mother. Even though people still dine and drink fine wines while enjoying an elegant ambience, unfortunately far too many of them have gone elsewhere for these pleasures. "Perhaps I should have listened to my mother. She wanted to move the Sterling House to a better, more amiable lucrative location. I did not then, nor do I wish to do so now. The gamblers are all gone, too, because Jonas, as much as you paid, I suppose I knew all along the day would come when you could no longer pay for the protection we needed to keep this part of the business flourishing as it did in Uncle Charley's time.

"This too has changed. I cannot pay the bribes, as all the money taken in must go for supplies for the restaurant and alcohol for the saloon as well as the legal licensing fees extracted on a regular basis.

"Erwin, the liquor license is well over $5,000 a year and ladies are not allowed in the saloon any more. Without them, many of the male clientele go elsewhere to places where they can have a drink with a lady friend." She sadly shook her head.

"But the woman are still allowed in the private dinin' rooms?" Jonas asked seeming to ignore most of what she had said yet wanting to make sure of one fact. "Is that correct?"

"Yes, but with great caution as to what they are served, even in the privacy of those rooms. Wine is allowed, but little else," Lillian added. "Plus, officers of the law watch us. We are patrolled for violations by those we don't recognize as officers of the law as they spy and snoop into our private affairs. Those temperance league woman would see us shut down in one's own heartbeat."

"I know," Jonas continued, still ignoring the issue of the law along with those who carried the temperance banners, "that Ming Su and Ling Su have both been carefully instructed about the bakin' and cookin' of all the good things Soolie once fixed here for people."

No one will ever be as good with all of this as Soolie, she thought, *even if they do follow Soolie's recipes.* But, she agreed with his statement with a nod of her head. This was certainly no time to quibble over the best cooks in a kitchen that was short of supplies required to do the cooking at all. *Jonas, are listening to what I am saying?* she wondered, but held the question.

"I have been thinkin' about something that might help us. I may have an idea for some changes, but I need ta talk ta someone first."

"Who might that be?" she asked.

"I don't want ta get your hopes up." *or scare you,* he thought.

"If you have a plan to get our compliment back in the Sterling House and the money to continue our lifestyle here on Larimer Street, then by all means implement it, and please," she implored, "do so quickly."

Jonas walked across the room and kissed her lightly on the cheek. "We will survive this, Miss Lillian," he said as he quickly left the room.

"That was certainly most strange and abrupt." she said somewhat surprised. " Erwin, do have any idea what he was referring to?" she asked.

Erwin's shoulders elevated slightly as he replied, "No, but you know how quiet he is about things all the time. There are secrets inside him that no one will ever know. Miss Lillian, he is a thinker." he said and then asked, "Just how bad is this?"

She tried to keep her voice calm as she responded. "You have seen the ledgers and you have seen the business drop more and more."

"Yes," he replied, pondering the last set of figures he had seen. "Still, the accounts are all settled as I recall."

Lillian took an unsteady breath. "That is true, but there is not enough money to replenish as we should be doing. Inventory says we have enough whiskey and beer to last about a month. Wine a little longer, but it is the barrels in the kitchen larders that I am concerned about, as well as the spices, sugars and delicacies to keep the standards of the Sterling House." She faced him honestly. "We may all be out looking for gainful employment if a reversal of this is not forthcoming."

"I can play the piano just about anywhere," he offered, "and make money with my talent, but I would rather play and entertain here."

"Yes, Erwin," she said.

"Miss Lillian."

She waited.

"I have some money put back, if you think that will help us," he offered.

It will take more than money. It will take a miracle, she thought, struggling to control the great caring emotion she felt for this young man who had always looked after her since her earliest memories.

Here he sat, and in his shy way, still offering to help with money. She felt certain he did not have that much. She shook her head as she fought back the tears. "You save your money," she said, turning away. "Perhaps some day we will need it more than today."

"As you say," he replied as he struggled with his own emotions. It was breaking his heart to see her this way.

Erwin Frederson had few needs and those he did have had always been met by the Sterling House, Charley Gaynor, Jonas Gregory and this wonderful woman he loved as a sister. A blood tie he had never truly known.

He had absolutely no intension of marrying and begetting a flock of children. He did not remember his mother or his father, only the stories told about them. He knew times had been hard and bitter for many during the early days in Denver. Yet he could not justify his father Elias Frederson's desertion of them and secretly faulted him for his mother's death. He had never been told what she died of other than what he presumed to be a broken heart.

He did not want or need a wife and young children frightened him in some strange way. He was, for all purpose and personal intent, married to the Sterling House. He loved Lillian in ways that were private and special only to his emotions. That was how he wanted it and how he wished it to stay.

The salary he had earned through the years, along with at sometimes lavish tips for his piano playing, had been wisely saved. By the advice of a shrewd banker, he had invested into what was rapidly becoming a profitable venture for him even though he had never seen the land, or the peach orchard, he owned on the west side of the Great Divide. The name of the town where he owned his land was Grand Junction, Colorado, and although a fairly new town, from all reports, it was rapidly becoming a garden of fruit orchards and Erwin Frederson owned one of them.

There was a home on the acreage and a caretaker family. He was assured, by the banker, the Grand Junction Frederson Estate was well tended by the Mexican family that lived there.

Erwin was satisfied and he trusted in the title and deeds he held on this property. Perhaps the day would come when he would see his investment and actually live there, but for the time being, it was enough for him to know that for the past two seasons he had received a tidy sum of money from the sale of the sweet peaches grown on this western slope acreage.

Offering this home on the western slope of Colorado as a place for all of them to go had occurred to Erwin before, but he felt certain Lillian was not ready to leave the Sterling House. He had observed her many times staring off into the far distance away from the Sterling

House. He was certain in her heart, she was still waiting for Paris Montoya to return.

Where are you, Senor Montoya? he questioned in silence as he continued to watch Lillian as she was again staring out the window into her own private thoughts.

She walked to where he sat. She stared down at him for a moment and then said, "Tell me I am right in my pursuits."

Erwin exhaled, slowly, and replied, "Yes."

"I am going to my room to rest for a while. When Jonas comes back with whatever miracle he seems to have in mind, and is ready to share, please come and get me."

Erwin did not answer, as he watched her walk out of the room, shoulders straight, head perfectly poised and could not help wondering how long she could stay here and wait? How long would the business allow her to wait? He knew from the bottom of his heart that, no matter what, he would wait with her and when the leaving was right, he would have a place for her to go and for them to live.

*   *   *

The short, blonde, plump and attractive woman quickly inventoried the elaborate, yet extremely tasteful, furnishings in what she assumed was a receiving room or parlor in the beautiful Denver Sterling House. There was little here, however, that she herself did not display in her parlor house from the gold leaf finials on drapery rods to the plush carpeting beneath her feet.

Yet somehow, inside these walls, it all seemed more refined, more dignified and more elegant. Inside her mind, in a place she seldom cared to visit, Mattie Silks knew it took more than the buying of fine furnishings to present a dignified, well respected appearance to Denver City's upper crust or the crust of any other city's society. In the spirit that made her who she was, she also was very much aware that she quite frankly did not care. Many of the husbands, fathers and sons of these elite society ladies had visited her "maison de joie" on occasion. Apparently, the appearance of her establishment did not offend the masculine senses as many were return patrons for the Scarlet Sisterhood's sexual favors.

Mattie was amused. Surroundings, be they in the richest part of town, this unusual Sterling House Saloon, or a parlor house of dubious reputation in the red light district on Market Street, all were the same when the lights dimmed and the clothes removed. Pretentious was pretentious and practical was practical.

One of Denver's most celebrated Madam, Mrs. Mattie Silks, considered herself to be a pretentiously practical business woman. If what her quiet friend, Jonas Gregory, had told her was true, there was money to be made here for both houses. Her parlor house, which she was only too aware was referred to by some as a house of ill repute, was not struggling. Why? Because, as she saw it, men would always seek sexual pleasures outside the Victorian sexual morality which seemed to separate, sexually, a husband from his wife. According to social convention, a wife's sexual duty was for procreation only.

Certainly not sexual pleasures.

However, the Sterling House was not so fortunate. What was offered behind its closed doors and well lit rooms could be found behind many closed doors and, in some cases, better lit rooms where culinary competition was extreme. Men could, and would, seek their sexual pleasures from their favorite women, but be equally satisfied by another when the lights were dimmed.

When it came to refined dining, society's women could be outrageously finicky as to where their palates would be satisfied and even more finicky as to what would satisfy them. It came as no surprise the Sterling House was struggling to survive.

Mattie had dined here when she sought quieter times than at her own opulent bordello. There had been times when arrangements had to be made for certain gentlemen callers who wished their anonymity in such houses where they appeased their sexual appetites. She had discreetly met them at such places as the Sterling House. Mrs. Silks knew her more favorable clients, knew their names, their bank accounts and how to protect them and their illicit pleasures. As she continued to assess her surroundings, she felt this house showed promise but in a different way to yet compliment her business. She looked up and smiled as the woman she knew to be Miss Lillian Anne Sterling, owner of the Sterling House, entered the room. She sat delicately on the edge of a finely tapestried chair across from her. Mattie felt herself pull up straighter in her chair. She knew she was being appraised by the most magnificent blue eyes she had ever seen, set in the face of a most beautiful woman. Somewhere in her mind a memory was triggered.

"I am Lillian Sterling. What may I do for you?"

Mattie winked and without reserve said, "It may be more what I can do for you." She somehow knew they would become friends despite their social differences. "Do you know who I am?"

Lillian slowly blinked and slightly nodded. Few if any, if they would admit it, would not recognize one of Denver's most famous madams. Her flamboyant reputation was on just about every street and some of her antics were widely known.

"I know of you, Mrs. Silks as your reputation does precede you." What had Jonas Gregory gotten her into and why was this woman of nefarious fame seeking her audience?

"As does yours, Miz Sterling."

The two women stared at each other, neither faltering.

Then Mattie smiled even broader, her blue eyes twinkling as she reached up and touched the diamond encrusted cross she wore around her neck "I never did hold much with reputations. Sometimes they can just plain get in the way of . . . ." she paused, " . . . getting to know a person."

Lillian's demeanor softened and she returned the expression. There was truth in the statement. She did not dislike the rather attractive, plump little blonde woman wearing a stunning silk day dress with more diamonds on that cross around her neck than Lillian had ever seen in one piece of jewelry.

In addition, value judgments were not hers to make based on gossip, hearsay or reputation. Lillian considered herself a moral woman, yet she was a saloon owner. In the eyes of many, that was a disreputable business. She pulled the bell cord. "Mrs. Silks, I assume are a tea drinker?"

Mattie beamed. It had been a long time since a lady had offered her a cup of tea. "Please, my dear girl, call me Mattie, and I would love a cup of tea."

Ming Su and Ling Su graciously served the tea and small sweet cakes, which Mattie tasted without delay. "Tasted these before," she said, wiping her fingers on a table linen, "and always wondered about the recipe that makes them so special."

"Family treasures," Lillian said. "One lump of sugar or two? Do you prefer cream?"

"I like my tea strong and undiluted by any kind of sweeteners," Mattie answered, savoring another cake. "Family secret, huh?"

"From as far back as I can remember from a woman who was a slave to my mother's family in the South before the great war and prior to my mother's coming here." Using a small pastry fork, she, too, savored one of the cakes and realized, again, how much she too enjoyed them.

"Are you from the South as well?" Mattie asked, sipping her tea and admiring the absolute beauty and charm of this alluring woman.

"No," Lillian replied, "I was born here. Actually, in an Arapaho Indian teepee out there on the plains the night of the great fire which almost destroyed Denver in 1863. My Father, Andrew Sterling, and a dear friend of the family took my mother to a place of safety the night of that fire and it happened to be where the Arapaho were camped."

Mattie's eyebrows arched as she said, "And the Indians let your mother stay there with no harm to her?"

"Seems the Arapaho were also very good friends of that old mountain man friend of this family as well."

"What an incredible story. So," Mattie continued, "how far back in Denver City's history does the Sterling House go?"

Lillian was proud to share the Sterling Family history with this woman, although she knew the woman's intent for being in the Sterling House was not to learn its history. "My father, Paw Paw, wagered and won in a Spanish Monte card game, two plats of land on this corner of Larimer Street. Back then, only prairie dogs, grasshoppers and an occasional snake or two were in residence.

"He, and his partner, Charley Gaynor, a fine gambling gentleman, built the Sterling House Saloon. My mother Abigale, with the aid of her freed slave woman, Soolie, created the rest of it when they arrived here from Georgia in 1862. It was all built around the charm of my Paw Paw, the gambling expertise of Charley Gaynor and the reputation of the finest of pastries in all of Denver City at that time, compliments of Soolie and her incredible way with spices. The original building has been here since about 1861 with additions and rebuilding as noted over the years."

"These people speak of, your family, are they all gone?" Mattie asked.

Lillian nodded with a silent acknowledgement.

"You have something to be very proud of, my dear young woman. Something, indeed. And what of you? Your mannerisms are not those of the young women of proper Denver City, trained and schooled as they might be."

Lillian recalled her days at Wibscott Finishing School of Refinement for Ladies. "I attended a very strict school of refinements in St. Louis, Missouri. But," she added, with a touch of strong pride in her voice, "I was raised in this house, on these streets of Denver City, along the banks of the Cherry Creek and Platte River with those mountains to the west of me. I have no home but this one. And," she added, her voice calming, "I never will."

"I knew it," Mattie said. Without asking, Mattie helped herself to more tea. "I have seen you before and, yes, it was on these streets when you were young. I remember your dark hair flying in the wind and those blue, blue eyes of yours shining upward toward the sun. Two boys were with you," she continued, smiling as she pulled from a long forgotten memory of her own wild carriage rides on the infamous Market Street. "One boy with red hair and the other with blond and dark skin."

Lillian relaxed her posture and, for a moment, studied Mattie Silks. "I, too think I remember you." she said, recalling the incident from her running free days. "I was with Erwin and my wild natured brother. As I recall, we were returning from the river trying to get back to the Sterling House, because we were late coming home. I knew mother would be very angry, especially if she knew we had been playing in the Platte. We came running up I Street and as we were about to cross Market, there were with your horses and carriage, racing so fast." Lillian stopped in the memory.

"I too remember the day." Mattie said. "I stopped the carriage just in time. But, what I remember was you and those eyes."

"Mother witnessed it all as she was coming after me. Her distraught nature was not due so much to the fact I had been swimming, but more so that I had been speaking with you. But I did not know that you were a . . ." She stopped in mid-sentence.

Mattie laughed. "You can say the word, Lillian. 'Madam.' I am quite sure your mother was appropriately concerned," she encouraged her and both women laughed together.

"Lillian, I am a business woman and I am in the business of women. Women who satisfy men. Before you think too unkindly of me, let me assure you, I have never taken a girl into any of my parlor houses who has not had experience in such matters. No innocents. These girls come to me for the same reasons I hire them. There is money in what we do for all of us. And that, my dear young lady, is why I am here today."

Lillian considered the woman's words as a large cloud of doubt crossed her face causing her to frown.

A smile crossed Mattie's face and she managed to hold back her laughter as she said, "Oh, my dear young lady, not to worry. Your modesty, virtue and chastity are all quite safe. Although," she daringly added, "I doubt if there is a man anywhere who would not pay handsomely for moments of your time."

Lillian thought for a moment she should be insulted by this comment, but just as quickly let it pass. It was this woman's way of paying her a compliment, although she had never thought of herself in just such a way.

Mattie caught the slight flicker of uncertainty in Lillian's eyes as to how to relate to the comment. Mattie almost wished she had not said it. She quickly continued her train of thought. "Jonas Gregory is a friend of mine. He came to me telling me of your plight in the business world. The lack of good business which once supported your

Sterling House. "I wholeheartedly agree that Larimer Street is sagging and sinking but there is still money to be made. Not that I mind the Orientals as well as the Mexicans who seem to be moving in on all sides of us, but they tend to take to their own kind. This is not the strong clientele you and I need. My money comes from the top of the deck and sometimes the bottom as well and so will yours." she said, shaking her blonde head of curls, " But it is up to us business women to know when and how to cut that deck."

"You have my attention," Lillian said and pulled the bell cord for more service.

"I have not seen all of this fine establishment and the way it is decorated, but from what I have seen, it would be a dirty, crying shame to let this all just fall away, because the class of patronage needed has gone elsewhere. So, I propose we, you and I, bring them back. At least the men folk."

"Frankly, I am not quite following your line of thinking." Lillian said, her mind racing to avoid the confusion. She thanked Ming Su and poured fresh tea.

Ming Su did not let on, however, she knew this woman and was concerned as to why she was in the Sterling House. She retreated from the room as quietly as she had entered not wishing to bring attention to herself.

"My thinking is of a logical business nature, my dear. Thank you for the tea. It is quite good." Mattie sipped and replaced her cup on the saucer. "To the point. Many of my patrons wish to keep their identify confidential during the early hours. I have fine dining at my parlor house, but it is open with little seclusion for those who don't wish to be seen with my lovely ladies even though they want to be with these same lovely ladies during dinner. This is to say nothing of later when the lights burn lower and the faces are not quite so easily recognized."

Lillian stirred her tea, as her mind slowly began taking in the direction Mattie had hoped it would.

"I know you have special, private dining rooms on the second floor just below us. I know they are elegant and would more than meet my eye's approval therefore, meeting the standards of my, shall we say, clientele."

"I see where this is going," Lillian said, agreeing with Mattie. "But," she questioned, "could you assure me there would be no illicit behavior in these rooms."

"Only dining with other arrangements possibly made for later, back at my parlors. My gentlemen clientele would be directed to come to the Sterling House for dinner and the lady of their choice would enter through one of your back doors, meet them in the appointed room and all would be kept secret and above anyone's immediate suspicion.

"I mean, if there can be tunnels all over this town to shuttle the unsoiled upper crust of this city's spoiled elite society, plus a lot of other dandy Dan's, back and forth to protect their sacred identity, I reckon we can use an alley."

Lillian was amused as she, too, was aware of the infamous tunnels leading from hotels to pronounced places of business, primarily those associated with the politics that ran the city. It was a puzzlement to her that if so many of the city's politicians spent so much of their time traversing these tunnels to be with the ladies of the night, then why were there so many ordinances to inhibit such businesses, especially the saloons.

She brought her mind back to the issue at hand. "And it would be only dinner?" Lillian emphasized again, convincing herself of the proprieties which would be involved. There was no tunnel under the Sterling House and that, if this proposal worked, the alley would have to suffice to maintain everyone's reputations including that of the Sterling House and her own.

"Only dinner," Mattie assured her, "served in a style and with all the decorum your Sterling House still has. Not many left like this in this part of town," Mattie said still appraising the room where she sat.

"What about the authorities and the payoffs that I can no longer afford? The serving of alcohol has become a very expensive business."

"My dear girl, don't worry your pretty head. Why don't you let Mattie take care of these trivial matters. Most of those taking these bribes owe me, or competing parlors, either money or favors for being discreet when their behavior, shall we say, crosses the street. I will pay for the privilege of my girls to come here and help provide you with the patronage the Sterling House needs to stay in business.

"You charge for your services, just like you always have. Serve your exquisite meals with all the specialties these fine gentlemen like to have. I will continue to serve them the other desires their bodies seem to crave."

Mattie Silks shrewdly appraised Lillian Anne Sterling sensing the young owner was carefully fitting the pieces together in her own mind as she assessed the financial wisdom of the proposition. She slowly removed her lace glove and held her hand out in Lillian's direction. "Deal?" she offered by the gesture.

Lillian rose to her feet, looked down at the most unusual woman she probably had ever known, or ever would know. With little to no reserve, she extended her hand and said, "Deal."

"Good." Mattie rose to her feet. "Here," she said, handing Lillian an envelope. "This will help you get your dining rooms ready, Miss Lillian. Your first patrons will be here tonight. With my help, and your good taste, we will put the Sterling House back on its foundation. I have much to do this afternoon. My carriage is just outside and I will take my leave of here. I would not want to sully your reputation, or elevate mine too much, by our being seen together."

Lillian took the envelope from her, but did not open it. "Will you come back and visit with me from time to time?" Lillian tentatively offered, not sure exactly what else to say to this woman. She wanted to ask her how it was she knew Jonas, but thought better of it. He was, after all, a man and, although a quiet, reserved man, a man nonetheless. Mattie Silks was obviously in the business of taking care of men, no matter what their demeanor. The envelope could wait. It was obvious it was money and would be put to very good use this very day.

"As time permits, but I am a busy woman. It has been my pleasure, Miss Sterling." With that, she sashayed across the room, her satiny petticoats rustling. "Consider that an investment in our future," she said, referring to the unopened envelope in Lillian's hand before she left the room, closing the door behind her.

What have I just done? Lillian thought. She sat down and put the envelope on the table. She had just made a business arrangement with one of Denver's, possibly one of Colorado's, most notorious women. Exhaling slowly, she stood up and walked to a mirror where she stared at her own reflection. Sometimes she knew the woman who stared back at her too well. Yet at times, not nearly well enough.

What had possessed her to stay in the same room with this woman, granting an audience with a nefariously well known woman of the purloin scarlet sisterhood. The Cyprians of the night. Oh, yes, she knew the terms for the ladies. She stared harder into her own intense blue eyes. It had been a point carefully, and yet covertly, addressed at the Wibscott School as she and the other young ladies in training for womanhood had been carefully instructed. Proper ladies and those of good breeding, proper backgrounds and greater education would have no concourse with those connected to those of immoral, immodest or improper consequence. Another of those not of 'accuracy of personality' issues.

But, Lillian reasoned, smiling at her reflection. *This is not a matter of accuracy.*

This is a matter of survival. The Sterling House needed patrons and business to survive. She knew that local social morality would not approve of this. In the pit of her soul, she felt a sting of this social morality, but her logic told her it was a struggle for survival in a section of 'old' Denver where the "moral female majority" of Denver's new money seldom, if ever, visited.

She picked up the envelope, opened it, and could hardly believe her eyes as her thumb riffled through the bills inside.

"Oh my God," she said aloud. There was easily $5,000 in that packet. She sat back down and counted the money again. It was there, it was real and it was the miracle she needed.

With the help of a madam, an assortment of women of a different moral fiber, the lustful desires of men, and this $5,000, the Sterling House would survive.

Chapter Twenty

At the turn of the century, Denver's deteriorating core city was past being pretentious, opulent or gaudy. Her exterior still glittered, beckoning to strangers. Those with daring and bravado to tempt every hand of fate ever dealt continued to swell the ranks of this city which had taken root at the base of the Rocky Mountains at the confluence of Cherry Creek and the South Platte River. However, it was those who continued the old traditions, trying to maintain the old structures and hold onto their lifestyles given by the generation before, that suffered the most from the social decay that had slowly moved into the heart of Denver.

About two years had passed since Lillian had agreed on her business relationship with Mattie Silks. Lillian had not seen the plumpish, blonde madam since that afternoon, but the beautifully dressed young ladies of the night began appearing with the first one showing up, as if on cue, that very same evening of their agreement.

Lillian had been delightfully pleased by their decorum and behavior as they graced the Sterling House and its private dining rooms. These ladies were always dressed in the most fashionable evening gowns, with their hair gracefully arranged and their manners quite acceptable. Many became regular patrons with only first names being revealed to Lillian, but each of them properly referred to her as Miss Sterling.

She never actually knew the names of the men who joined them for dinner although she recognized many of the faces of not only law enforcement agents but local politicians as well. The bribes were silently taken care of, the soup was ladled, the wine flowed and the Sterling House was, for the most part, financially stable.

All around them were many tawdry saloons and wine rooms, shops of pornography, houses where the homeless and near homeless flopped for the night. This was all adjacent to the second hand clothing stores and businesses where people could pawn trinkets and treasures for cash to be spent on whiskey or beer or a night's flop over. The three-story Sterling House held its firm foundation at the corner of 19th and Larimer, maintaining its upper class decorum behind its brick walls. With the help of Erwin, Ming Su took care of the reservations as well as the upper level dining rooms with her impeccable attention to the most minute detail. Jonas still continued to tend to the saloon. Ling Su saw to the proper serving of the meals with a new small staff of people who worked not only the kitchen, but the large dining area as well.

This was a time when having a position that paid a reasonable wage was a luxury for those who wanted a fulltime state of employment in this somewhat less than desirable section of Denver.

Lillian attended to the ledgers appearing usually once during the dinner hours to greet familiar clientele. It was a formality only, as she chose to recluse herself more and more as the days, weeks and months passed.

On the exterior, the Sterling House appeared most respectable, but she knew it was being supported and was financially dependent on the participants of one of the greatest vices in Denver. Prostitution.

Lillian rarely sought the view out any of the front windows. If she did, it was to let her gaze travel upward to the sky, away from what she was struggling so hard to maintain. Her place and status in a city going sour with age.

She was not the only one struggling to hold on to what they considered to be theirs. Although she rarely read *the Rocky Mountain News,* or any of the other Denver tabloids, she knew there had been a war with Spain over Cuba an island in the Caribbean near the coast of Florida. Spain wished to continue its rule over the Cuban people and the United States wished to protect its American claims. When talks reached an impasse, Spain declared war on the United States. On the evening of February 15th, the USS Maine, which had been stationed in Havana, Cuba's harbor, mysteriously blew up and sank. President McKinley had no choice but to openly return the declaration because although not a proven fact, many were certain Spain had been responsible.

At the onset of the conflict and disagreements with Spain about Cuba, with war eminent, a camp had been set up in City Park to house the First Colorado Infantry. When the news reached Denver that war had been declared on Spain, the soldiers had marched down the streets of Denver to Union Station to be transported away to fight what many politicians had called a "Splendid Little War." In reality it had lasted just a bit over 100 days.

Lillian had tried to listen to the political talk about who owned what and who controlled where but it was all a jumble to her. She saw it as a way for one government to control the fates of others, with or without their consent.

All she knew was that, based on the greed of some, the lust for power by others, the Spaniards were no longer welcome in the United States or its territories. Just as in California, they had been ousted.

Paris Jacob LaRoche de la Montoya was a Spaniard. Lillian had no idea how long it would be before he could safely return to the United

States. In her heart, it did not matter, because she would continue to wait at the Sterling House, where he could find her when the day of his return came.

The Sterling House saw the stroke of midnight, when there had been great celebrating in the streets, in every saloon and restaurant that had an open door, as many were awake to welcome the dawn of a new century.

The turn of the century was with them and every light in the Sterling House was lit as the small hours of the new day came upon them. The champagne had bubbled and the wine had flowed with food delicacies served on each table.

The patrons had finally all left and the front doors had been locked firmly against late revelers. Lillian, Jonas and Erwin sat in the kitchen area with Ming Su and Ling Su at a small corner table, eating bowls of rice. They listened to what was being said, but understood little of the conversation. They were warm, dry and well fed. To them, January 1st was just one more day as it certainly was not the Chinese New Year.

"Happy New Year, again," Erwin said and drank a little more coffee.

"The same to you, Erwin," Lillian responded, also sipping a cup of coffee. She had imbibed only one small glass of champagne at midnight, preferring to keep a straight mind. "And Jonas, what do you see for us in this brand new year?"

Jonas smiled slightly as he sipped on a rich bodied cognac. "More of the same." he said and was silent. He was aware that if the ladies of the night stopped coming for the secluded dinners, the Sterling House might become too silent to survive.

There was silence for a few moments and then Erwin spoke up, trying to lighten the mood. "I was sitting here, trying to think of the most remarkable, interesting or notable thing I can recall from the past few years. I suppose it would have to be what happened over at the Stock Yards." He frowned and then smiled as he recalled the slap in the face, and municipal embarrassment the promoters had received from this purported stock show.

"Oh, I remember that." Jonas said, recalling that cold day in January. "It would not have been nearly so bad, if they had not advertised a free barbeque an' free beer. " He kind of laughed. "As I recall readin', over 20,000 of Denver City's finest, right off these very streets, broke down the barricades an' rushed the place. The *News* claimed they ate every bite of the tons of meat that had been prepared for all those visitin' stockmen an' dignitaries. Of course, what better ta wash it all down with than ta swill the free beer that was also there for the takin'?"

Erwin leaned back in his chair as he too recalled the reports from this disastrous affair. "From what I heard," he added, "when the whole thing was over, there was nothing left except a lot of broken boards, some gnawed bones and a bad reputation for the people who tried to put together a livestock show.

"Those bummers apparently carried off the beer barrels, over a 1,000 steel knives, all the tin cups and platters, to say nothing of the meat cleavers and hatchets that disappeared.

"So much for their showing of stock at the Denver Stock Yards. I am surprised the livestock survived it all. Somehow they did and the ranchers took their prize cattle home the next day."

"Do think they will ever try such a thing again?" Lillian asked.

"Not very soon if they are smart," Jonas said. "Maybe, when Denver City matures an' the officials sweep this bad memory under the Colorado rug, where it can be forgotten. We might be civilized in a lot of ways with Denver comin' a long way since I first set eyes on it, but She can still be an unruly an' wild place to live."

"Speaking of wild things," Lillian said, in Erwin's direction, "the wildest thing I can recall doing was when we all would run off to the river to go swimming. You always scolded me and told me not to go because Mother would be upset if she found out."

"And she always found out, too," Erwin noted and then grinned, recalling how impossible Lillian had been to control during those years.

"Remarkable, your mother," Jonas said.

"And you, Jonas?" Lillian asked, moving away from that subject.

Jonas hesitated for a moment as he watched Ming Su and Ling Su. "I suppose it was respondin' ta the plight of those two young ladies over there," he said. "Seems I have adopted two daughters an', of course, I have my son sittin' here at the table."

Erwin flushed, grinned and managed to say, "Yes, my father."

"I seem ta have three children an' I think that is most remarkable for someone who has never been married."

Ming Su had carefully listened to what was being said and whispered to her sister. Their faces were radiant because they knew they were loved by this man and blessed to have a home such as the Sterling House.

Jonas very quietly asked, "An' you, Miss Lillian? What is your most notable memory?"

She thought for a moment and her incredible meeting of Paris Jacob Montoya entered her mind. She quickly returned that memory to its secret place in her heart and said, "Besides the obvious floods, fires, swarms of insects, increased rat infestations in the basement causing me not to go down there any more and seeing too many drunks in the alley, the most notable thing was granting an audience with Mattie Silks and agreeing to the business arrangement that has helped keep us financially sound." She laughed. "Now, gentlemen, that was notable, remarkable and most interesting."

Erwin knew he was blushing and refused to look at Lillian. He was naive about many ways of the world, but not completely innocent about what passed between men and women. Indiscreet sexual pleasures had no place in his life as he chose not to indulge.

He knew the reputation of Mrs. Silks and it was obvious what business the beautiful ladies were in that came through the kitchen doors to find their way to the privacy of the upper rooms and the company of their gentlemen callers. In his opinion, it had taken great courage for Lillian to meet with this woman of the "other" lifestyle, let alone conduct business with her girls.

Jonas held back a smile. He could only imagine what the reaction had been between these two women from vastly different backgrounds when they had met. He knew Mattie Silks to be a shrewd woman, good with business affairs. He also knew Lillian to be equally shrewd when it came to survival.

Nothing more was said on the subject.

"Are ya sure everyone has left?" Jonas asked Erwin.

"I believe so. Before all the lights are out, I will double check."

"What was that?" Lillian said directing her attention toward the back door as they all heard the loud thump against the bolted door.

Jonas was immediately on his feet and drew his pistol as he headed for the door. "One more drunken bummer ta be sure," he said. In a louder voice, he demanded, "Who is there?"

There was another thump and a muffled voice could be heard. "My sister."

Lillian leaned forward and asked, "What was said?"

With a frown on his face Jonas turned and looked back at her. "Sounded like someone said 'my sister'!"

Lillian's voice caught in her throat as she stood and took a few steps toward the door. Erwin grabbed her arm and said, "Wait, Miss Lillian. Let Jonas do this. It might be bad."

Jonas cocked the pistol and unbolted the door. "Be aware. I am armed," he said before he opened the door to reveal a tall, very thin man with blond curly hair, wearing leather pants, a capote blanket coat and moccasins on his feet.

"Lillian Sterling." he said, "Is she here?"

With caution, Jonas stepped aside and Lillian faltered in her steps as Erwin caught and supported her.

Charley Paul Standing Horse Sterling stepped into the light and back into Lillian's life.

"Charley Paul!" she exclaimed. She pulled lose from Erwin and rushed to him. "Charley Paul." she repeated. "My brother."

"My sister," he said and opened his arms to her.

Ming Su and Ling Su stared with great curiosity at this strange man, whispering to one another as they backed into the shadows of the room. They had seen this kind of person before, but never in this house. They wondered why the young Missy was holding him, crying and laughing all at the same time?

Lillian cradled him in her arms and wept tears of relief, tears of joy and tears of feeling his body alive in her arms. "Come in. Come in. Ling Su, Ming Su, quickly. We need coffee and hot soup immediately. "Where have you been? How far have you come?

Let me look at you." She stepped back, scarcely believing her eyes.

Charley Paul stepped fully into the room and found himself immediately surrounded by Jonas, Erwin and Lillian. "My family," he said and then looked straight at Jonas or rather at the gun he held. "Are ya gonna shoot me?"

They all laughed as Jonas quickly holstered his pistol. Without hesitation grabbed Charley Paul and hugged him. "It is good to see you, boy." He let him go and stepped back "Damn, but it is good to see you."

Charley Paul let his eyes rest on Erwin. "I see your hair is still just as red as it always was," he said, tousling the man's full head of hair. "Do still plink an' plunk on the old piano?"

"Sure do," Erwin replied, running his hand through his hair to smooth it back down.

"An' you, my sister," Charley Paul said, as once again blue eyes met dark brown.

In that instant, the bond, which had truly never been broken, was strongly renewed between them, "are more beautiful than a nighttime sky filled with the wonders of the stars only as I imagined you to be."

"Such a compliment. Thank you."

"Are ya goin' to keep me standin' here in the middle of the kitchen or do I get to set a spell?"

"By all means, please sit down. Here, have some hot coffee. Ming Su is the soup ready? Are you hungry? Where have you been? Can you stay?"

They all started laughing as Lillian stepped out of her perfect ladylike control and began tripping over her own questions.

"Whoa, little sister," Charley Paul said. He took off his coat, tossed it into a corner and sat down. He looked with curiosity at the Chinese girl who cautiously served him coffee. "Thank you," he said, but she had already silently and quickly crossed the room to be away from him.

"No need to be fearful, Ming Su. This is my brother Charley Paul," Lillian said moving the sugar and cream toward him.

Ming Su nodded in his direction, but made no motion to come near him. She knew of these people of the half worlds of the white and Indian, more so of the half world of the Chinese and white. She also knew they usually brought nothing but trouble as they did not belong in either world.

How could this barbarian be of kinship to her Missy Lillian? she wondered. Many things she did not understand about these white people with no way of finding out. She encouraged Ling Su to serve the soup and they quietly retreated to their own little table, listening as they could to the conversations that had not stopped since this strange man with the unruly blond hair had stepped into the room.

"How long has it been?" Lillian asked and then answered her own question. "I was sent off to school just the year after you left here with Buckland and Soolie and that has been 20 years."

"Near to 22 years." Erwin added.

"Close enough," Charley Paul said, as he alternately drank the coffee and spooned the soup. "Wasn't sure any of you would still be here after all this time, but it was worth a try. Good to see ya, Jonas, an' you, too, Erwin." He returned his attention to Lillian, who was still smiling at him. "Rest of the family?" he bluntly asked.

Lillian's smile disappeared as she slowly shook her head. "Gone," she said. "All gone."

"I see," he said and was quiet. "Soolie died." he said rubbing at a scar that ran the length of his cheek.

"I know," Lillian responded. "Buckland told me when he came here just before he died."

"So after Soolie's death, the old mountain man came back here to die. I wondered what became of him." Charley Paul said and dropped the subject. Lillian sensed there might be more he wanted to say, but didn't.

Jonas stood up and walked to where Ling Su and Ming Su sat. He excused them and then said, "I think this is a time for close family talk." He walked back to where Charley Paul sat and shook his hand.

"Good ta see ya home. I will take my leave. Best of New Years, Miss Lillian," he said and left the room.

Charley Paul watched him go and then said, "Same Jonas I remember. Always quiet an' always in another room."

"Some things never change," Erwin added. He then yawned behind his hand. "Suppose I should take my leave, too, if I can trust you two not to take off and go swimming or get into some other trouble."

Charley Paul and Lillian laughed, recalling those days when Erwin had insisted, to no avail, they not do things he knew would cause them trouble with Lillian's mother. "A little too cold to go swimming," Lillian said.

"That it is," he said, delighted to see the two of them together. "Besides, I think both of you are old enough to know better. It is late and believe I will leave you to the family talk."

"Erwin, it is good to be back. We will talk more."

Erwin also shook his hand and then put a protective arm around his shoulder. "Lillian, shall I turn down a bed perhaps in your mother's old room?" he offered.

"Yes, please," she answered, "And also bank a fire in the fireplace as well."

"As you say. And again, Charley Paul," he repeated, "good to have you home." It was quiet for a few moments after Erwin left as if both Lillian and Charley Paul were rebuilding the years they had missed due to the willfulness of others and the passage of time.

Lillian refilled his coffee. She could not stop watching him as many questions formed in her mind. She knew this man as the brother she had ran wild in the streets with and who had been taken from her because of her mother's harsh ways. She was also wise to instinctively realize she did not know the grown man who, after 20 years, sat in the kitchen of the Sterling House.

There could never be mistaking him as the son of her father because of that incredible blond hair, just as there was no denying his Indian heritage. His dark skin and eyes reminded one of seeing the night coming straight at you. Yet, she could also see a grim harshness about him and her Grand Paw Paw's words echoed in her memory. *"He never did quite fit, no matter what me an' Soolie did fer him. His torment bein' from two worlds caused him ta do bad things sometimes."*

As she watched him, she wondered just what bad things Buckland Kavanaugh meant. She sat back down. "How did get that scar?" she ventured.

He reached up and rubbed the scar again. "Some Crow stole horses from some white people an' the Cheyenne I was livin' with got the blame for it. The Whites come searchin' for their horses an' would not believe us when we told them the Crow had done it. A fight came about an' some young white man said I didn't need this blond hair. Said he wanted it in place of the horse he had lost. His knife missed what he wanted but I have this to remind me of him."

"And what happened to the man?"

"Some things, little sister, ya don't ask."

Lillian's blue eyes widened as the darkness of his eyes and his expression told her the answer. "So, where have you been?" she asked, changing the subject of the scar and what happened to the man who had given it to him.

"When we left here," he said, "Buckland took us up to the Bitter Root in Montana. He trapped some an' built a cabin. We were happy. Soolie loved it there. She loved him an' she loved me. That was all I knew or cared about.

"Then, some Indians came an' said a white man could not live with a black white woman an' have a son like me. They said it was a bad omen an' bad medicine for them. "They burned us out. Buckland

239

wanted to go after them, but Soolie begged him not to go. He calmed down an' took us to a fort somewhere up even more north. We stayed there for a long time. Soolie cooked for the men an' they loved her cookin' just like everyone always did."

Lillian nodded in agreement recalling the woman's incredible way with foods. "Buckland trapped an' helped make maps of the area. I tried to go with the men, but I was no use out there. I always seemed to be in trouble or causin' it. The government finally closed the fort. We had no choice but to leave. The government put people together that did not belong together, but the tribes managed.

"We lived with some Cheyenne an' Lakota. They were doin' well in that camp, fendin' for themselves an' plantin' a garden. Buckland went on the hunts with the warriors but the soldiers always went with them.

"Soolie learned how to tend to the meats that were brought in. Scrapin' hides with the best of the Indian women. I mostly hung around with the older boys an' young men. Buckland warned me not to get too close to them listenin' to the stories of past war victories. I did not heed his advice an' kept persuadin' myself I would do better on my own with these men who bragged of their exploits an' the exploits of their fathers an' grandfathers.

"I thought better than diggin' in the dirt with Soolie or goin' on supervised hunts with Buckland. I finally left with Young Thunder an' his brother Tall Trees. That was about when I took out on my own."

"You left them there?" she asked, trying to follow his story.

"Yes," He said, still recalling his memories from the past.

"We headed on up to Canada. Lily, I went on some raids, burned out some settlers an' miner's camps an' I stole a lot of things that did not belong to me. I was good at stealin' an' sellin' the stolen property to the whites. If I kept my hair cut short an' wore the white man's trappin's, I could pass, but I didn't like it. I knew it was wrong but I had no place to go. I could not go back to Buckland an' Soolie an' bring my shame to them.

"Those young Indian renegades were usin' me an' convincin' me at the same time that Buckland an' Stoolie were better off without me." He frowned.

"I got arrested for stealin' some bread out of a window. I remember we could smell that bread as we rode past the old farm an' Young Thunder dared me to steal it. Said I was a coward if I did not do it. That dare an' my not being a coward cost me about five years in jail."

Lillian took a shuddering breath. "You spent time in prison for a loaf a bread?" "It was actually two loaves of bread an' one peach pie." he laughed and then leaned forward. "Probably the best thing that could happen to me when it did before somethin' worse came along the path I was on." He leaned back in the chair and stretched his body out. "Could have been longer the way I figured it, but the peach pie was long gone before they caught me, so they couldn't prove I had taken it." He rubbed his stomach and smiled at his own humor.

"When I got out, I went back to the Cheyenne camp. That was when I learned Soolie had died an' Buckland was gone. I wandered the woods an' mountains north of here since then not certain where to go or what to do. But I find those trails are closed for me now an' I must go somewhere else where the wind blows an' hope for the best." He stopped talking, tired of living it all over again.

"Enough about me. What of you an' this Sterling House? Where is our Paw Paw?"

Lillian avoided telling him about their father's death. "Mother was never interested in what Denver City had to offer. The schools here were not refined enough for me to attend.

"After you left, she insisted I go back East to school. As much as I am reluctant to admit it, the refinements were good for me. I am able to maintain where I feel a less qualified woman would have failed here in the Sterling House."

"Well, little sister, your refinements are pretty obvious an' your beauty is without question."

"It is the Sterling quality bloodline," she said.

Charley Paul lifted his empty coffee cup toward her in a toast. "But you still have not told me what happened to Paw Paw."

"The most terrible day of my life was the evening of my returning home from school reception. There was a man from Paw Paw's past that had held a grudge for many years and he chose that night to attack Paw Paw with a knife."

"What!" Charley Paul exclaimed.

"He came charging out of the crowd. I don't remember the words he said. All that has ever been in my mind was that he plunged a knife into Paw Paw. Uncle Charley shot and killed him but it was too late. The knife had found its mark and the poison that followed killed our Paw Paw." Lillian hung her head as the sorrow of her father's dying once again clouded her mind.

Charley Paul sat motionless, his mind numb from what she had told him. He slowly pushed his blond curls off his forehead and then looked away. This was something he was not expecting to hear. Because it had been so long, there could be no words of comfort he could give her for the loss of their father. It was also apparent the time for anger toward the man who had done the killing was also long past. It was over. It was done. His mind returned to what Lillian was saying.

"Mother was not capable of taking charge of the Sterling House. I had to learn how to manage it and keep it alive if we were to survive.

"Charley Paul, I did it. My eastern schooling was perfect for the task. Uncle Charley and Jonas Gregory helped with the saloon, Erwin helped me with the ledgers and books, Mother helped me learn the restaurant and we have, as you can see, survived." She stopped short of telling him about Mattie Silks and what it had required to survive during the past few years because of what was threatening her business.

"Lily, my sister, you have no man to help take care of all this?"

Lillian gently put the death of their father back into its resting place. She held up her left hand and said, "Oh, there is a man, but he cannot be with me as destiny and fate have taken him away.

"Then you have married?" he asked.

"Yes," she replied. "In my heart and soul, yes, but he is far away and I can only hope he returns soon."

"He is a fool to leave ya unprotected." Charley Paul got up and walked to the potbelly, where he tried to stoke life back onto the dying embers.

"He will return." she said with complete confidence. "In the meantime, the Sterling House is my protection."

She watched his futile efforts. The embers were barely glowing. Lillian also rose and pulled her shawl closer to her shoulders. "Perhaps we should seek the comforts of my mother's old room as I am sure Erwin has the fire banked perfectly for us."

Charley Paul fully closed the damper. "What about your mother?" he quietly asked.

In one word, Lillian responded, "Also gone." And they left the subject with that answer.

*   *   *

The Sterling House was dark and quiet as Lillian and Charley Paul climbed the spiral staircase to the second and third floors. Each was lost in childhood memories of racing up and down these stairs as they played games only they understood, always watchful for Abigale. Inevitably, she would halt their playful antics for a few moments before another scheme could be conjured up to avoid her and her watchful, critical eyes. Lillian opened the door to her mother's bed chambers and for a moment Charley Paul hesitated.

"Only her angry spirit remains and even that is faint," Lillian said as she stepped into the room and turned on more light.

Charley Paul cautiously entered the room which had at one time been forbidden to him. He still expected to see Abigale standing in the shadows, waiting to pounce or verbally rebuke him for being there.

Lillian pushed the logs closer together to stoke up the fire. "Come closer to the fire, where we can stay warm." she said. "I see Erwin has thought of everything," she said and poured them each a snifter of brandy. "This and the fire will keep us warm."

Charley Paul cross-legged on the floor and leaned closer to the warmth. "It seems strange to be in this room,." he said. "I keep lookin' over my shoulder to see if she is goin' to swat me."

Lillian lowered herself to the floor beside him. She, too, remembered how her mother had reacted to Charley Paul when he was in her presence, taking swipes and swats at him when she thought no one was watching.

"Her hand never found you too often, now did it?" she said.

"Too fast for her," he said and they both smiled. "Kind of thankful for those big skirts she wore, too, 'cause she couldn't kick at me either. Guess no body has wanted me around much 'cept for Soolie an' Buckland." He picked up his glass of brandy and gulped it."

"Nonsense, Charley. I always wanted you with me. I cried for days after they took you away. Then I cried harder when I was separated from my father after my mother insisted I go to that school of refinement back East. It was as if it was all some kind of evil plot to keep us apart and keep me away from my father."

"It was all the way it was meant to be, I suppose. I was meant to go with Buckland an' Soolie an' you were meant to go off to that fancy school." Once again, dark eyes met blue and he knew, just as he had known as a child, that he could trust her with how he was feeling.

"Lily, there is so much I need for you to understand an' how can I make you understand what it is like to have both sides of the world around you hate you for what you are? There is one thing I have learned an' learned well. I have no place in any white man's town. Even thought I can pass, an' have done so, my skin is too red. I have been told by too many that I cannot live on the reservations to the north either as my heart is too white.

"This scar on my face is not the only one I carry. There is a greater one on my heart," he turned to stare back into the fire. "Buckland told me that Paw Paw killed that man that butchered my mother at Sand Creek. Maybe this is part of what is wrong with me. I swear, Lily, if he had not killed that man, I would have found him an' his end would have come at the point of my knife." He stopped for a moment and let his thoughts calm. "There is something in me, in my blood, that riles too easy."

"I know." was all she said.

Lillian was silent for a long while, but looked at him out of the corner of her eye. Her brother was a handsome man by any standard.

Why not, he was of Sterling blood, she thought. Yet she also saw something more in his steady gaze into the flickering fire. He had a coldness in him that had been fostered somewhere back in time, perhaps even a time before he was born.

She said, "Charley Paul, you can stay here with me. Help me take care of the Sterling House. I can help make up for that which was lost to you so long ago." She realized her words were thin but it was all she could offer.

He sadly shook his head, the firelight playing off his blond curls. "There is no place here for a breed like me, either. You don't know the trouble this would bring, if I stay. I cannot change what I am.

"I think the Nations, somewhere in Oklahoma, will be the place for me. More of my kind there, they tell me an' I have heard the Cherokee take kindly to people, sometimes. I needed to see you, the only family I have, before I disappeared into the Nations."

"You talk as if you will never return."

He was silent, staring into the flames of the fire. "Chances are, I will not." Lillian's heart broke again, because she felt that he could not stay and as with so many others, she could not go with him. He was a man on his own, as he had been for many years and would probably stay that way. She rested her head on his shoulder and let the words become quiet between them. Her brother was of Sterling quality, strong, firm and stubborn in his own convictions.

Charley Paul Standing Horse put his arm around her and they watched the fire burn lower. He was glad he had came this way and Lillian was happy to have his strong shoulder to lean on, if but for just a short time.

*   *   *

January 1st's predawn cold swirled through the city and settled onto the streets of the sleeping city. The warmth of their memories had seen them through the first small hours of the new year. Much had been recalled with a few of each one's private memories not disclosed, but Lillian Anne Sterling, and her brother by a different mother, Charley Paul Standing Horse Sterling, had reunited their childhood bond. He had finally let her fall sleep undisturbed.

Lillian knew before she opened her eyes, that he was gone. She snuggled closer under the warm comfort blanket she knew Charley Paul had used to cover her where she had fallen asleep in front of the fireplace. The fire was out, with only a few sparse, faintly glowing embers to remind the room of the warmth the fire had once produced. Lillian sat up and realized her backside was stiff from sleeping, not only in her confining clothing, but also on the floor.

"Charley Paul," she whispered to the cold room and then moved to the fireplace to stir the embers, add a log and try and rekindle not only the warmth but the memory of his being with her. It was then she noticed, written in the cold, grey ash on the hearth, the message he had left for her.

"My love stays with you, but I must to go."

Lillian pulled the blanket tighter to her body. She shivered, more from her uncontrollable sadness than from the cold, as she sat down on the edge of the hearth and reread his message.

You did not have to go, she thought as tears flowed down her cheeks and fell from her face to mingle with the dust of the ashes and what he had left. His words.

Chapter
Twenty One

Notable things happen to important people in noteworthy places. There was not a newspaper that did not carry the most notable fact that President Theodore Roosevelt was in Colorado on one of his famous bear hunts in the mid-spring of 1905.

In the minds of many, however, he had missed the prize trophy, "king of the grizzlies," which had been killed just a year before south of Pikes Peak on Black Mountain. Old Mose, as the marauding bear had been named, was given credit for the slaughter of at least 800 sheep and cattle, as well as a number of human deaths. This gargantuan bear, weighing in at over 1,000 pounds, was given his day of notability with his picture printed in the news. The meat from this bear sold for ten cents a pound during the Christmas week. If President Roosevelt knew of this kill, he would have certainly commented on its being a notable event.

Lillian, too, was experiencing a most notable event with significant consequence in her life. Jonas Gregory, after 45 years in Denver, Colorado, was leaving. He had spent 40 years of his life in the Sterling House. He had informed her he wanted to leave. From her earliest recollections of this man, Lillian had always found him to be quiet and somber. Smiling did not seem to be part of who he was. Yet on this warm Colorado afternoon, sitting in the still richly furnished, but slightly fading, front living room on the third floor of the Sterling House, many slight smiles played across his features.

Strange, Lillian thought, as she had never seen it before, *he could be considered a handsome man when he did smile.*

"I can not believe I am actually doin' this," he said, his hands nervous with the stack of advertisements he held in his hands. "But, Miss Lillian," he continued, holding the papers out to her, "I am 60 years old an' never been anywhere except Missouri, where I was born, across Kansas ta come here an' then here ta the Sterling House."

"China!" she said, taking the papers and beginning to read them. "Why, of all places, China?" She knew the answer before he told her. Lillian had seen them talking, had actually seen Jonas smiling as the three of them read through many pamphlets and books about this country so far away. All along, she had thought him only to be helping with their education. She never dreamed they were planning on leaving.

"Ming Su an' Ling Su," he said. "want ta see their homeland."

"This is their homeland. Weren't they born here over in the old Hop Alley?"

Jonas realized there might be a bit of desperation in her voice, but he also knew there was a bit of desperation in what he was needing and planning. "As far as I know. Still, they have a homeland, too.

"Their parents came from China. They may have some kinfolk left there. They want ta go an' see an' I want ta go with them. It is not safe for young women ta be travelin' alone, especially in some foreign land where women are not that highly regarded." He stopped himself, realizing he might be saying a bit too much. But then thought, *No*, and continued. "From what we know, they were left behind the night of that riot. Had they not been taken in by Lizzie Preston, Mrs. Mattie an' then you, who knows what would have become of them."

"Yes, Jonas, we are all grateful no harm befell them. "China?" she repeated with greater emphasis. "That is so far away," she said with concern in her voice.

Jonas became very somber again. "Before I die, I want ta do something worthwhile. I believe helpin' these girls find their true homeland an' possibly their family is worthwhile."

"You raised Erwin. That has been most certainly worthwhile. You manage the saloon which is also very worthwhile."

Jonas shook his head. "The Sterling House raised Erwin. He is married to it an' most devoted ta you. The saloon nearly runs itself an' Miss Sterling," he sadly added, "I don't have ta tell ya how business has dropped an' continues ta do so. Our leavin' would lessen your responsibilities. Hired help cannot possibly cost you as much as we do."

"I see," she said. "It does appear that your mind has been convinced to do this."

Without further defense of his intent, he said, "Yes."

"I suppose this day had to come. All I can do is wish you, Ming Su and Ling Su the very best. I do offer my gratitude to you for all the devoted years."

"They were years well spent," he said, rising. "When I came here, how could anyone have guessed these two unusual girls would come into my care. It may not be the right thing ta do at my age, but it is what they want an' I want it too."

Lillian rose to her feet and walked to him. "Jonas." she said, as she gently embraced him, "I cannot imagine my life without you but, if you must go, then go with my blessing." She stepped back. "The Sterling House will survive and be here when and if you wish to return."

Jonas nodded his head in her direction and left the room.

Lillian had years to remember with this man. Although he had never said much, Jonas Gregory had always been a part of her life as well as the life of the Sterling House.

*   *   *

When her thoughts were the heaviest, Lillian found a window where she could stare out over a bustling Larimer Street. Now, however, it seemed it bustled to a different rhythm. A pulse intensified by the onslaught of more vice and more crime. There was more unscrupulous gambling and con games, uncontrolled back alley prostitution where it was sometimes a challenge to outmaneuver the rats that came out at night to feed. It was not only the four legged creatures that came to feed on the waste of mankind. Two legged ones also roamed Larimer Street, prowling for easy prey.

Lillian knew that most of the saloons had side or back entrances that were marked "Ladies." These entrances led to lurid dens of iniquity. If a lady did enter, she would not return the same.

Although she wore social blinders most of the time, Lillian was not blind to these things. She was also aware, that in her own way, she abetted some of the immorality.

None the less, the ladies of the night who came through her back doors were, in her eyes, exactly that. Ladies. There had never been misconduct at the Sterling House and its integrity would always be maintained. Without Jonas and the girls, it would become more difficult, but she would manage.

As she continued to watch the street below, Lillian realized she had become far too complacently reclusive, relying on the old ways as she slowly became out of step with the times. Perhaps the Sterling House was out of step as well.

Denver most recently boasted a wondrous thing called a motion picture. She was yet to see one with no desire to go. Her motion picture was the ever changing life on the street below and the Sterling House all around her. Secrets had been kept from her, such as how fatefully ill her uncle had been, and now Jonas was preparing to leave.

She had also heard that men flew through the air due to the endeavors of the famous Wright Brothers at some place back east known as Kitty Hawk. The third floor of the Sterling House was as high as she cared to be and wondered how long it would be before powered aircraft would be seen in the skies over Denver.

Perhaps if they flew high enough, they would not see what Larimer was declining into. Granted, plans were being made to renovate around Cherry Creek as well as along the Platte River, but would any of these plans cure what plaguing Larimer Street? It was as if the city officials were overlooking this part of Larimer Street as though it did not exist, while decent businesses and decent folks continued to move away.

She, too, had been attracted by the lure of the bright lights over on the "Great White Way," Curtis Street, where the upper echelon of society went for the theater, dining and entertainment. Unfortunately, she did not have the means to get there. All she could do was struggle to hold on where she was.

Perhaps this was part of what Jonas had seen. In any event, it was his decision and there was nothing else to do but be supportive of that decision. She would not wallow in the self pity that was trying to engulf her.

*   *   *

Union Station was much as it had been when Lillian returned from St. Louis after her schooling. However, seeing the huge steam engine that would pull the train out of the station, she saw where it had changed and was certainly not being the one that had brought her home.

She did not care. It did not matter. All she knew was that this smoking, belching, clattering, whistle blowing iron horse was going to take three people away from her. After the train pulled away from the platform, and out of sight, it did not matter which direction it went. The people would be gone.

Erwin stood back, as he always did, silent and reserved as always. Lillian let her mind go to a dim place as she wondered, *How long will it be before leave me. too?*

Many of Erwin's thoughts remained unspoken. He knew he would never leave her, but he too had mixed feelings of joy for Jonas. Where the man was going and what he wanted to do with what was left of his life.

He had tried to talk to Jonas about what seemed like a perilous journey to places unknown, but he quickly realized Jonas was firmly set on this venture. Erwin was happy for the man, so he had to set him free with no guilt or remorse for Jonas to look back on by his knowing of Erwin's sympathies for Lillian. Jonas had dedicated a lifetime to the Sterling House. It was time he saw his life in a different place. Far be it for Erwin to discourage him in this endeavor. His place was to continue encouraging Lillian in all ways possible.

"Will you please write and let us know are all right?" Lillian asked of Jonas. "Not much of a hand ta do such, but I will try," he said, realizing that even in his eagerness and joy to leave, he was feeling a strange loss beginning to form in his mind. He would miss this beautiful woman, and the Sterling House, which had come to mean so much to him. He walked the small distance to where Erwin stood and shook his hand. "Take care of her, Erwin."

Erwin, choked with emotion, gripped Jonas' hand and could only nod his head. Ming Su bowed toward Lillian. When she rose, she said, "I thank you most kindly for all you give to me. It was my pleasure and my life to serve you and your Sterling House. May the kind winds always find you."

Lillian smiled but her own intense emotions would not let her answer. She watched Jonas and Ming Su climb aboard as they began to wave farewell.

Lillian felt a tugging at her sleeve and turned to see Ling Su standing beside her looking straight into her eyes.

"Thank you, my Missy Lillian," was all the young Chinese girl said as she quickly walked away to board the train behind her sister and Jonas. "Thank you," she said again as the train began its lurching movement forward.

Lillian's eyes clouded with tears. These were the only words Ling Su had ever spoken to her.

Chapter
Twenty Two

When too much snow falls in the high country, and conditions become primly rich, the snow will move and tumble down in an avalanche of destruction.

That was exactly how Lillian felt, as if an avalanche of destruction had rolled over her. She was not the only saloon owner to feel this gut wrenching blow to all their livelihoods. The Women's Christian Temperance Union, along with other supposed morally, ethically and, in some case, legally correct groups had finally won their long war with those who would provide and to those who would imbibe.

The bartenders in Denver City had tapped their last glass of beer, jigger of gin, shot of whiskey or drop of any type of alcoholic beverage at the stroke of midnight, December 31, 1915. The sale and consumption of alcohol had become illegal. Prohibition had become a reality in the State of Colorado!

With an anger she had never been known to express, she had slammed closed the doors of the Sterling House refusing to open them to anyone. She dismissed the kitchen staff promising to pay them for the day as she had turned them away from their work. She had slowly climbed the stairs to the third story sitting room to wait. Wait for what, she was not sure as she angrily stared through a window down to a cold empty, street below. With so many businesses closed all around them, few people were venturing out. Even though there was defiance in her every thought, she knew there was no way to circumvent what had fallen down around them.

Erwin had followed her and when she turned toward him, he sadly shook his head, agreeing with her without saying a word. He was aware she had to work through the anger she was feeling toward a society she felt had betrayed her.

"There have been rumors of this for years, but I never thought those pious wretches could actually close the doors of the decent businesses here in Denver City." she raged. "I could understand closing down the saloons that only serve alcohol and what passes for tidbit meals, but not stop us from serving fine wines and champagnes with our meals in the Sterling House restaurant. We are a decent establishment which has stood for quality since my Paw Paw and Uncle Charley opened the doors so many years ago. "Furthermore," she added, "when my mother came here, she saw to that quality being maintained against all adversities." Lillian folded her arms across her chest and returned her angry gaze to the street. *To say nothing of what I have endured,* she thought.

Erwin quietly waited.

"Erwin," she continued, toning down her voice, "You are the only one left, the only one I can talk to. It has all changed so much. I fear even some of the quality has vanished as well because of the changes."

"Come have some tea," he said in a quiet manner, trying to soothe her as he poured the dark liquid into a cup.

"Perhaps my mother was correct in how she coped by her indulgences of sherry and laudanum."

"I cannot see you doing that." he responded and watched her stir her tea while she added a few grains of sugar.

"Nor can I, but what am I to do? Erwin, you will never know the anger I felt at having to leave here for that dreadful school. And then how poorly prepared I was for what I came home to.

"All I wanted was to come home and have my life return to normal," she said, "but that was not allowed.

"What I learned while away was invaluable and without that schooling, I could not have taken to task the management of this business along with all that waited for me upon my return.

"My Paw Paw's death, so soon, so sudden and Uncle Charley's dying the way he did. To say nothing of my mother's objections and constant criticism." She sipped her tea, recalling far too much. "There was no other place for me to go and no other thing for me to do. This," she said gesturing around her, "is all I have ever known. There is not much gainful employment for knowing which napkin to use or how to gracefully set one's teacup back in one's teacup saucer."

With that moment of pure rebellion, Lillian deliberately set her teacup on the table beside the saucer and let her napkin flutter to the floor.

Although not a laughing matter, Erwin inwardly smiled at her subtle rebellion, but did not retrieve one or set the other in its proper place. It was true, they were facing a very serious situation with what would only be a more decided decline of business without the serving of alcohol.

He had an idea, but wanted to know what Lillian truly wanted before he presented it. "What about the ladies who come here?" he ventured. "The lack of serving drinks will probably not prohibit their entertaining ways."

Lillian sadly shook her head. "It has been over 15 years since my business arrangement with Mrs. Silks and, as with the continual aging and decline of Larimer Street, I have also seen an aging and decline with the ladies who come here and the gentlemen who seek their services. You know as well as I do, that fewer and fewer reservations are being made to accommodate the privacy they once required.

"I know Mattie Silks now owns that House of Mirrors right across the alleyway behind us, but I never see her. I think most of her clientele stays secluded behind those four walls.

"In reality, Erwin, I have never seen her since that first meeting. I was aware she was only doing Jonas Gregory a favor to keep us in business. This, too, is declining. Without the luxury of serving refined drinks, we will have little left to offer.

"This insidious prohibition, Bone Dry Act as they call it, is cutting us all to the bone of our existence. Although men will continue to be men with their lustful ways, this is bound to also affect her business as well." Lillian paused. "Her house is not my problem. The Sterling House is and I don't know what to do with it."

Erwin studied her for a long moment before he began offering what he hoped would be an answer for her. "Do you want to try keeping the Sterling House open on its food limited basis?" he asked.

Lillian struggled for an answer. One from the heart and one from her busine teaspoon in its spoon rest and ss logic. "When Ming Su and Ling Su left, they took a bit of the sterling quality of how the food was prepared with them. We were incredibly fortunate to have them with their impeccable deportment and gift for learning the culinary ways left behind by Soolie and the recipes I read to them from her writings. I have tried to instill those proper ways into the heads and hands of those who bake and cook for us. Yet, I feel the final culinary repast is sadly missing what was once here and I don't know how to get it back.

"Erwin, I will soon be 53 years old. Quite frankly, I do not have the patience to teach the skills any more. As I said, a small thing," she bent over to pick up the napkin, "to know how to fold a napkin. Quite another to teach others the ways and means of how to manage it."

He watched her as she delicately folded the napkin, placed it beside the teacup saucer, properly positioned the teaspoon in its spoon rest and returned the teacup to the saucer. "I cannot answer your question, as I do not know what to do." She slumped in the chair.

Erwin studied her for a long moment before he spoke. "I once offered money," he said, "and you refused it saying we might need it more at some other time. I was careful with my wages and some years back, I made an investment that some might have thought to be foolish.

"A pig in a poke, as they say. Yet the investment made sense. Rather than just leaving the money in a bank, which I don't always trust, I bought some property across the mountains.

"I have never seen it, Lillian, only some badly taken photographs, but there is a home there, and a nice one from what I can tell. What makes the money is the fruit orchard that is also on the property. Peaches. You know, those really sweet ones we like. I own a peach orchard across the mountains in a place called the Palisades near Grand Junction. Lillian, we can go and live there."

"Do what?" she questioned, wondering if she was truly hearing what she was hearing. "Leave Denver and the Sterling House? I can't do that."

"Under the circumstances, can you stay here?"

Lillian just looked at him but not answer.

"I agree with you wholeheartedly," Erwin said. "The quality of life here has diminished considerably. We both see it. It seems the very business that put food on our table has been reduced to the serving of food only.

"The people who work here now, merely work here. They have no vested interest except to be paid on a regular basis and that base is getting smaller all the time.

"I paid and dismissed the bartenders last night and all they did was shrug and walk away." He stopped for a moment and then reasoned,

"I highly suspect the kitchen staff would react much the same way. People don't care anymore. Not the way they once did."

"Are you proposing I sell the Sterling House?"

Erwin reached across the table and took both her hands in his. "I propose," he said, "you sell what you really don't want, even though I fear it will not bring much in light of all that has happened. You can put into storage what is left and take only our personal belongings. We will board up the Sterling House and go to this peach orchard until these politicians come to their senses and repeal this Bone Dry Act. We can come back and start over when all of this nonsense about no drinking of alcohol is over.

"I have enough money to accomplish this move and the sale of peaches, and whatever else we might see fit to raise and sell, will tide us over until we can return to the Sterling House."

Lillian stared at him for the longest moment, emotionally confused by points beyond her ability to reason. Yet she heard the logic in what he proposed. "My formal training did not prepare me for horticulture. I know nothing about raising peaches." she said and a small twinkle reappeared in her blue eyes that had been filled with tears, "How big is the house?"

Chapter
Twenty Three

Over the expanse of time from its humble, almost innocent conception, the skyline of Denver had changed many times due to the ravages of Mother Nature's floods, windstorms, and violent acts which could never be predicted or stopped.

Added to this was the carelessness of man's insistence on civilizing, taming and controlling what he thought to be his with roadways dug into the earth, buildings blocking the sky and humanity's byproducts polluting the air.

The Sterling family, with all its members, those of choice and those by chance, had also changed the earth beneath the foundation of the city, the alleyways of stone and the streets of clay.

If there could be thought and mind to any of this, it would wish to be free of the weight of time. Just as Lillian Anne Sterling wished to unburden the troublesome memories of a life, in odd and strange ways, unlived. Her life weighed on her heavily as the City of Denver weighed on the Breast of Mother Earth.

As far as she knew, she was the last of the Sterling lineage with only one half brother, who had disappeared into the Nations to find a place where he could be at peace with the world. She had no sisters, no aunts, no uncles and no cousins with only vague memories of stories of a Southern heritage, also dead and buried somewhere back in Georgia. These were dim, distant stories of times and places she could never be close to. A way of life destroyed by man's greed and constant penchant for dominance.

I am facing the very same things where I am trying to live, she reasoned, being aware she too had challenged the doors of time, but also was fully aware that her passing would leave no mark on time to tell she had ever existed.

With the help of what was left of the kitchen staff, she and Erwin had inventoried, sorted and sold many things from the Sterling House. The dining room furniture was carefully stacked and the linens packed away. All the fine crystal, china and silver had been put into storage on the second floor under strong lock and key.

After the first spring thaws, they had shipped many of their very personal things across the mountains via the rail lines. They had notified the caretaker family that the owner would soon come to occupy the house.

Erwin had shown her the telegram stating that the family who had been living in the main house had very quickly set about to move into a smaller house on the lower end of the property and were "anxious to have the new owner come home."

Come home? This is my home, she thought as she walked the length of the cherry and mahogany wooden bar in what was left of the Sterling House Saloon. She turned and let her eyes travel the full length of the darkened room, made even darker by the wooden slabs nailed not only to the outside of the windows, but the inside as well. Erwin had insisted there be iron bars installed between the wooden slabs to add to the security. The front doors were secured by tight bolts.

In her mind, she could still hear it, still see it. *Where had it all gone?* The men laughing and talking as they leaned against the bar. Charley Gaynor tempting the gamblers to play that all but long lost game of cards he was so famous for dealing. Most of them knew they would lose to him. Most of them did not care, as there was always the chance he would forget a card or two as he dealt Spanish Monte and they might win a little of their money back which he sometimes let them do.

Before she turned out the lights, she looked up at the blonde nude still staring down over the room with her painted blue eyes seemingly fixed on the artist who had originally painted her, not knowing she would reign over the Sterling House Saloon for so many years.

Lillian thought she saw sadness in that forever young face, but realized it was only her own sadness mirrored in everything she saw.

She walked on and stopped at the foot of the stairs. For a moment, she heard a young girl's laughter and she could visualize the little dark haired girl as she ran to her Paw Paw or her Grand Paw Paw to be lifted high in the air. Lillian could still smell the leather and tobacco odor her Grand Paw Paw always had and the sweet, delicate aroma of shaving soap her father used. Then there would be her mother, scolding and angry, because her baby daughter was in the saloon.

She shook her head to clear the images from those times long past.

She started up the spiral staircase and then stopped to turn back. For a moment, she was swept back to another time when she had descended these stairs on the arm of her proud father. In a memory, clouded by age, she saw once again those dark eyes watching her. She remembered how that man's gaze had caused her to actually stop on her descent. "Lillian," her father had questioned, "are you all right?"

She remembered her answer. *"Yes father. I am . . . I am wonderful."*

For a moment, her blue eyes misted with tears, but there were none left for her to cry. She had longed for, prayed for, the conception of a child with Paris Jacob Montoya. The seed he had left with her, the seed of life he had planted, had been at a time of her infertility.

She had his one and only letter. She had his promise. She had two rings she still wore, but she did not have his child. She did not have him.

Perhaps that had been for the best. All the waiting in the world would not have given a child his father, just as all the waiting she had done had not brought him back to her. In a few more days, she would be gone. If, just if, he ever did return, he would not be able to find her as there was no one who would know where she had gone.

She would keep the letter and wear the rings, but the waiting was over. In her heart, she knew it was time to leave the skid row Larimer Street had become. She also knew it was time to stop waiting for a man who was not going to return.

Upon reaching the third floor front sitting room, she once more peered down at the stillness of Larimer Street as the streetlights slowly came to life. They created a very hazy effect as they illuminated the street below.

Opening the window, she felt the damp, chill in the air from the afternoon's spring thunderstorm. She knew the indigents along Larimer had sought early refuge in whatever doorway or empty building they could squeeze into. Their alcohol was gone, too, and many of them had gone into frenzies to find whatever was left of it to be found.

This had turned into a time of panic for many whose sole reason for living was to find that next cheap bottle of booze. Their existence had been to stand in first one soup line and then another. They waited for the thin sustenance that passed for soup or the stale breads that were being doled out all the while pondering where and when they could get that next drink.

All of this was sinking Larimer Street deeper into its own decay, making Larimer Denver's old age home for lost winos and indigents as well as those who had no where else to go.

Every beer brewery had closed their doors, throwing hundreds of people out of work while Coors, Walters and Zang's rapidly searched for ways to stay in business with Zang's production of Zang's Snappy and Zang's Wuerzberger near beer.

Many ice cream and soda shops opened. Unlike the bottomless pits of drinking, where the thirst for alcohol was never quite satisfied, Denver could only support so many of these businesses of a sweeter nature. The sweet tooth could easily be satisfied. The craving for alcohol never felt that.

All over the city, alcohol related businesses were closed with shutters on the windows and boards nailed to the doors to keep out those who would seek even a mean shelter for the night or pilfer a drop left in an empty or unbroken bottle. Erwin had assured her they were safe due to all the security measures they had installed. She knew he patrolled the house on a very regular basis and wore a gun.

For some odd reason, she thought of Mattie Silks and wondered if she, too, might not be looking down over Market Street, thinking many of the same thoughts about how their respective worlds had disappeared. Their businesses were no more than minor ripples in the complex civic stream of where they lived in Colorado. The high minded, stiff necked, overly moralized, conservatives thought the elimination of alcohol would eliminate lawless lewdness in Colorado. When the women had received the vote in 1893, the members of the Temperance League had pushed and pushed for laws they felt would end drunkenness as well as what they considered other vice driven crimes and social ailments. Even as reclusive as Lillian had become, she could hear the underground murmurings of those who were using an old word with a new meaning. Bootlegging!

What had once meant the upper part of a boot now meant to make, transport and sell alcohol illegally as ways were being devised and invented to slip around the law for a substance no one was going to do without.

Alcohol would still be served, but it would be in ways, and with financial means, she did not have. As always, the rich could skirt the law and the poor would go to jail for infractions of a lifestyle someone had changed for them by the signing of papers in a courthouse under the guise of protecting everyone from their own vices.

Lillian had sent a small note to Mattie Silks telling her of the decision to close the Sterling House and the proposed leaving of the Denver area. There had been a short note returned in response.

My Condolences ~ M. Silks

Shivering, Lillian pulled her shawl tighter around her shoulders and continued to watch the night reach into, and along, Larimer Street. She preferred the darkness as it was somehow surrealistic to her when she could not see the cracks in the sidewalks where weeds protruded, see trash littering the streets lining the gutters or buildings shuttered and boarded as they cracked and crumbled from disuse and disrepair.

The only movement on the street below was that of a lone vehicle. She watched it stop on the far side of the street and a man in a long black coat got out. He appeared to pay the driver and the vehicle pulled away, leaving the man standing on the street corner, walking cane in one hand and a small satchel in the other.

The man looked both ways on Larimer, crossed the street toward the Sterling House and disappeared from her view. Not that she could see him or the street all that well without her spectacles, which she preferred not to wear most of the time. It didn't mattered that she could not see him clearly. The man was just one more soul wandering the streets of old Denver with no intent, no purpose and no destination.

Lillian closed her eyes for a moment and remembered the handsome cabs and carriages that once filled the street, when people had intent, purpose and destination with much of that intent, purpose and destination being to visit the Sterling House.

Will the time ever come again? she desperately wondered, *but how can it, if I leave?*

It was the same thought that had tormented her since the decision had been made to leave. Erwin had been wise in his investments and the Western Slope of Colorado would be her home at least for awhile.

She sat down in front of the mirror and stared at her reflection. It was a hard truth, but her investments of emotions and monies were gone. She had to keep convincing herself that Paris Jacob was not coming back just as the Sterling House business was not coming back. Logic and reality told her she must move on if she was to survive.

Peaches, she thought. She knew nothing of them, except that she loved to eat them. She would simply have to learn how to grow them. They could not be any more difficult than learning the business of a saloon and restaurant.

There was a knock on the door and she said, "Yes, Erwin, come in." It could not be anyone else, as there truly was no one left.

Erwin opened the door and stood there, at first not saying anything. Finally, he managed to say, "Miss Lillian."

"Yes, Erwin, what is it?" Lillian turned slightly on the dresser bench and waited.

"It is late, but . . ." and he faltered, " . . . you have a caller."

"What?" she questioned. "There is no one I wish to see and, as you said, it is late. As you can see, I am preparing to retire. Send them away. I wish to see no one."

Erwin took a few steps toward her and held out a small china plate. "The gentleman asked for one of the silver calling card trays but they have all been stored away. All I could find was this plate. He said it would be all right to use."

Lillian looked down at the china plate and it was not a card she saw but a small silver chain with an ivory snowflake on it. Her hand flew to her mouth and she took several quick breaths as she felt her heart flutter.

Her hands shook as she took the plate from him and stared down at the Sterling family heirloom lying so quietly on the cool china. She was afraid she would drop the plate and set in on the dressing table.

"What shall I tell the gentleman?" Erwin asked, barely able to keep his own emotions under control.

In a very quiet voice, she said, "Show the gentleman in."

Lillian was frozen, unable to move. She was not ready. Not properly attired. Hair not styled. Candles not burning. Tea and sweet cakes not ready to be served. Beyond her these formalities, and racing through her mind, was a lifetime of expectations, a lifetime of waiting, desiring and longing. As the door opened, she rose on her unsteady feet.

"Miss Lillian Anne," Erwin said, stepping aside, "may I present Senor Paris Jacob LaRoche de la Montoya. Senor Montoya, Miss Lillian Anne Sterling of the Sterling House."

With those words, combined with a most gracious smile Erwin could no longer control, he quietly backed away and left the room to let these two people find where they had left one another so many years before.

"Senorita Sterling," Paris Jacob Montoya said, looking into the blue eyes he had waited to see for what seemed like an eternity. He lifted her trembling hand to his lips, but not before he noticed the small gold and silver bands she still wore. "Lillian, my love," he said as she collapsed into his arms.

Their waiting was over.

*   *   *

His cane rested comfortably in an ivory trimmed, wooden stand beside her parasols. His long, black, wool coat was carefully hung on the hall tree bench, along with her day and evening wraps.

His boots were off and her slippers were beside them. Her dressing gown and lace trimmed, satin nightgown lie beside his trousers and shirt on a low bench.

As time, space and miles were no longer between them, neither was any article of clothing, as they wrapped around one another in the darkness, under the luxuriously thick comforters on her bed.

They did not share intimacy immediately. Rather they enjoyed love in the ways of complete acceptance of the physical touch as their lips explored and gentle hands found secret places, barely recalled from years before. It was as if all of this had been held in secret waiting to once again be revealed.

The daylight hours would be the time for them to talk and begin to erase the years. Where had he been? Why he had not returned to her until now? He would learn how she had struggled to maintain where she was in a house dimming by age and the ravishes of rules applied by others.

The most important thing to Paris was the fact she was still in Denver, on Larimer Street in the Sterling House and had waited for him.

"I promised I would wait," she said.

"My love, I promised I would return," he replied stroking the inside of her thigh as she lay next to him, her head nestled against his chest.

She kissed his bare chest and then lay back on the pillows. "You have no idea," she said in the darkness, "how close this all came."

Paris sensed her urgency to talk, but pulled her back down to him. "I thank God you were still here," he said, smoothing back the hair from her forehead and kissing her face. "I prayed you would be safe and that I would find you."

Lillian drew closer to him, wanting to talk, but wanting more for him to make love to her. Needing to feel him inside her. She was not sure she would remember how, but trusted her emotions to lead the way. It had been so many years and no other man had touched her.

"Make love to me," she whispered. All the rest could wait as there was nothing more important than the love making that was finally theirs to share.

Paris Jacob pulled a little away from her and said, "I waited for you." He rested his hand on the mound of her womanhood. She felt fire burn through her.

"And I for you," she whispered, pulling him back close to her. "We will learn again what we once knew."

Lillian slowly let her lips move over his body, her hands exploring, touching and finding. Cautiously and with great curiosity, she kissed the tip of his extended manhood and tasted a hint of the salty honey lying just below the surface. She heard him moan low in his throat.

Paris Jacob started to rise up and pull her under him, but she pushed him back down against the pillows and crossed her leg over him. Not exactly sure of what she was doing, but driven by all that possessed her, Lillian delicately, gently continued on letting her body slide down over his until he was completely inside her.

Paris put his hands on her hips and gently rocked her body back and forth against his until he thought his mind could not bear more. He wanted to hold this feeling forever, never letting her go as he became one with her and she with him.

She responded to his hands, letting her body move with his, opening herself to a depth of womanhood she had only imagined. As the eroticism and complete ecstasy of their passion slowly subsided, they knew this was no longer the dream they had held. It was their reality with a pure expression of the love they had for one another.

They were as one, as it had been meant to be from the beginning.

Lillian's breath slowly returned to normal. She moved her legs down between his and relaxed her entire body on top of his.

His breathing, too, became steady as he stroked her hair and kissed her forehead. "Did you remember to bring a cloth to clean with?" he asked, feeling their combined wetness between them.

"No," she replied, feeling a bit embarrassed, but then quickly said, "I also forgot to lock the door."

They both laughed and let this become but one of many intoxicating and private memories yet to be created between them.

Chapter
Twenty Four

With no thought of its own, there was a light rain falling to cleanse the air over a city dirtied by time. Larimer Street and its buildings, sullied by the passage of too much time and too little care, felt the rain, but the stain was too deep to be cleansed by a spring rain. The Sterling House, with its once proud whitewashed bricks and copper trim, stood dingy beside its sister buildings on the once proud Larimer Street.

Paris Jacob LaRoche de la Montoya had returned to a city and a place he scarcely recognize. Much had changed in the many years he had been gone. Many things had changed for him as well.

He did not know where to start, where to begin to tell her all that had happened. On his return, a more than an anxious fear had swept over him when he had found the front of the Sterling House boarded up and securely locked.

Fortunately, he had seen a light in an upper window and he had gone around to the back to see if he could find anyone who could tell him what had happened to the Sterling Family. He had felt great relief when Erwin opened the back door to him and he learned all had not been lost.

Erwin had expressed the greatest of joy that Paris had returned practically on the eve of their leaving. Had he been a few days delayed, Paris's would have found a completely deserted Sterling House.

With great patience, Lillian had only one question for him as she quietly asked, "What took you so long?"

Paris began to fill in the distance of the years between them. "When I left here, I became quite ill on the voyage back to Spain. The doctors said it was a fever with no explanation other than it left me in a weakened state.

"I had to stay in Madrid, Spain, for several weeks before I could go on to Cordoba, where my family had gone. When I got there," he continued, "my mother was very sick. I was still so weak from my fever, about all I could do was sit beside her bed and hold her hand."

Paris averted his gaze as he could not control his emotions. "I think her heart was just too broken from all she had lost, to keep beating. She cried for her home in California and all that had been taken from them." His focus came back to her.

"My father promised to take her to Paris, France, if she would find the will to live and regain her strength. It did not happen. Her kind, gentle heart stopped beating. I wrote and told these things. Did you not get my letter?" he questioned.

Lillian walked to her writing desk, where she kept the special box she had treasured for so long. She brought it to the table and opened it for him. "This was all I ever received. From the many marks on it, it was a long time in coming. Maybe two years."

Paris frowned at the water smeared letter packet and recognized it from so long past. Picking it up, he carefully opened it and read what few still readable words. "This is the only one you ever received?"

"Yes," she answered.

"I sent several other letter packets to you, trying to let you know what was happening to me and in my country. When I received no response, I wondered if your mother . . ." he hesitated, judging his words before saying them. "She did not receive me well," was all he said.

"My mother was cruel in many ways," Lillian responded. "No, she did not favor you," she recalled, remembering her mother's bitter, angry words against this man. "But, to the best of my knowledge, she never intercepted the mail, as no mail ever truly came here."

"I never received but this one letter," she said, replacing the packet in the box. "I treasured this one, as can see. I have saved it all these many years. I was going to hand carry it with me when I left here, trusting no one to care for it as I do and have."

"My love," he said, holding his hand out to her.

"How could answer my letters if you never got them? But, I do wonder what happened to them?"

Lillian walked to him and cradled his head against her breasts, as she kissed him on the forehead. "Who is to say. Lost forever I suppose, but, I answered them every day in my heart even though I never received them." she responded and then sat back down across from him. She knew there was more he had yet to tell her, because there were still missing years.

With great sadness still in his dark eyes, he continued. "After my mother died, I took my father on a long journey away from Spain and all the grief he was suffering from too much loss.

"Two years, Lillian, two years we traveled. I knew we were spending what was left of the Montoya Estate. Yet I could not deny his grieving days. When we finally returned to Cordoba, we were broke and there was so much civil unrest in our motherland of Spain.

"There were small revolts and bigger ones. All those who worked our land for us, raising our cattle, tilling the fields and caring for the Montoya Estate either died or left. There was no money and many debts.

"Then my father died." He stopped for a moment and swallowed hard. "I had no way to return to Colorado. All I could think about was and how to get back here, With no money, I had no way to do this. My uncles, along with their families, came to the Montoya lands. With hard work, we were able to renew our estate."

Paris Jacob walked, without the assistance of his cane, to the window. He did have a noticeable limp, but Lillian did not rise to assist him. With great respect, she kept her distance allowing him the time he required to tell his passage of years.

"And then," he said, in a tone so low she could barely hear him, "there was a time when I was not sure I would be welcome here or anywhere in the United States. I could not openly state my feelings in my home for fear of being labeled a traitor. Spain did a very foolish thing declaring war on the United States over an island.

"Many of us felt the government was still smarting because they lost their foothold in California and northern Mexico. The land grants, the very same ones that caused us to lose so many of our homes in California, were also still a very stinging sore between our two countries. Spain wished to keep control of something they thought the United States wanted. Spain was blamed for the sinking of that ship in the harbor but I don't think they had the bravado to do such a thing. Still no one knows for sure who was responsible. Men on both sides wanted the war."

"I knew of the war," she said, "and could not help but wonder what the affect would be, not only on your country, but on you as well."

"Quite frankly, Lillian, Spaniards were not welcome in this country," he said, "and I am a Spaniard. It was a politician's war, fed by bitterness, resentment and greed. Men will always enjoy dressing up in uniforms and parading their intent. In my country, many chose not to be involved unless forced to go. And the affect on you?" he asked.

"Other than the parade to see them all off to fight the 'Splendid Little War', as it was called, and the parade when they all came home, the biggest celebration was the parade they had for a young man who died of a spinal disease before he left San Francisco to go to the war." She wearily shook her head. "I did not witness much of it; however, our elect uses any reason they can find to celebrate."

"As in my country, a lot of flag waving and marching bands went from one end of the street to the plaza and back again to where old men sat and told their stories of old wars and waited for this one to end."

"Did you want to go?" she asked out of courtesy for the complications that drew men into situations they did not always want to be a part of.

"No," he said, turning back to the window. "I became quite ill and had to leave Spain to regain my health."

Lillian frowned, but again, waited.

"Lillian," he said, turning to face her, "I had a stroke."

"You had a what?" she said, her blue eyes widening.

"A stroke, Lillian." He walked over to her and laid his hand on her shoulder. "All I remember is what I was told once I could understand what was being said. I almost died.

The doctors said my mind stopped working, because of the fever I had. When I regained my thinking, I was left paralyzed. I had to come back from all of that to get well enough to come back to you. I could not eat on my own. I could not walk, I could not stand. I had no memory. I was all but dead."

A shuddering sigh escaped her "The cane?" she questioned.

Paris sat back down. "For more than two years, I did not recognize where I was or much of anything else. I had lost my ability to speak and was paralyzed on my left side. When I was able to travel, the family sent me to Switzerland and a sanatorium for my recovery.

"All I could think about was getting well and did not really understand why. When the memories started to return, all I could think of was you and I knew I had to get well. I had to be a whole man before I could come here.

"I was an invalid, a cripple. A man who could not speak and barely walk, a man who could write only small notes to those who cared for me as my mind fully returned."

"Oh, my God, Paris!" Lillian exclaimed, hardly believing what she had heard. Paris looked down at the floor and then back at her. "Lillian, it took five years in Switzerland before I could come home. I was extremely weak in my left leg and I still must rely on the cane as see, but I had my voice and my mind. I also had my determination. My uncles took care of me, but again, the money was gone. Switzerland was not without its high price."

Lillian could hardly believe what she was hearing. The Sterling House problems diminished to nothing as she realized this man, this man she had loved and waited for, had literally fought for his life to be able to come back to her. "If I had been made aware, I would have come to you, putting aside all the adversity I had here."

"I had no way to let know. As I grew stronger and once again became aware of world affairs, I feared your life was not easy, as rumors of hard times in the United States came to me.

"From the little time I had spent with you, I knew you were strong willed, of a good, logical and sound mind. I should have come back to help a lot sooner, but this," he tapped his left leg, "and this," then his temple, "would not permit it.

"While my mind repaired itself, I jabbered like a baby, but the hardest thing was to walk again.

"And, Lillian, I would not come back to until I could walk to you on two good legs. Even in that I must be supported by the cane part of the time."

Lillian honored the pride in the man, but felt compelled to say, "Paris, don't you know none of that would have mattered?"

"When I saw the look in your eyes last night when I came into this room, I knew that, but a man can be stubborn and filled with far too much pride for his own good. I was blessed, Lillian, blessed to have my life returned to me and then have my life spared."

"Spared?" she asked.

"I was finally sound enough to make the journey, and Lillian, you will not believe this, but I missed the boat." he continued, with a touch of irony to his words.

"You missed the boat?" she said, questioning his statement.

"The *RMS Titanic.*"

Lillian's hand flew to her mouth and she said not a word as the horror of the world's greatest shipwreck flashed into her mind.

Paris let another memory of a twist of fate come to his mind. "I arrived in Southampton, England, one day after the *Titanic* had put to sea. I was still in England, arranging my travel back to Cordoba, when the tragic word of that ship's great sinking came to us." He looked back at her. "If I had made that port, if I had been on board that ship . . ." He stopped, not wanting to let his mind go completely to that place of great tragedy in the cold North Atlantic.

For a moment, Lillian was speechless as she let his words take full form in her mind. "The *Titanic!*" was all she could say. The mental image of the frozen bodies that floated in that icy ocean water crowded into her mind. *The Rocky Mountain News* had been quite graphic in its description of the disaster of the White Star Lines prized ship.

"I was spared, Lillian. My life was spared so I could come back to you. Now that I am here, I see that your struggle has come to an end here in this house your father left for you. I am not sure what I can do, but I am here to help you."

Lillian let the mental image of the *Titanic*'s sinking leave her mind. So many had died with so much being lost.

"I am so glad you missed that boat," she said and they both let the thought settle.

"Some things are meant to be and some are not," was all he said wanting to change the subject away from the tragedy of *Titanic* which was still a raw wound for so many. She had no idea how many times he had thanked God he had missed that departure.

Paris was silent as there was not much more he could tell her. It had been a long, complicated journey for him to finally return to her.

It was obvious by the condition of the Sterling House that the passage of time had not been kind to the Sterling family. "Lillian, my love, what has happened here? What happened to the Sterling House and your family?" he asked.

Lillian blinked a few times and let her mind come back to the present. "Denver City," she began, "has seen many changes since my return from school. My father had wisely built in a profitable area of what once was the majesty of this city.

"My father's dying thrust me into a world that was beginning to drift away from Larimer Street and all it once stood for.

"Paris, I had to learn and learn quickly if we were to survive. Mother could not take care of all of this. I quickly began to learn the good businesses were beginning to move away from this street of many origins. A lesser class of people moved in. Many of the smaller businesses, such as the Sterling House, were broke beyond financial repair due to the coinage acts which changed our monetary systems from silver to gold.

"Many people of the influential, wealthy families, lost everything they had. Some men committed suicide or turned to strong drink to numb the thoughts of complete loss. "So many were living in the Sterling House who wanted answers I did not have. Their very survival seemed to rest in the rooms of this house. I had to keep it alive by whatever means I could. I had nowhere to go and only those who lived here to help me.

"Mother wanted to move away from Larimer Street as she could barely tolerate the blight that had taken over. There was no place to go and not enough money to go there if we could have moved the business."

She sadly shook her head and closed her eyes. She searched her mind for all to tell him. "Always, there were those who wanted the saloons closed and the politicians who did not, because they received money back in their own pockets out of money from each and every license, fee and bribe we were forced to pay to stay in business. Somehow the temperance ladies moved into places of city prestigious power and with the curse of the women's power to vote, they voted in Prohibition.

"It would have made no difference where the Sterling House had been located. Without the serving of alcohol we could not survive."

"I wonder," he said, "if those who saw fit to do this understand the depth of destruction their actions have caused. This is truly a great loss for you and for many." He was silent. What words could he say to her to ease the grief of her loss of the Sterling House and all it had once represented.

"Your family?" he questioned, "I know Erwin is still here, but what about everyone else? Charley Gaynor? Your mother? Is there truly no one to help you keep all of this?"

"No one," Lillian answered. "Charley succumbed to a disease of the body that no one can seem to explain. Something known as cancer, of which there is no cure, only death."

Paris frowned deeply at the news of the death of Charley Gaynor. "I will miss Charley," he said. "He was a good man that I can only wish I could have been with him more. His passing saddens me."

"Erwin and Jonas inherited that big house of his and they decided to sell it in preference to living here. When it sold, they moved to the Sterling House.

The next winter, my Grand Paw Paw, returned to the Sterling House to live out his final days. He had lived a full, rich life and it was his time to pass but it was none-the-less a sad passing for me. He is buried next to my father."

Paris was quiet to let her reflect for a moment on the three men buried at Riverside and memories only she held.

Lillian continued. "Somehow, we stubbornly survived. It was about ten years later when Jonas left the Sterling House with two Chinese girls who worked here. He had more or less adopted and cared for them. The girls, Ming Su and Ling Su, even though apparently born here, wanted to go to China, their ancestral homeland. Jonas told me he had never been much of anywhere or seen much of anything. He said he would attend to them and what they wanted. "Paris, I never heard from him again."

"I did not know Jonas Gregory except to see him here behind the bar. Charley had told me he was a good man, a steady and faithful man. China is a long way from here and just who was this grandfather you mention?" Paris asked, not sure he recalled her mentioning another relative living at the Sterling House.

Lillian realized there was so much he did not know about her family, just as there was so much about him and his family she did not know. "Not a blood grandfather, but the only one I ever knew. He was a trapper of furs, a mountain man, a pilot and a guide for those who would come West when west was more than a direction on a compass or chart. When it was a destination.

"His name was Buckland Kavanaugh, the man who helped to bring Paw Paw, Uncle Charley and a lot of other people out here when there was no safe way of doing this. He was my father's best friend second only to my Uncle Charley. He too left here such a long time ago only to return when it was his time to die."

"It seems I recall your Uncle Charley mentioning this man." He was thoughtful for a moment and finally had to ask, "what of your mother?"

Lillian looked away. "She died of bitterness and loneliness, too much drink and too much laudanum. She never belonged here but there was no place for her to go until death released her."

He softly responded, "It is a sorrow in our hearts to lose our parents."

Before he could say more, there was a soft knock on the door.

"Yes?" Lillian answered and Erwin entered the room, bringing breakfast for them.

"I thought you might need some nourishment," he said as he presented the trays he had brought. "We still have some of the service left unpacked." His eyes went from Paris to Lillian and his heart was happy with what he saw. "I cannot begin to tell you how happy I am that we were still here for your return." he continued as he poured steaming cups of coffee.

"And I cannot begin to tell you how happy I was when it was you that opened that door last night," Paris said. "Only two cups of coffee? Please, Erwin, sit with us so we can talk."

"Oh, no sir, Senor Montoya. There is still much to see to and much to attend to for us to be able to leave here as planned. I am not a strong judge of people," he said, looking away to keep the blush from his face, "but I believe you will be joining us on our journey?"

Lillian laughed, sipped her coffee and said, "Yes, Erwin. That he will be."

Erwin was overjoyed as he left the room shaking his head in a very positive way, feeling great happiness.

Lillian said, "I have no idea what I would have done without him through all these years. Now he is my salvation and our future is with him."

"What journey?" he asked. "It appears obvious you are not planning on staying here, but where are going?"

"Erwin may be a quiet, shy and a bit of a reclusive man in many ways. Yet he is shrewd," she answered. "All these years that I paid him a salary, he did not waste his money. He invested it into land and property on the western slope of our state. A place called Grand Junction, where much fruit is being grown. From what he tells me, many orchards are planted there."

"He has a home there?"

"Yes," she continued, "and apparently a lot more, as there are peach orchards there, too. It is from this he says we will survive."

"You knew nothing of this before now?"

Lillian shook her head. "He said he knew the day would come when he would want to retire and had planned on my old age care as well. I never thought I would leave here and especially not under the circumstances that have caused boards to be nailed to the doors and windows."

For a moment Paris frowned slightly and then had to ask, "This is a difficult time in your life and I am sure he was not planning on my returning here as I have. He is more than gracious to invite me, but I have no rights of interference."

Lillian's blue eyes were very somber and her voice very serious as she said, "Erwin Frederson has cared for me since I was a child. He knows my heart and he knows I have waited a lifetime for you. As always, he says very little and probably never will, but to see him smile the way he just did is in the strongest of favor for you."

Paris hesitated before replying. "I am not as well as I would like to be and I have no great fortune with only a modest sum coming from the Cordoba Montoya Estate. But, I will work as hard as I can to make our lives successful. If raising peaches is what we must do to survive, then raise them we will. All that is important is that I have never stopped loving you. If will allow me to stay, Lillian, I promise I will never leave again."

Her gaze never wavered as she spoke. "You made a promise once before and kept it. You promised to return and did. I made a promise too and I kept it."

Lillian reached for his hand. "I promised to wait for you and I did. On this day, my love, I promise this. I will never let you leave me again."

Paris Jacob LaRoche de la Montoya raised her hand to his lips and lightly kissed the double set of rings she wore. "As promised, my love, this is forever." he said and then with all the love his heart had for her, he added, "until death do we part."

With that, the Woman of Sterling Quality . . . . Lillian Anne Sterling . . . . smiled!

Of
Sterling
Quality

Epilogue

To the west of Denver, Colorado, solidly set in a tremendous corridor, is a barricade. Not one made by man, but rather fashioned by the Powers of the Universe and the awesome forces of Mother Nature. In the beginning, when man first witnessed the ruggedness of this barricade, only the bravest, or the most fool hardy, dared venture too far into the vast lofty unknown.

It was a wise man who recognized his limitations to penetrate a wilderness whose vastness seemed endless. Perhaps it was wisdom combined with arrogance that allowed man to believe he could ultimately conquer the massiveness of the Rocky Mountains. For the most part, this domain was left for God and Mother Nature. But as with the spread and the progress of civilized man, those who would engineer passages, rights of way and roadways, had found ways to penetrate, travel through across and around these once formidable mountains.

Although passable roadways over the high mountain passes of Colorado existed in 1916, the rails were the most reliable and easiest mode of transportation. It was the choice of travel Lillian had selected for her departure.

As Lillian Anne Sterling boarded the train at Union Station that would take her away from her home, she was strangely quiet. She felt the tug of invisible bonds were holding her, pulling her back into a time when it all had been so different.

They had paid for a private Pullman seeping car to allow their privacy. She, Erwin and Paris sat in silence, waiting for the train to begin its movement to their destination of choice across the mountains and to the west.

Once again, as in years long past, she tried to wipe the dirt from the window, only to realize it was still on the outside of the windowpane. As the train began to move, and in those final moments, through the smears, the soot and the grime, she saw them all. Andrew Wesley Sterling, her father. Blond and blue eyed, a handsome man from Georgia, seeking life and running from it at the same time.

In the beginning, he had walked the hard packed earthen streets, stepped gaily around the mud holes and avoided the sticky gumbo mud in the streets he had prowled up and down along Larimer Street in those uncertain days.

He had longed to cross Cherry Creek or follow the Platte to the veins of gold he could only dream about, but his footsteps never wandered that far from what he, too, had come to love.

Lillian knew it was more than the Sterling House and the many people who had passed through its opulent doorways, walked across its plush Pakinstani carpets to enter its elegant chambers for food, drink and gambling. Her father's love had been for early Denver, as She had struggled in Her youthful arrogance to become Queen of the Plains.

Abigale Westmoreland Sterling, her mother, whose prideful Southern haughtiness had clung to her as so many cobwebs in an old attic. She had marveled at the first paved streets which protected the hems of her fine lace petticoats and kept the mud off her kid leather slippers.

She had seen the gaslights come to light her way and watched the towering five, seven, and even nine-story buildings mushroom above her to block her view of the mountains.

She had refused to acknowledge anything over seven stories. "God lives up there," she said and she was not ready to meet him on the top of a building in Denver City. Some of her old hoop skirts and bustle dresses were still packed in trunks somewhere in the Sterling House's attic along with her yearning for the more genteel Southern lifestyle she had at one time wanted to escape and then longed for when it was no longer available.

She had never truly forgotten, or forgiven, a way of life that created her values. In many ways, she had seen Denver much differently than her husband Andrew and blamed it and him, for developing calluses on her hands and in her soul.

Her survival had been based on those calluses, but inwardly, in her own stubborn ways, she had remained a Southern aristocrat and had never let anyone forget there was a more genteel manner in which to live. She had professed an intolerance abhorrence for slavery, but expected to be catered to when it suited her stubborn mind. Abigale had never truly released her hold on Soolie.

Soolie's dark face and almond shaped eyes floated into Lillian's memory. She had been a part of Lillian's childhood that could never be forgotten and those special New Orleans pastries had left an even sweeter memory.

Her special recipes had been tediously written down on little cards and were carefully packed away in a wooden box. Someday, they would be of value again. That old black woman had, unfortunately, lived at the wrong time. She was free to come and go, but chained to a past that had shackled her to attitudes which did not speak of freedom. She had been freed of physical slavery at a time when freedom could not be a true state of being if one possessed a tiny drop of African blood. Her mental comforts had finally came in the form of Buckland LeRoy Kavanaugh, a mountain man who was out of step with time as he had outlived his own time.

There had been a precious half-breed Indian boy, the only male offspring that could have carried the Sterling name into another generation had the child been permitted the honor.

He, too, had been tainted, cursed by Indian and white alike. In his lifetime, he had experienced the white world's brutality in more ways than just a name denial. Soolie's black race might have felt the whip, but Charley Paul's red ancestors had been brutally butchered.

Charley Paul Standing Horse Sterling, the only brother Lillian had ever known, had been raised by a freed slave and a mountain man, away from his true blood family because of the slaughter of his Indian mother and her people at Sand Creek. This was all because Abigale would not tolerate Andrew's indiscretion with Pale Star Rising. In all reality, Andrew had no choice and she had been forced to leave the sanctuary the Sterling House had provided.

This Indian woman had died tragically a long time back. Lillian did not know all the details. She did not want to know them. All she knew was that the man who had killed Pale Star had died at her grieving father's hands. Somehow, she knew it was not an easy death. All she cared to know was that her father had loved this woman. Had never stopped loving her.

Charley Paul's people, the Arapaho, floated past Lillian's thoughts and disappeared into the mist, their drums long silent and their teepees forever gone along with the buffalo and a freedom only they understood. Sand Creek was but a tarnished memory and most people didn't know where it was or what had truly happened out there on the plains less than 200 miles from Denver.

No blood relatives from either side of her family, the Sterlings or the Westmorelands, remained to come to Colorado. There had been those who, by faith or loyalty, had attached themselves to the Sterling House.

She thought of Charley Gaynor, and how he had been her uncle by choice. Two things stood solid in her mind when it came to her Uncle Charley. How he always seemed to be smiling and how his hands were always busy shuffling and ruffling a deck of cards or carving wooden toothpicks, a smile on his face no matter which he was doing.

Then there was Jonas Gregory, who had sought to change his destiny by leaving. Would it have made a difference to the Sterling House if Charley Gaynor had lived and Jonas Gregory stayed? Somehow, she thought not.

Lillian continued to watch familiarity slip away as the rails began to move her away from the place of her home for over 50 years. She thought of the beautiful building on the corner of Larimer and J Streets, or 19th Street as it had come to be known. A small change in a name that someone, somewhere in a nondescript office, thought would be advantageous to the sum of what Denver was or what it was destined to become.

Laws had been passed and levied by those who thought to rid Denver of what they considered to be improper and infectious to the morals of those who chose to live their lives as they saw fit.

The Sterling House had been her life. Even though faced with problems of management and managing, the Sterling House had become her joy of living. Her pride. Even with their personal emotional differences, it had also been her family's pride. In those early years, many people had come to Denver City, a place so remote on the plains. They all had struggled to survive against odds of the greatest magnitude. Only a rare few had survived those pioneering days.

Others who had followed had taken over with their complete renovations of a quality of life only remembered by a few. It was in establishments, like the Sterling House, the true Denver had been born.

From the night of that Monte game so many years gone by, when her father had won—*Lock, Stock and Barrel*, that which was to be his beginning, he had known where his future would be. When he had lifted the canvas door flap, smelled those rotted pickled eggs, cast his eyes on the blonde nude, he had envisioned a business that could be lucrative and a lifestyle of his choosing. He had rolled up his sleeves, poured his first drink and officially claimed the Sterling House as his own, his destiny, and the destiny of those around him, had been set.

With sound suggestions from others and a few of Andrew's own ideas, the Sterling House had grown into the beautiful, elaborate, three-story building which had become more than respected as a fine house of excellent quality food, good spirits and honest gambling.

Many neighboring taverns, groggeries, saloons and even some eateries supported and fostered immoral behavior behind closed doors and drawn draperies. The Sterling House was of sterling quality, as was she, as was her father and her mother along with everyone associated with the Sterling House.

Lillian thought of Mattie Silks with her golden curls, diamond cross necklace and covey of soiled doves. Their reputations might be a bit dark, but they were for the most part, as Lillian knew them, honest, hard working women surviving against the odds of the demoralized ones around them who kept secrets in back rooms and projected qualities that were false.

Each of them, herself included, had fluttered too closely to the flame of life until the flames had consumed them. Mattie Silks was a survivor. Lillian knew this woman would outwit them all in her own way. She would continue to thumb her nose at a society that would not accept her as it had bloomed and blossomed as people came and went each adding their own elements of charm.

Lillian's thoughts were fading just as the City of Denver disappeared behind them while the train gathered steam and power to take them away from a past that could not be their future.

She looked at Erwin and asked, "Will it always be there?"

Erwin shifted his gaze out the window and then back at her. He somberly nodded. She felt Paris beside her and again her heart leapt with a joy she thought she could never have. There was no place for him to go except with her. They would have hours and days and weeks to fill in all the missing pieces in both their lives.

Sensing her thoughts had been many miles, and many years away, he left her the silent space she needed in these last moments. He took her gloved hand in his and lifted it to his lips, lightly kissing the back of her hand as he gently pulled her back to the present. Lillian Anne Sterling smiled at the man she had loved from the first moment she had seen him and then looked back out the window.

"It all has to do with quality of like minded people," she said. "Far too many seem to have forgotten the quality of those who came first." She paused, reflecting on where she came from and the quality of what had made her who she was as she allowed all the bitterness to fall behind her to lie scattered in the cinders along the railroad tracks that led both east and west out of Denver.

"Denver City's quality may have changed," she quietly added, closing her magnificent blue eyes, "but mine never will. When the quality returns, so will I."

Lillian Anne Sterling allowed the passage.

The end of a great saga for a family
That truly was
. . . . . of Sterling Quality

Previous Books of

* * *

Spirit Vision of a Grandmother
Path to the Spirit
Writing on the Teepee Wall
Tucker The Troll
Chilblains

* * *

Visit the Website at

www.BarbaraWyckoff.com